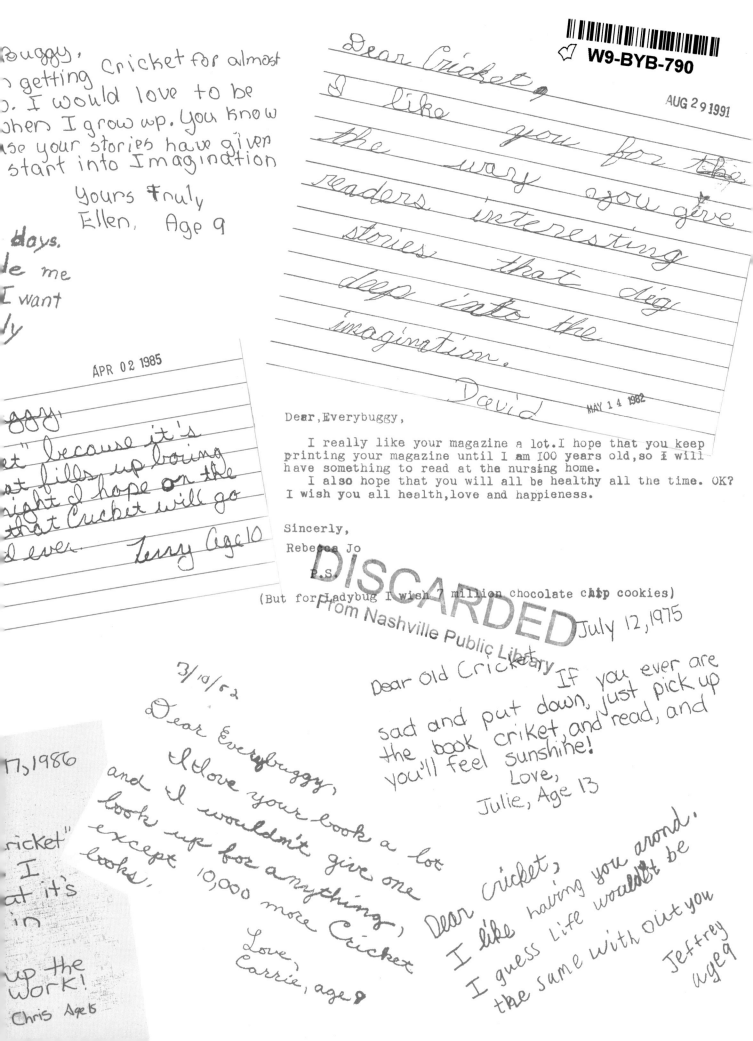

buggy,
getting cricket for almost
. I would love to be
when I grow up. You know
se your stories have given
start into Imagination

Yours Truly
Ellen, Age 9

days.
le me
I want
ly

☞ W9-BYB-790

Dear Cricket,

I like you for the
way you give
readers interesting
stories that dig
deep into the
imagination.

David

AUG 29 1991

MAY 14 1982

APR 02 1985

ggy,
" because it's
at fills up boing
ight I hope on the
that Cricket will go
d ever.   Terry Age10

Dear, Everybuggy,

    I really like your magazine a lot. I hope that you keep
printing your magazine until I am 100 years old, so I will
have something to read at the nursing home.
    I also hope that you will all be healthy all the time. OK?
I wish you all health, love and happieness.

Sincerly,
Rebecca Jo
P.S.

DISCARDED
From Nashville Public Library

(But for Ladybug I wish 7 million chocolate chip cookies)

July 12, 1975

Dear Old Cricket,   If you ever are
sad and put down, just pick up
the book criket and read, and
you'll feel sunshine!
Love,
Julie, Age 13

3/10/52

Dear Everybuggy,
I love your book a lot
and I wouldn't give one
book up for anything,
except 10,000 more Cricket
books.
Love,
Carrie, age 9

Dear cricket,
I like having you arond.
I guess Life wouldn't be
the same with out you
Jeffrey
age 9

7, 1986

ricket"
I
at it's
in

up the
work!
Chris Age8

CELEBRATE
Cricket

CELEBRATE Cricket®

30 Years of Stories and Art

Edited by Marianne Carus

Cricket Books

Chicago

NASHVILLE PUBLIC LIBRARY

To my husband Blouke, my best friend and loyal supporter.

Compilation copyright © 2003 by Carus Publishing Company
All rights reserved
Printed in Canada
Designed by Ron McCutchan
First edition, 2003

No part of this publication may be reproduced in whole or in part, or stored in a retrieval system, or transmitted in any form or by any means, electronic, mechanical, photocopying, recording, or otherwise, without the written permission of the publisher. For information regarding permission, write to Carus Publishing Company, 315 Fifth Street, Peru, Illinois, 61354.

The Library of Congress Cataloging-in-Publication data for Celebrate Cricket *is available under LC Control Number 2003010284.*

"Only the rarest kind of best in anything can be good enough for the young."

—**Walter de la Mare**

"A child is not a vase to be filled, but a fire to be lit."

—**François Rabelais**

Table of Contents

CONTENTS

Genesis
by Lee Bennett Hopkins

In the beginning . . .

one cricket
was born

who rubbed its wings
who chirped
to let us know

how
worlds of reading
can
change
us
so . . .

Art by Trina Schart Hyman

Lee Bennett Hopkins has published more than seventy-five books for children and young adults, including the poetry anthologies *I Think I Saw a Snail: Young Poems for City Seasons* and *A Song in Stone: City Poems.* He founded the annual Lee Bennett Hopkins Poetry Award in 1993 and the Lee Bennett Hopkins/International Reading Association Promising Poet Award in 1995.

Let's Celebrate *Cricket*

*C*RICKET, THE MAGAZINE for children, invites you to a very special birthday party! As of September 2003, *Cricket* is thirty years old, and all of you are invited. It doesn't matter if you're young or old, or somewhere in between, we want you to help us *Celebrate Cricket* with this book that gives you a taste of thirty years of great stories, poems, fabulous illustrations, letters, and very special memories. This celebration may be a nostalgia trip for many of our first readers in 1973, who wrote to us then that they would keep their *Cricket* magazines for their own children, who now may be subscribing to *Cricket* themselves. And our current *Cricket* subscribers will find many wonderful stories—some of them my personal favorites—in this book.

It's difficult to believe that thirty years have flown by, because *Cricket* is still just as lively, perky, and exuberant as it was in September 1973 when the first issue stirred up great excitement in the press and in the children's book world. At that time, *Cricket*'s

**by
Marianne
Carus**

Marianne Carus in 1976

1

format was 6″ x 9″, it was bound like a small paperback, and the illustrations were black-and-white with one-color overlay. The first issue had stories by Isaac Bashevis Singer, Lloyd Alexander, Sid Fleischman, Astrid Lindgren, Gianni Rodari, Arnold Lobel, Jean Craighead George, Julius Lester, and poems by T. S. Eliot, David McCord, Nikki Giovanni, Gwendolyn Brooks, and James Reeves.

HOPELESSLY NAIVE LUNATICS

I'd like to think back a bit and tell you how it all began. What sparked the idea to start a new children's magazine when there were already eighty-five or ninety such magazines saturating the market? Many people shook their heads and felt sorry for us, such hopelessly naive lunatics, who wanted to publish yet another magazine. But the idea was really not as crazy as it may have seemed. In the sixties I had edited the Basic Readers for the fourth, fifth, and sixth grades of the Open Court Correlated Language Arts program, which introduced thousands of children to worthwhile literature. Teachers begged my husband, Blouke (publisher of the Open Court Publishing Company), and me for more high-quality, literary reading materials, not books, but shorter selections. In order to find good stories for these young readers, I looked at all the existing children's magazines, hoping to find just what I wanted. But I searched in vain. There was not one literary children's magazine among all those being published in the 1970s. The stories were dull, mostly staff written, the illustrations mediocre. Not one of all these children's magazines offered *original contributions* by *contemporary authors!* Only one, *Children's Digest,* published excerpts of some of the best contemporary children's books.

I was disappointed but continued to do some intensive research in the University of Chicago's collections of old readers, where

I came across many stories taken from a children's magazine called *St. Nicholas,* that was started in 1873 and edited by Mary Mapes Dodge, the author of *Hans Brinker; or The Silver Skates.* After her death, *St. Nicholas* sadly ceased publication in the late 1930s. In *St. Nicholas* I finally found good literature—great stories and poems, well-written nonfiction articles about all kinds of subjects—and there were great illustrations.

Mary Mapes Dodge wanted to "inspire children with an appreciation of fine pictorial art. Pictures for children should be heartily conceived and well executed," she wrote. "If it only be the picture of a cat, it must be so like a cat that it will do its own purring, and not sit, a dead, stuffed thing, requiring the editor to purr for it. One of the sins of this age," she continued, "is editorial dribbling over inane pictures!" (This was written in 1873!) I began looking through many bound volumes of *St. Nicholas,* and it was *St. Nicholas* that inspired my first thoughts and plans to create a new magazine, a magazine for children that would aspire to the same high literary standards, the same excellence that could consistently be found in *St. Nicholas.*

Our magazine would include only stories, articles, poetry, and illustrations of the highest quality. The layout and design had to be excellent. We wanted to develop in our readers not only a feeling for good content and style, but also a rudimentary aesthetic sense or taste for fine graphics. Exposed to good writing and good illustrations we believed that children would eventually develop a taste and appreciation for good literature and art. We still find it extremely important to present the young child with literary and artistic experiences that have integrity, beauty, and humor, because we believe that good taste can be developed and nurtured.

More important even than development of artistic tastes, however, were the educational ideas, the philosophy, if you want to call it that, behind the publication of this new magazine. We wanted it to be lighthearted, delightful, funny, amusing, nondidactic, but at the same time we were determined to introduce the basic values of our own and important other cultures throughout the world with the great stories in our new magazine.

We wanted our readers to find out about great events in history and we wanted to publish well-written stories about these events, stories that would be so alive and so exciting that young readers could not put them down. In our new magazine we planned to introduce the great and famous people who shaped history—not just statesmen, kings, and queens, but also great writers and poets, scientists, explorers, composers, artists, and naturalists. We wanted to give our readers a feeling for other countries by offering them stories translated from other languages, stories that would awaken their respect for other traditions and customs and stimulate their curiosity, their imagination, and their sense of wonder. What is important about education of young people, Plato said in his *Republic,* is to create in children an imagination. Imagination, he implied, is the machine with which we create the world for ourselves, and without imagination, education is more or less useless.

A MISSION AND A BUG

In 1972 I wrote a mission statement for our new magazine, and we have faithfully adhered to it in all these thirty years. One of our main commitments was and always will be to create in children a love of reading by sustaining a lively, witty, and cheerful tone and a sense of humor. In the late sixties at the Frankfurt Book Fair, I had by chance come across a small book *How Six Found Christmas.* The author/illustrator was a certain Trina Schart Hyman. I fell in love with her art, and shortly after our return, Blouke and I visited her and asked her to illustrate several stories for our Open Court readers.

In 1971 I phoned Trina and asked her to consider becoming the art director of our new magazine. "I've never art directed a magazine before," Trina objected. "And I've never edited a magazine before," I answered. "We'll make a good team." Trina drew a very nice and natural-looking cricket, who would become the main character in the magazine, and his various friends, Ladybug, George the earthworm, Sluggo the snail, and, of course the antagonist Ugly Bird. They all explain the difficult words in the stories and have their own hilarious and exciting adventures in the margins. "The bugs," as we call them, or "the gang," all great characters, each one of them, were a huge success right away and enchanted not just our readers, but also our entire staff, which then consisted of one editorial assistant, a part-time secretary, and myself.

For each issue Trina drew and wrote the bugs' comments and their small adventures, comedies, and tragedies with her unfailing and delicious dry sense of humor. When she came to Illinois for our first Editorial Board Meeting in 1972, she surprised us with a live cricket in a little cricket cage and brought several drawings of Cricket's friends Ladybug, Charlie the young cricket, George the earthworm, Sluggo the snail, and Ugly Bird. She also brought the absolutely wonderful first cover for our magazine. You'll find a conversation with Trina on page 50.

But why a cricket? How did this new magazine get its name? It was difficult to find just the right one. I made long lists, and so did Trina, Kip Fadiman, Kaye Webb, and my entire family. I liked *Troubadour* or *Taliesin,* the wandering, storytelling bards of old, but everyone found these names too foreign, too unfriendly, and not accessible enough for children. Many long discussions and

HI LADYBUG!
DID YOU WRITE
A LETTER SAYING
HOW MUCH YOU
LOVED CRICKET?

I COULDN'T.
UGLY BIRD
ATE MY PENCIL!

BURP

phone calls later—one week past the deadline, I was reading Isaac Bashevis Singer's *A Day of Pleasure* about his childhood in Warsaw and his little friend Shosha. He wrote: "There was a tile stove in Shosha's apartment behind which there lived a cricket. It chirped the nights through all winter long. I imagined that the cricket was telling a story that would never end." That was exactly what I wanted our new magazine to do: "tell stories that would never end," and here was our name: *Cricket!* Hurrah!

In 1971, when we discussed the idea of creating a children's magazine at one of our Open Court Editorial Advisory Board meetings, we had found to our great surprise and delight that Clifton Fadiman and Isaac Bashevis Singer, two Board members, were extremely enthusiastic and supportive of the idea.

Clifton Fadiman, who insisted on being called "Kip" (he didn't like the name "Clifton"), a judge of the Book-of-the-Month Club and book editor of the *New Yorker,* had always wanted to start a literary magazine for children. He had a great interest in children's literature and was working on a critical history of that genre. He completely agreed with our ideas for the new magazine and was delighted when we asked him to become a member of the staff. He wanted to be senior editor and insisted that I had to be editor-in-chief. With Kip's great knowledge of authors in the United States and abroad (he was on a first-name basis with almost all of them), he was a tremendous help in spreading the word about *Cricket.* The press knew him because of his years as host of the popular *Information, Please* radio program. Teachers and librarians knew and adored him. Together we wrote to three hundred of the best authors for children as well as for adults here and abroad and asked for any kind of story they might have tucked away in a drawer. We asked adult authors such as William Saroyan, Mary Renault, James Herriot, and many others, if they could possibly turn their talents to writing for children. And slowly manuscripts started to come in.

THE BRILLIANT BOARD

In the meantime we had invited the luminaries in children's literature to join *Cricket*'s Editorial Advisory Board: Isaac Bashevis Singer, one of the world's most distinguished novelists and short-story writers for adults and for children. He received the Nobel Prize in 1978 after he had won the National Book Award for his children's book *A Day of Pleasure;* Lloyd Alexander, one of our best children's writers who had won both the National Book Award and the Newbery Medal; Eleanor Cameron, an author of children's fantasy and science fiction novels as well as an excellent critic in her books *about* children's literature; Sheila Egoff, the grande dame of children's literature in Canada and author of *The Republic of Childhood;* Virginia Haviland, the head of the children's section of the Library of Congress, and well-known author and anthologist of the world's folk and fairy tales; Paul Heins, editor of the *Horn Book Magazine,* the periodical devoted to the serious examination of children's literature; Walter Scherf, then director of Munich's world-renowned International Youth Library, and also lecturer and translator; and last but by no means least Kaye Webb, a well-known British TV personality and director and editor of Penguin Publishing in London, but mainly the founder and editor of the Puffin paperbacks and of *Puffin Post,* a charming, lively, child-friendly magazine. Blouke and I were great admirers of Kaye's vast knowledge of British writers, illustrators, and their books.

In November 1972 we had our first Editorial Advisory Board meeting in the lodge of our beautiful local Illinois state park Starved Rock, and they came from all corners of the world. What

Editorial Board meeting 1972 at Starved Rock Lodge. At the center table, clockwise from left: Lloyd Alexander, Eleanor Cameron, Blouke Carus, Marianne Carus, Clifton Fadiman, Kaye Webb, Walter Scherf, Virginia Haviland, Paul Heins, William Caroll, Marcia Leonard, Sherwood Sugden (back to camera), Trina Schart Hyman (back to camera)

we had in common was a great passion for children's literature and the desire to give our children only that "rarest kind of best in anything" that Walter de la Mare, a famous British poet, once said is good enough for the young.

I had invited a recently hired editorial assistant to the meeting, Marcia Leonard, just out of college, who tells you on page 74 about her impressions of that meeting. So does Eleanor Cameron, who wrote an article for her local newspaper in 1973. You'll find it on page 86. I am sad to say that many of our brilliant and wonderful first Board members have passed away already: Kip Fadiman, Isaac Bashevis Singer, Eleanor Cameron, Virginia Haviland, Paul Heins, and Kaye Webb. Others just as accomplished and capable, children's literature critics and authors, have joined our Board throughout these thirty years: John Rowe Townsend, author and critic; Ann Thwaite, author and biographer; Nancy Larrick, author, critic, and anthologist; Betsy Hearn, Professor of Children's Literature at the University of Illinois, critic, and author; Virginia Hamilton, author and winner of the MacArthur Genius Award, the Hans Christian Andersen Award, and the Newbery Medal; Seymour Simon, author; Jim Trelease, author and lecturer; and Trina Schart Hyman. After fifteen years, Trina had passed on her magic wand and her bug characters to Jean Gralley, who tells you about her experiences as *Cricket*'s staff artist for the last fifteen years on page 167.

WE SEND OUT A PILOT

During the summer of 1972, I had put together a *Cricket* pilot issue, which we wanted to send out to the media, literary critics, authors, illustrators, librarians, teachers, and other distinguished people. But first we sent it to our Editorial Board members for their comments. We wanted them to critique the as yet unillustrated selections for the pilot issue, suggest alternates if they didn't like them, discuss different features like an editorial page, a page for letters from children, and a section for children's own writing, which I had tentatively called *Cricket League,* a name and idea shamelessly stolen from *St. Nicholas.*

Most of the selections for the pilot issue were reprints, but I had also received four original contributions: a greeting from Snoopy, together with an illustration from Charles Schulz, one of Kip Fadiman's friends. Sid Fleischman sent me a new McBroom story that later became part of a book, "McBroom the Rainmaker" (see page 94). Nonny Hogrogian wrote and illustrated a story just for the pilot, "The Unhappy King of Gargantak."

The greatest challenge came when Isaac Bashevis Singer sent me his manuscript called "Why Noah Chose the Dove," the story of Noah's ark. Unfortunately, the manuscript was much too long for our magazine, and I had to cut it in half. I had edited and cut many, many stories in my former life as textbook editor, but this was the first time I worked with a world-famous author and I wondered how Singer would react to my severe cuts of his manuscript. But I shouldn't have worried. He was wonderful, kind, and

Sid Fleischman's McBroom, as drawn by Quentin Blake

supportive. He said that he liked what I had done and would use this version for his upcoming book *The Bird of Peace.* I wish I could tell him again how much confidence he gave me for the long years of editing that lay ahead. Isaac was a loyal friend and great admirer of *Cricket.* He read every issue from cover to cover and told me that he liked *Cricket* much better than any of the contemporary adult novels he had to read. He continued his support with friendly letters and many stories he wrote just for us, stories that were later published in anthologies by Farrar, Straus & Giroux.

Lloyd Alexander sent me "A Hungry Reader," a short article about his childhood, and, to our great surprise, he added his own illustrations. Lloyd was just as supportive as Isaac. He has written many exquisite stories for *Cricket* over the years, and we always celebrate their arrival. Not only does Lloyd write beautifully, he has a great sense of humor, and an often hilarious tongue-in-cheek insight into human foibles and weaknesses, and strengths. We also celebrate Lloyd's stories because we hardly ever need to edit anything at all—he is not only an exquisite writer but also a very careful one.

We had named the last selection in our pilot "Old Cricket Says." It is an editorial written for both adults and children. Kip Fadiman wrote the first one for the pilot and also "A Letter to All Young Crickets from an Old Cricket."

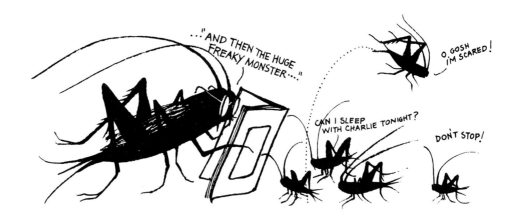

· A LETTER TO ALL YOUNG CRICKETS FROM AN OLD CRICKET ·

Dear Crickets,

On your mark! Ready! Set! Go!

We're off!

This is the start of Cricket. It's your own magazine. You'll get it every month, for nine months of the year. (The people who make it up have to have a vacation, too.)

What will Cricket be like?

Well, look it over now quickly. Then read it slowly.

It will have stories. Lots of stories. Funny stories. Scary stories. Stories about things that could really happen. Stories about things that could *never* happen. (Sometimes they're the best.)

It will have riddles and puzzles and tongue-twisters.

It will have rhymes for fun, and verses that are just nice to read out loud, or that make you dreamy, or that make you form pictures in your head.

It will have tales from far countries and strange peoples.

It will have stuff about great men and women of the past and the present, and stuff about the earth and the sea and the stars, and stuff about science and machinery and travel and space and sports.

It will tell you about things to make and do, outside the house and inside the house.

It will have a lot of nonsense in it.

And—*loads of pictures.*

And there's more I want to tell you about, but that's enough for *Cricket's* first chirp.

Happy Reading!

Old Cricket

P.S. Please write us.

I had asked all of our Board members to write the "Old Cricket Says" editorial now and then, but pretty soon Lloyd became our loyal and brilliant Old Cricket, coming up with information and topics that amazed and entertained not just our readers but their parents and our entire staff. On special occasions I became Old Cricket and wrote the editorial myself, but in the pilot I only wrote the introduction to our "Letterbox" and to the "Cricket League." Both of these were, and still are, the children's own sections, which they write themselves. Each month the issue editor creates a contest for our readers to write either a poem or a story, draw a picture, or take a photograph. We publish the best entries three months later and give surprise prizes and certificates for the best entries.

Trina's bugs cavorted in the margins of the pilot issue to the greatest delight of all readers. They introduced the artists and explained difficult words, always witty and creative, and often ridiculously funny. Here is Trina's first cartoon; she called it "Cricket and Fat Ladybug."

NEW YORK MEETS *CRICKET*

In order to introduce our new venture to the publishing world in New York City, we planned a big launching party in the St. Moritz Hotel and invited all children's publishers, editors, art directors, agents, critics, the press, and of course, authors and artists. And they all came. New Yorkers love a good party, Kip said, and he was right. We had a great time, even though it was crowded, and we spilled over onto the balconies of the roof garden high above the city. Kip, several Board members, and I gave short talks about our goals and hopes for the magazine, but Isaac Bashevis Singer brought the house down with his ten reasons why he likes children. Here they are:

1. Children don't want their mothers to be liberated.
2. Unlike their fathers they can fight without talking about peace.
3. They can hate their parents without the help of psychoanalysis.
4. They can sin without making long and boring confessions.
5. They have no use for equality.
6. They don't give a hoot about progress.
7. They don't want to be profound.
8. They don't flatter the young.
9. They don't worry about the old.
10. They don't feel guilty for being healthy, beautiful, and charming.

One artist wrote to me after the party, "If a bomb had gone off during your party, the entire children's book world would've been wiped out."

Well, now New York knew about us, even though nobody in the New York publishing world could really understand how anybody in publishing could survive in the middle of Illinois cornfields, of all places! I reassured them during my many visits to New York later on, that crickets need wide open, green spaces to survive.

Cricket

the magazine for children

January 1973

Cover for the pilot issue, illustration by Trina Schart Hyman,
acrylic paint and india ink

In January 1973 the pilot issue was finally published in black and white with a green overlay because of Arnold Lobel's "Frog and Toad" story. I am happy to say that it was a huge success. Not just with the media—all major newspapers ran articles about this unusual new literary magazine for children—but also with professional children's book people, librarians, teachers, authors, and artists. They loved it, but some found the hand-lettered table of contents difficult to read (especially for children), and several commented that the magazine had a homemade look because of all the hand-lettered titles.

We needed a designer. Somebody who could work with production in LaSalle on page layout, design, and type. Open Court Publishing had hired John Grandits, a young designer, for their textbooks and part-time for *Cricket*. John had type in his blood (his father owned a print shop) and a good background in Bauhaus design. He got along famously with everyone, and even though his heart always longed for New York, he stayed in LaSalle, Illinois, with his wife and baby son for six years, first as designer for textbooks and *Cricket,* and from 1979 on as full-time art director of *Cricket.* Read John's memories on page 50.

Manuscripts kept coming in, and we needed more help in editorial. In 1974 I hired two new editors, Kathleen Leverich and Charnan Simon. Charnan tells you about her first years at *Cricket* on page 80. We also had acquired two consulting editors. Our masthead grew from three people, Kip Fadiman, Trina Schart Hyman, and me on the pilot, to six in 1974. Manuscripts and portfolios began pouring in, and Marcia, who was now first reader as well as proofreader, permissions editor (for reprints), and after a while editor, became my "good girl Friday." Trina also got help. Dilys Evans, originally from Wales, joined her in Lyme, New Hampshire, as her assistant art director.

ORANGE CRICKETS AND STACKS OF MAIL

Despite somber and threatening warnings from magazine and financial consultants who said that *Cricket* was a literary and artistic success but a financial failure and a high-risk publishing venture that could not possibly succeed, especially not without advertising, we were well on our way. The *Free Enterprise Magazine,* however, agreed with our publishing consultants, and we were amazed to read the following in their winter 1976 issue on collecting children's books: "But let's not forget children's magazines. One in particular, *Cricket,* is the kind of artsy, high-class publication that I imagine will be fairly short-lived. It will definitely become a collector's item, when it does perish, because of its famous writers and illustrators. So, if you start subscribing now (and happen by the three earlier volumes), you may put away a small gold mine for the years to come."

At that time we also had a basic disagreement with our direct mail consultants. (Direct mail is the brochures you receive in the mail, advertising a product and encouraging you to buy it.) The consultants didn't like Trina's black cricket. And worse, they had gotten rid of it and replaced it with a lame, stiff, stylized, completely unnatural green-and-orange bug that looked more like a tired grasshopper than anything else. We were all of the same opinion: the green/orange cricket had to go! And even though they accused us (the entire staff and Board) of not having any marketing sense and frightening our poor little readers with a black and ugly (!) cricket, and we would be sorry, and on and on . . . we won. The grasshopper disappeared, and our good, old black cricket took over. When we sent brochures with this cricket to a million households with kids, asking their parents to subscribe, we received so many huge sacks full of replies that we had to hire more than twenty people to help sort all that mail. Almost overnight we got at least 100,000 subscribers.

It all sounds like a huge, wonderful success story, but remember, kids outgrow their magazines, even though our readers assured us that they would read *Cricket* until "the world comes to an end." We needed to send renewal notices, bills, new direct mail efforts. Finally we had to find a company that specialized in fulfillment (all these details to get the magazines to the right kid at the right address, to send bills, etc.).

In September 1973, thirty years ago, the first subscription issue of *Cricket,* which had the same contents as the pilot, was finally published. Marcia and I were jubilant. It had been a long wait—and a lot of work.

CRICKET CHIRPS IN ENGLAND

In 1976, another important event happened. *Cricket* crossed the ocean to England to be published there as *Cricket and Company.* We couldn't use the name *Cricket* for the British edition because of the favorite British cricket game. Ann Thwaite, who tells you about *Cricket and Company* on page 181, and John Rowe Townsend, both British, were editors for *Cricket and Company*, and Ann was also in charge of the British "Cricket League." We had received so many letters from British *Cricket* readers, asking us to publish *Cricket* in England that we finally fulfilled their dream. But, alas, the British *Cricket and Company* didn't last long, only fourteen months, because it was too difficult and too costly to conduct marketing campaigns both in England and the U.S., and to oversee the operation from the U.S. So, even though we already had 45,000 British subscribers after a year, we had to close down the operation.

Many years later, in 1988, Blouke and I attended the biannual

International Board on Books for Young People (IBBY) Congress in Oslo, Norway. We met Jacqueline Kergueno there, who was an editorial director of children's magazines at Bayard Press in France. We had several interesting talks about magazines, production, content, and art, and found that we had the same visions for our magazines. Bayard was publishing fourteen children's magazines at the time, and Jacqueline asked us why we were doing just one. We considered publishing a younger magazine for 2–6-year-olds, but we also knew that a younger magazine needed four-color

illustrations. After Oslo we agreed to work with Bayard, buying from them a few stories and art for each issue of a new magazine we launched in 1990, called *Ladybug*. The name for this second magazine had been determined long before the launch, because of Cricket and Ladybug's long friendship and their cartoon in *Cricket* magazine. *Ladybug* had four-color illustrations throughout, and it was beautiful.

We are no longer with Bayard, but we enjoyed our association with them.

Cover for the first issue of Ladybug, *September 1990, illustration by Marylin Hafner*

BUGS GALORE!

After *Ladybug* we started in January 1994 *Spider* for 6–9-year-old beginning readers, and in September 1994, we began publication of *Babybug,* a small board-book magazine with rounded corners for the youngest, 6-month–2-year-old crowd. A "looking and listening magazine," with beautiful illustrations, Mother Goose rhymes, easy stories, and poems.

Marianne Carus

Finally in 1998, at the request of countless "*Cricket* alumni," we began publication of *Cicada,* a magazine for readers 14 and up. *Cicada* is for teens who appreciate fine literature and like to read excellent fiction and poetry. We also accept teen poems and stories if they measure up to the content from adult writers. We call these five, *Cricket, Ladybug, Spider, Babybug,* and *Cicada,* our "bug magazines." They all have a variety of fiction and non-fiction stories and articles, poems, and activities. They all have the best illustrations we can get here or abroad and the greatest stories we can find anywhere. One important point in our mission statement was and still is to find and publish excellent young authors and artists and give them a start in their careers. I am very happy to say that we succeeded in doing that. You can read Jim Giblin's story on page 122, Eric Kimmel's on page 154, and David Wiesner's on page 151. But there are many, many others who got their start with a story or illustration in *Cricket.*

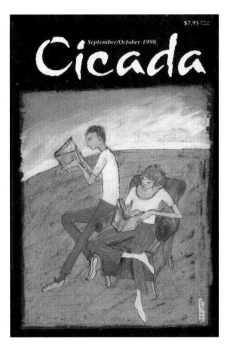

Cover for the first issue of Cicada, *September/October 1998, illustration by Natali Fortier*

With the cooperation of the Smithsonian Institution we started three nonfiction magazines: *Muse* in 1997 for 9–14-year-olds, *Click* in 1998 for ages 3–7, and *Ask* in 2002 for 7–10.

In 2000 we aquired the Cobblestone Group of nonfiction magazines: *Cobblestone* (American history), *Faces* (anthropology), *Dig* (archaeology), *Odyssey* (science), *Calliope* (world history), *Footsteps* (black history), all for 9–14-year-olds, and *Appleseeds* (general interest) for ages 7–9.

And, finally, in 1997 we started a book division, Cricket Books, first with Stephen Roxburgh of Front Street Books, and since 2000 with Marc Aronson, who now is publisher of Cricket Books and of his special division for teenagers, called Marcato Books. Among other awards, Cricket Books has won the Scott O'Dell

Award for the best historic fiction in 1999, and the Batchelder Award for the best translated book from a foreign language in 2002.

Thinking about the good old times, I especially remember all the smart and brilliant young people who worked with me on *Cricket* over the years. Several of the early editors are now writers, publishing their own books. They made do with dingy, small, and windowless offices above a bar and did their best to find the few jewels in the piles of unsolicited manuscripts they had to read. They put up with life in a small town because they shared our vision to give children "only the rarest kind of best in anything." Several of them stayed five or six years, others only two or three, but we always had a good team. I want to take this opportunity to thank all of them, and especially our present editors and art directors and all of our fantastic authors and illustrators for giving their best and doing such excellent work for *Cricket* magazine. Let's celebrate *Cricket,* and may it go on "until the world comes to an end."

Congratulations! from Eric Carle

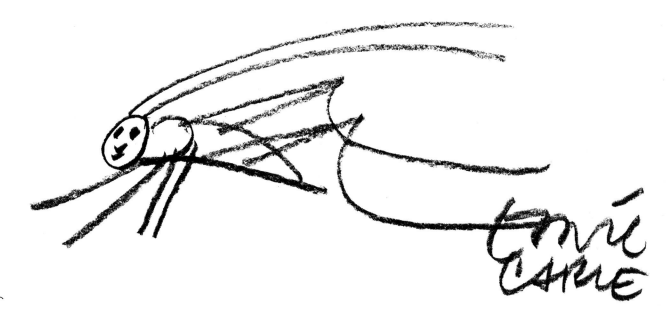

ISAAC B. SINGER
209 WEST 86TH STREET
NEW YORK, N. Y. 10024

Jan. 19, 1973

Miss Mariaane Carus,Editor in Chief
Open Court Publishing Co.,
Box 599
La Salle, Illinois 61301

Dear Friend Marianne Carus,

THE CRICKET is beautiful!, The more I look at it
 and the more I read it, the more I enjoy it. If
it will continue to be like this it will soon become world famous. As you know I did nothing as
an "editorial adviser", but I'm proud to have contributed to it. My wife and my secretary who is
writing this letter share my elation for the new
magazine. Thank you for the three copies you
sent me and since you were gracious enough to offer
more I would like three more just to be able to
give them as gifts to people who are interested
in literature for children. I suspect that you have
done all the work yourself. I always believe that
good things are done by one person.
With my very best regards to you and your dear husband.

Cordially,

Isaac B. Singer

the Fools of Chelm and the Stupid Carp

**by
Isaac Bashevis
Singer**

*Translated by the
author and Ruth
Schachner Finkel*

*Illustrated by
David McPhail*

THIS TOOK PLACE in Chelm, a city of fools. Where else could it have happened? Every housewife in Chelm bought fish for the Sabbath. The rich bought large fish, the poor small ones. They were bought on Thursday, cut up, chopped, and made into gefilte fish on Friday, and eaten on the Sabbath.

One Thursday morning the door opened at the house of the community leader of Chelm, Gronam the Ox, and Feivel Ninny entered, carrying a trough full of water. Inside was a large, live carp.

"What is this?" Gronam asked.

"A gift to you from the wise men of Chelm," Feivel said. "It is the largest carp ever caught in the Lake of Chelm, and we all decided to give it to you as a token of appreciation for your great wisdom."

"Thank you very much," Gronam the Ox replied. "My wife, Yenta Pesha, will be delighted. She and I both love carp. I read in

Cricket, November 1973

a book that eating the brains of a carp increases wisdom, and even though we in Chelm are immensely clever, a little improvement never hurts. But let me have a close look at him. I was told that a carp's tail shows the size of his brain."

Gronam the Ox was known to be nearsighted, and when he bent down to the trough to better observe the carp's tail, the carp did something that proved he was not as wise as Gronam thought. He lifted his tail and smacked Gronam across the face.

Gronam the Ox was flabbergasted. "Something like this never happened to me before," he exclaimed. "I cannot believe this carp was caught in the Chelm Lake. A Chelm carp would know better."

"He's the meanest fish I ever saw in my life," agreed Feivel Ninny.

Even though Chelm is a big city, news traveled quickly there. In no time at all the other wise men of Chelm arrived at the house of their leader, Gronam the Ox. Treitel Fool came, and Sendor Donkey, Shmendrick Numskull, Chazkel Pinhead, and Dopey Lekisch. Gronam the Ox was saying, "I'm not going to eat this fish on the Sabbath. This carp is a fool, and malicious to boot. If I eat him, I could become foolish instead of cleverer."

"Then what shall I do with him?" asked Feivel Ninny.

Gronam the Ox put a finger to his head as a sign that he was thinking hard. After a while he cried out, "No man or animal in Chelm should slap Gronam the Ox. This fish should be punished."

"What kind of punishment shall we give him?" asked Treitel Fool. "All fish are killed anyhow, and one cannot kill a fish twice."

"He shouldn't be killed like other fish," Sendor Donkey said. "He should die in a different way to show that no one can smack our beloved sage, Gronam the Ox, and get away with it."

"What kind of death?" wondered Schmendrick Numskull. "Shall we perhaps just imprison him?"

ISAAC BASHEVIS SINGER

"There is no prison in Chelm for fish," said Chazkel Pinhead. "And to build such a prison would take too long."

"Maybe he should be hanged," suggested Dopey Lekisch.

"How do you hang a carp?" Feivel Ninny wanted to know. "A creature can be hanged only by its neck, but since a carp has no neck, how will you hang him?"

"My advice is that he should be thrown to the dogs alive," said Treitel Fool.

"It's no good," Gronam the Ox answered. "Our Chelm dogs are both smart and modest, but if they eat this carp, they may become as stupid and mean as he is."

"So what should we do?" all the wise men asked.

"This case needs lengthy consideration," Gronam the Ox decided. "Let's leave the carp in the trough and ponder the matter as long as is necessary. Being the wisest man in Chelm, I cannot afford to pass a sentence that will not be admired by all the Chelmites."

"If the carp stays in the trough a long time, he may die," Feivel Ninny, a former fish dealer, explained. "To keep him alive we must put him into a large tub, and the water has to be changed often. He must also be fed properly."

"You are right, Feivel," Gronam the Ox told him. "Go and find the largest tub in Chelm and see to it that the carp is kept alive and healthy until the day of judgment. When I reach a decision, you will hear about it."

Of course Gronam's words were the law in Chelm. The five wise men went and found a large tub, filled it with fresh water, and put the criminal carp in it, together with some crumbs of bread, challah, and other tidbits a carp might like to eat. Schlemiel, Gronam's bodyguard, was stationed at the tub to make sure that no greedy Chelmite wife would use the imprisoned carp for gefilte fish.

It just so happened that Gronam the Ox had many other decisions to make, and he kept postponing the sentence. The carp seemed not to be impatient. He ate, swam in the tub, became even fatter than he had been, not realizing that a severe sentence hung over his head. Schlemiel changed the water frequently because he was told that if the carp died, this would be an act of contempt for Gronam the Ox and for the Chelm Court of Justice. Yukel, the water carrier, made a few extra pennies every day by bringing water for the carp. Some of the Chelmites who were in opposition to Gronam the Ox spread the gossip that Gronam just couldn't find the right type of punishment for the carp, and that he was waiting for the carp to die a natural death. But, as always, a great disappointment awaited them. One morning about a half a year later the sentence became known, and when it was known, Chelm was stunned. The carp had to be drowned.

ISAAC BASHEVIS SINGER

Gronam the Ox had thought up many clever sentences before, but never one as brilliant as this one. Even his enemies were amazed by this shrewd verdict. Drowning is just the kind of death suited to a spiteful carp with a large tail and a small brain.

That day the entire Chelm community gathered at the lake to see the sentence executed. The carp, which had become almost twice as big as he had been before, was brought to the lake in the wagon that carried the worst criminals to their death. The drummers drummed. Trumpets blared. The Chelmite executioner raised the heavy carp and threw it into the lake with a mighty splash.

A great cry rose from the Chelmites. "Down with the treacherous carp! Long live Gronam the Ox! Hurrah!"

Gronam was lifted by his admirers and carried home with songs of praise. Some Chelmite girls showered him with flowers. Even Yenta Pesha, his wife, who was often critical of Gronam and dared to call him fool, seemed impressed by Gronam's high intelligence.

In Chelm, like everywhere else, there were envious people who found fault with everyone, and they began to say that there was no proof whatsoever that the carp really drowned. Why should a carp drown in lake water? they asked. While hundreds of innocent fish were killed every Friday, they said, that stupid carp lived in comfort for months on the taxpayers' money and then was returned sound and healthy to the lake where he is laughing at Chelm justice.

But only a few listened to these malicious words. They pointed out that months passed and the carp was never caught again, a sure sign that he was dead. It is true that the carp might have just decided to be careful and to avoid the fisherman's net. But how can a foolish carp who slaps Gronam the Ox have such wisdom?

Just the same, to be on the safe side, the wise men of Chelm published a decree that if the nasty carp had refused to be drowned and were caught again, a special jail should be built for him, a pool where he would be kept prisoner for the rest of his life.

The decree was printed in capital letters in the official gazette of Chelm and signed by Gronam the Ox and his five sages—Treitel Fool, Sendor Donkey, Schmendrick Numskull, Chazkel Pinhead, and Dopey Lekisch.

Isaac Bashevis Singer wrote novels, memoirs, short-story collections, children's books, and plays. Most of his fiction is set in Jewish, Eastern European villages that were destroyed in World War II. In 1978 he was awarded the Nobel Prize in literature. He was a member of the *Cricket* Editorial Board from 1973 to 1991, the year of his death.

Meet Your Author

Isaac B. Singer — About Myself

Isaac Bashevis Singer, circa 1973

I WAS BORN IN the village of Radzymin, Poland, in 1904. When I was three years old, my parents moved to Warsaw, the capital of Poland.

My father was an orthodox rabbi, and our house was a house of holy books and learning. Other children had toys; I played with the books in my father's library. I began to "write" before I even knew the alphabet. I took my father's pen, dipped it in ink, and started to scribble. At school I amazed my fellow students with fantastic stories. Once I told them that my father was a king, and they believed me.

I came to the United States in 1935 and learned to speak English. But I write all of my books first in Yiddish, and then I translate them into English. I have written eleven books for grown-ups and ten for children. I like to write for children. I think they are the best readers. All of my works have been translated into a number of languages.

I live in New York with my wife, Alma. Our son, whose name is Israel, lives in the land of Israel. He is a teacher and a journalist. I have three grandchildren, one girl and two boys.

My hobby is taking long walks in New York. I love birds and all animals, and I believe that men can learn a lot from God's creatures.

Cricket, November 1973

*Clifton Fadiman,
circa 1973*

Clifton Fadiman and the Beginnings of *Cricket*

by Anne Fadiman

THE OLDER my father got, the younger his favorite people were. By the time he died in 1999, at ninety-five, his most unalloyed affection was reserved for babies—the only people who, as he put it, "hadn't yet harmed anyone." He had a horror of war and meanness, so this was a high compliment.

During much of his adult life, my father's beau idéal was between eight and twelve years old: a smart but un-nerdy boy or girl who was capable of disappearing for hours into a corner of the attic with a copy of *Tom Sawyer*. This was the kind of reader he had in mind when he wrote, in a 1945 essay called "My Life Is an Open Book,"

> The child does not interpose a continuous, fuzzy, wavering screen of personal desires and wishful visions between himself and the page. On the contrary, he and the page are one.

Young readers interested him far more than grown-up readers;

he believed them capable of far deeper responses to literature and endowed with far better taste. This interest expressed itself in many forms: four children's books of his own; several essays on children and reading; a long article on children's literature in the *Encyclopaedia Britannica;* afterwords to a set of classics for young people; a three-volume anthology of international children's literature; and, at one glorious point in my early childhood, a job judging a children's book contest—glorious because dozens of books were delivered to our house daily, and my brother and I were permitted to help unpack them from their Jiffy bags and array them alphabetically on shelves and (after they overflowed) on window sills and bureau tops and floors. And of course we got to read them.

You can imagine my father's excitement when, in 1972, he got a call from Marianne Carus asking if he'd help found a new magazine for children, one that (in the words of Jeffrey Hart, a syndicated columnist who reviewed its first issue) would be based on a tripartite premise: "that there are powerful anti-reading trends at work in American culture (true), that it is terribly important for these to be resisted (true), and that they can be resisted by literature properly selected (to be decided)."

My father wanted to be one of the deciders. As senior editor, he spent much of that year working with the Caruses to plan just what kind of trend-bucking magazine this was to be. Its name, he told me, was to be *Cricket;* its entomological theme would be carried out by a young artist named Trina Schart Hyman, whose crew of highly educated bugs (assisted by an occasional snail or bird) would patrol the margins, explicating abstruse words. His own comments to the readers would appear in several of the early issues under the name "Old Cricket."

My father was delighted that *Cricket* had no interest in restricting its vocabulary to monosyllables. After all, in 1964 he had written a book called *Wally the Wordworm,* in which a voracious bookworm was unsatisfied by eating the words in

> a picture book with only seventy different words in it—all
> > short,
> > flat,
> > bare,
> > dull,
> > poor,
> > thin,
> > old ones that kept repeating themselves. They were
> > good enough for a stupid worm, for a slow worm, for a
> > worm who didn't care about real nourishment. But not
> > good enough for Wally.

They weren't good enough for my father either, and he was therefore highly gratified that *Cricket*'s first issue contained the word "terpsichorean." (It appeared in T. S. Eliot's "Song of the Jellicles" and was glossed by a small insect who raised its leg in an arabesque and explained that "Terpsichorean means dancing.")

He was also overjoyed that *Cricket,* as an enthusiastic critic named Leslie Hascom observed, did not "smack of 'relevance'. . . . It is literary in the sense that what it purveys is imagination." Imagination! That was the thing—the heart of every great piece of children's literature. He himself had written:

> The so-called "better" juveniles that flood the book-
> dealers' shelves every year—the skillfully constructed,
> highly educational, carefully suited-to-age, morally sanitary,
> psychologically impeccable children's books—don't really
> make much of a dent on the child's consciousness. They
> are constructed for "the market." I don't mean the commer-
> cial market, but the market that is supposed to be the child's

brain, as if that brain were a kind of transaction center in which each transaction was expressible in definite educational quanta.

It was clear that *Cricket* would never regard a child's mind as a transaction center. To put it another way (in a lovely line from Rabelais that my father quoted in an early ad for *Cricket,* an open letter addressed to "Dear Fellow-Parent"): *A child is not a vase to be filled, but a fire to be lit.*

With Marianne Carus, my father wrote three hundred letters to writers around the world asking for manuscripts. He read stacks of stories and poems, sometimes until 3 A.M. And he talked widely to the press. As I look at the old clips from 1973, I can hear his voice, rising with enthusiasm:

> Unless children's tastes are degraded and altered, they are naturally good. We have two basic notions for *Cricket.* The first is based on maintaining standards of the highest quality in both text and art, and the second is delight in the surprise and fun and laughter that should be part of being a child.
>
> A child who never has the opportunity to compare values will settle for what he's given now and later in life. If shoddiness is all you know, how can you learn to reject it?

At the end of that interview, he told the reporter: "At the risk of sounding sentimental, I must say I like children because to be young is to have hope, to have almost infinite options. Children are malleable and plastic. Adults are frozen." But *he* wasn't. Old Cricket, who was sixty-nine when he said that, was as malleable as a child of ten, for the simple reason that that child still lived inside him. His years with *Cricket* breathed further life into that child, and ensured that he would never become frozen.

Anne Fadiman is an award-winning essayist, author, and editor. Her first book, *The Spirit Catches You and You Fall Down,* won the National Book Critics Circle Award and the Boston Book Review Anne Rea Jewell Nonfiction Prize. Since 1998 she has served as editor of the quarterly journal *The American Scholar.*

Old Cricket's Family Album

by Lloyd Alexander

Lloyd Alexander at the first Board meeting in 1972

MARK TWAIN ONCE said that his brightest, most vivid memories were of things that never happened. In my case, I have to admit that a lot of the snapshots in my internal photo album are a little out of focus, with occasional double exposures.

For example, I'm not absolutely sure exactly where Marianne, Blouke, and I first met. The background is fuzzy, but I think it's a reception following a conference at Drexel University, Philadelphia. The location isn't significant. The consequences are.

In my mental snapshot, we're at the fringe of a crowd, in close conversation while everyone else is assaulting the refreshment table, with Marianne calmly talking about a bold and daring project: creating a children's literary magazine. An amazing venture. As far as I knew, there had been nothing like it since the legendary *St. Nicholas Magazine.*

The sandwiches were vanishing rapidly, but I was too caught up in Marianne's project to care much about food. The idea of a magazine of genuine literary quality fascinated me. Marianne

34

added one thing more: Would I be on the Board of Advisors? I had never advised anybody about anything. I also suspected it might involve work and thought, two occupations I always make great efforts to avoid. Marianne has a way of making things irresistible, so I agreed. Marianne told me she'd be in touch, and we left it at that.

Time, in the literary world, is elastic. It shrinks too short when a deadline looms. It stretches to painful infinity when an author, say, waits to hear his editor's reaction to his manuscript. In general, though, the literary pace tends toward the leisurely. I expected to hear from Marianne in, oh, maybe a year or two. No, after only a few months I had a letter from her announcing an upcoming board meeting. I had not a clue what to prepare for or what advice I could give. I certainly had not the least inkling of what lay in store over the next thirty years.

We gathered in a river resort at Starved Rock Lodge in northern Illinois. In the course of time, we would meet in other venues: conference facilities on the University of Chicago campus; in Tarrytown, Washington Irving country in upstate New York; in Manhattan's St. Moritz Hotel. Starved Rock, I think, was everyone's favorite. The air was clear and crisp, the atmosphere conducive to mental effort and sharpening the appetite for great meals. The scenery was spectacular.

The advisory board was pretty spectacular, too. Marianne, who seems to know everybody in the world by their first names, had invited the most knowledgeable people in children's literature from England, Germany, Canada, and the United States. Several of these I knew by reputation; Paul Heins, editor of the *Horn Book Magazine,* Eleanor Cameron, splendid novelist and essayist, and I had been fond friends for some years.

Marianne was editor-in-chief. Senior editor was Clifton Fadiman, host of my favorite radio quiz show when I was a boy:

"Information, Please" was surely the most sophisticated and wittiest of programs, and one of the most popular (refuting the idea that intellectual content and mass media are mutually exclusive). Fadiman had a truly encyclopedic mind. If there was something he didn't know, it probably wasn't worth knowing. And there he was, sounding exactly like himself; and there I was, addressing him by his nickname, "Kip."

As for the rest of the staff, I hadn't seen so much creative energy and bright, young talent all in one room at the same time. My best plan, I decided, was to keep my mouth shut and look as if I were thinking brilliant thoughts, too deep to express.

The art director was no less than a genius: Trina Schart Hyman. Her work had always dazzled me. But, never in my wildest imaginings could I have foreseen, over the years, that she would illustrate most of my stories in *Cricket.* More than that, Trina would do superb jacket illustrations for a good many of my novels.

Here, I can't resist turning the album pages nearly twenty years into the future. Trina and I had collaborated on *The Fortune-Tellers,* the most magnificent picture book I had ever seen. We were, that year, at the American Library Association convention, signing books in our publisher's booth, when a young woman hurried up.

"I'm so delighted to see you," she told me. "Wonderful! I thought you were dead."

I was at a loss to come up with any kind of reply. Trina, who has a wit that operates at the speed of light, took less than a nanosecond to speak up:

"He is. And he's looking better now than when he was alive."

Forgive the digression. I'll turn the pages back to our first board meeting.

Marianne welcomed us graciously and spoke a little while

LLOYD ALEXANDER

about *Cricket,* as the magazine was tentatively called: her vision of it, what she hoped we could accomplish. A kind of mission statement of goals, content, level of quality.

Two things gradually dawned on me. First, quietly and confidently, Marianne was, in effect, talking about creating nothing less than the world's best magazine of children's literature. Second, she was really going to do it. It was going to happen. I think we all knew it would happen. I had the sense of being present at a historic moment.

For the rest, we discussed contents, editorial mix, general principles. There would be regular features: letters from young readers, an ongoing cartoon strip with a permanent cast of characters: Ladybug, Sluggo, Ugly Bird, and others, all with their unique personalities.

The last page in the book was to be called "Old Cricket Says," a kind of editorial page with a number of functions. It would be the one place where *Cricket* could express opinions, comment on some particular situation, expand, or offer sidelights on the magazine's contents. It could also be sheer fun, ranging freely over any subject in the world. Old Cricket would speak in his own tone of voice, his own persona; a familiar, recognizable character. As if he really existed. (I would come to believe he did exist.)

Marianne invited us all to contribute an "Old Cricket Says" on whatever subjects interested us. I swear she turned a glance on me, indicating it would be a good idea if I made myself useful from time to time. (I think she must have noticed my tendency to woolgather and sidestep doing actual work.)

Caught up in the spirit of the moment, I rashly promised to see what I could do.

I had never written literary magazine articles. "Old Cricket Says" was not an easy form. For one thing, it was short—always more difficult than a longer piece where there's room to wander around. It was, of necessity, limited to a single page, a couple of dozen lines. A mini-essay where every word had to pull its own weight. But I tried my hand at it. Marianne liked it and even suggested my writing a few more. Which I did.

For some while, many of us took turns being Old Cricket.

Depending on deadlines and other circumstances, Marianne and her editorial staff would write the essay. Little by little, however, I found myself writing the pieces more or less regularly. I relished taking on the guise of Old Cricket. In the course of thirty years, I think I gradually turned into Old Cricket himself.

Maybe it's a good thing that we can't foresee the future. It would spoil the surprises. I would, over time, have many of them. One of the biggest: Marianne and Trina let me realize a secret ambition.

It was an ambition I never dared to admit openly. Too shocking and ridiculous: I had always yearned to be an artist. Trina discovered my terrible secret more or less by accident.

We had been sitting together at the table during one of the board meetings, as often happened—Trina as the mischief-maker of the class, and I as the classroom dullard. Marianne, that afternoon, had brought in a technical consultant who talked in detail about readership, demographics, distribution—serious, nuts-and-bolts questions that every publication has to consider.

No matter how hard I tried to grasp these subjects, my mind began drifting. I reverted to a disgusting habit that had been my downfall from the days of my fifth-grade arithmetic classes. Instead of taking notes on the yellow pad in front of me—I'm sorry, I couldn't help it—I doodled silly pictures.

Trina glimpsed what I was doing. My secret was out. I had been caught red-handed; worse, caught by a world-famous artist.

I braced myself, ready to be mocked, taunted, scorned, and dismissed as a bumbling incompetent.

Trina peered at my scribbles. She had a wicked glint in her eyes, which I should have recognized as a fiendish plan being hatched.

"Not too bad," she said.

Be careful what you wish for. You might get it. Soon after that, Marianne wrote asking if I'd write a short piece about my childhood reading. It would even be illustrated. Trina, she told me, thought I'd be just the one for the job.

Naturally, I panicked. I had never been given a real artistic assignment. After I picked myself up from the floor, I did manage to produce a drawing. Marianne accepted it along with the article. I suddenly became a published illustrator.

Marianne let me illustrate a couple more pieces, including about a dozen line drawings for a long, wildly comical poem by William Cole. I considered that my finest achievement.

"Just don't quit your day job," Trina said.

Riffling through a few more snapshots, I see how many connections *Cricket* would have with much of my work. In fact, two novels grew from stories I wrote for the magazine.

One example: Marianne thought it would be fun to begin a story and let readers suggest their own ending for it. I worked out the tale of Miklan, a young scamp who spins a preposterous yarn for the town baker as a scheme to get free pastries. There were plenty of story elements and raw material for any number of endings. I myself had no idea how it could end. Since I wouldn't have to write the conclusion, I didn't worry about it.

The first installment had been published and the second was in production when Marianne changed her mind.

"We'll really need a third part," she told me.

But, I asked, what about the end?

Two spot illustrations by Lloyd Alexander for William Cole's "A Boy Named Mary Jane," January 1974 Cricket

"Ah, that," she said. "I think you should be the one to do it."

Ouch! I had, so to speak, written myself into a corner. In desperation, I finally did come up with a surprise ending—surprising myself more than anyone else.

But—the unforeseen consequences. A good many years later, when I was in a mood to write a comic novel, with interconnected trickster tales, I remembered that rascal Miklan. Instead of a boy, the trickster would be a girl: *Gypsy Rizka.*

Another example: For years, I had been flirting with the idea of something involving my odd assortment of relatives, but had never found a way to deal with the material. I had given up on it. Marianne, however, urged me to do something autobiographical. That started me thinking again. For Marianne, I wrote an affectionate memoir of my father's box of ancient artifacts. It stirred up long-forgotten family dramas. I finally understood what I wanted to do. The result was an autobiography pretending to be a novel: *The Gawgon and the Boy.*

Just a couple more snapshots. Long after that first Board meeting, Trina and I were at presentation ceremonies in Burlington, Vermont: Trina to accept the Boston Globe–Horn Book Award for her illustrations; and I for the text of *The Fortune-Tellers.* Trina's daughter Katrin was there with her husband, Eugéne, and firstborn son, Michou. All had served as characters in the book. (Trina had sneaked me into one of the pictures, too.)

"When I was a little girl, I wrote you a fan letter," Katrin told me. "You didn't write a letter back. You only sent me some kind of booklet."

I hung my head. It was true. I remembered. I hadn't realized she was *the* Katrin Hyman. I stammered that I had been tired, up to my neck in work that day. Lame excuses, I admitted.

"It's all right," Katrin said. "I forgive you."

LLOYD ALEXANDER

A last photo, a musical one. Blouke is a first-rate cellist. Marianne plays the violin better than I ever will. So, when they visited Drexel Hill one evening, I borrowed a cello and an extra violin from the local school, and we played chamber music. One of the Carus daughters, Tina, joined us with her flute. As my Paris-born wife, Janine, listened uncritically, we tried a Mozart flute quartet, K. 285. (We made do without a viola and doubled up on the violin part.)

Marianne and Tina had an animated, mother-daughter discussion whether to count "and *one*" or "*one* and." That got sorted out; and, in the slow movement, with the rest of us doing a hushed pizzicato, Tina took the leading voice in those haunting passages. Beautiful. The notes still linger in my mind.

These snapshots have been altogether personal. I leave it to the experts to deal with the complexities of running a magazine. Scholars could write doctoral dissertations on the paperwork covering Marianne's desk. One impudent wiseacre—let him be nameless—called it "The Leaning Tower of Peru."

Old Cricket's family album, I hope, gives at least a hint of the general atmosphere. During three decades, we grew to be friends as well as colleagues. From the beginning, I think all of us agreed with philosopher-essayist Dr. Wayne Dyer's principle: Do what you love, love what you do. To which, add: And do nothing but your best.

It worked. It always will.

Lloyd Alexander has written over thirty books for children, including the Prydain Chronicles. His many awards include the Newbery Medal for *The High King* as well as the National Book Award for *Westmark* and *The Marvelous Misadventures of Sebastian*.

A HUNGRY READER

by
Lloyd
Alexander

I WAS ALWAYS A hungry reader—in more ways than one. I gobbled up stories and never had my fill. At the same time, I wanted a real taste of whatever food the people in the stories were eating. Reading about the Mad Tea Party in *Alice in Wonderland,* I pleaded for a cup of tea, bread and butter, and treacle (treacle, I guessed, was something like pancake syrup). My poor mother! How did she ever find patience to put up with her son's reading-and-eating habits!

In *Treasure Island* (you'll be reading it soon), bloodthirsty pirates nearly find young Jim Hawkins hiding in an apple barrel.

Cricket, September 1973

So, of course, I had to munch an apple. The flavor of those pages and the flavor of that apple were both delicious.

However, when Robin Hood and his Merry Men dined on venison washed down with flagons of brown October ale, I could only make believe with a hamburger and a glass of root beer. A dish of cornmeal mush took the place of Indian maize when, sitting cross-legged under our living room lamp, I devoured *The Song of Hiawatha.* Our neighborhood grocer never sold—nor had we money to buy—anything like the rich feasts at *King Arthur's Round Table.* Instead of the roast goose of *A Christmas Carol,* I gnawed a chicken leg. The pages of *Winnie-the-Pooh,* along with my fingers, got sticky with honey. My mother's cookbook held no recipe for the nectar and ambrosia of Greek mythology; I settled for cornflakes and grape juice. Zeus must have smiled at that.

In time, to sighs of relief from my parents, I lost the habit of eating what I read about; but never my hunger for reading. I think the stories we love as children stay with us, somewhere in our hearts, to feed our imaginations. We never outgrow our need for them, any more than we outgrow our need for food. But, to me, the books I love are better than a feast.

A Gift from Gertrude Stein

**by
Lloyd
Alexander**

*Illustrated by
Mike Eagle*

ARTISTS AND WRITERS have always fallen in love with the beautiful city of Paris. Many American authors have chosen to live there, and one of the most famous was Gertrude Stein. As for the least famous, I could easily have claimed that distinction in the autumn of 1945. I was in the Army then, supposedly a translator, mainly a jeep driver. I preferred to think of myself as a writer, though I had written very little and published nothing at all. I admired Gertrude Stein's books, longed for a chance to meet her and pay my respects in person. Whether she wanted to meet me was open to question.

Cricket, January 1977

There was one way to find out. Her telephone number was in the directory, like any common mortal's, and I made up my mind to call her. However, when the moment came to do it, I began quaking in terror. A dozen times I picked up the phone and put it down again. Finally, telling myself that a writer must be courageous in all circumstances, I managed to dial, praying nobody would be home.

When a voice answered, my carefully worded speech of introduction immediately flew out of my head. I stammered and babbled, realizing it was Gertrude Stein herself on the other end of the line. To my amazement, she invited me to visit her the next afternoon at her apartment on Rue Christine, Number 5.

The invitation terrified me as much as it thrilled me. She had been friends with painters like Picasso and Matisse, novelists like Ernest Hemingway and F. Scott Fitzgerald, and so many other artists, poets, and composers that I couldn't imagine myself setting foot into this magical world.

That night I couldn't sleep, trying hopelessly to imagine what to say at our meeting. According to all I had read, she was a brilliant conversationalist and sharp-tongued with people who annoyed her. Born in Allegheny, Pennsylvania, she had lived in Vienna, San Francisco, Boston, London, New York, and had traveled throughout Europe. She had studied philosophy, psychology, literature, history, and art; she once planned to become a doctor and had been one of the first women admitted to Johns Hopkins School of Medicine. Her goal was to use language in ways never used before. Even people who hadn't read her books knew the famous line from one of her poems: "Rose is a rose is a rose is a rose."

Many critics at first made fun of her work, judging it meaningless and foolish. But she answered, "Now listen! I'm no fool. I know that in daily life we don't go around saying '. . . is a . . . is a . . . is a . . . .' But you have to put some strangeness, as something

IS GERTRUDE STEIN REALLY VERY FAMOUS?

OF COURSE! LLOYD ALEXANDER WOULDN'T HAVE BEEN SCARED TO VISIT JUST ANY OLD BUGGY!

GEE! . . . I WONDER HOW YOU GET FAMOUS!

WELL, I GUESS YOU HAVE TO BE VERY, VERY SMART — AND VERY, VERY TALENTED, AND VERY AMBITIOUS . . . .

. . . AND VERY LUCKY!

A GIFT FROM GERTRUDE STEIN

unexpected, into the structure of the sentence in order to bring back vitality to the noun."

When a journalist asked her, "Why don't you write the way you talk?" she replied, "Why don't you read the way I write? I do talk as I write, but you can hear better than you can see. You are accustomed to see with your eyes differently to the way you hear with your ears, and perhaps that is what makes it hard to read my works."

Many of her books were indeed difficult, and understanding them demanded a mind as complex as her own. Yet I knew she disliked formal education. At college, during one final exam, she had simply written, "I am so sorry, but really I do not feel a bit like an examination paper in philosophy today." Anyone who hated final exams as much as I did would surely be sympathetic.

I also knew that Gertrude Stein had been warmhearted and welcoming to American soldiers, had visited them in Army camps, had eaten with them in mess halls—eager to talk and delighted to listen.

But on the afternoon of our meeting, none of this did anything to calm my nerves. When I reached Rue Christine, a little street on the left bank of the River Seine, I had to fight the temptation to turn and run. I knocked at Number 5. There was no mistaking the woman who opened the door.

She wore a long skirt of dark, heavy wool and a sleeveless jacket over a workaday shirt. Her iron gray hair was cropped even shorter than my military cut. Gertrude Stein had been described as looking like a Roman emperor or an Aztec figure carved in rock. But to me, as we shook hands, she seemed not at all stern or monumental. The deep lines only gentled her face, instead of making it severe and forbidding. Her eyes were clear and penetrating, her glance shrewd but full of good humor;

BUT YOU HAVE TO WORK HARD, TOO!

JUST THINK! ONCE LLOYD ALEXANDER WAS ANY OLD BUGGY, JUST LIKE US!

AND NOW HE'S FAMOUS!

MAYBE FAME IS CONTAGIOUS, AND HE CAUGHT IT FROM GERTRUDE STEIN!

DO YOU REMEMBER SEEING THIS LLOYD, WHEN WE LIVED IN PARIS?

NO, BUT I DO REMEMBER THE HONEY!

LLOYD ALEXANDER

though she was in her seventies then, her smile was quick as a young girl's.

I was still too flustered to take in much of this, and altogether bedazzled when we stepped into the living room. What seized me first, as surely as if it had taken me by the shirt front, was the huge portrait Picasso had painted of her. To me, it is a masterpiece and one of the most striking portraits in modern art.

And more masterpieces covered the walls. The room sang with the colors and shapes of a hundred paintings and drawings by nearly every great modern artist, most of whom she had known personally. Sculptures, figures, objects, sprang to life on the mantel over the fireplace. I could scarcely take my eyes away.

Gertrude Stein was watching me, enjoying my enjoyment; she urged me to look as closely as I wanted. More paintings were stored in the basement, she told me; but, fine though they were, she had no room for them all.

Suddenly I realized I was still clutching the gifts I had brought: a jar of honey my parents had sent me, a box of cornflakes I had saved out of my breakfast that morning. These were all I could find in the way of presents. I blurted out my compliments and handed her the packages.

She beamed as if they were lavish offerings. She adored honey, impossible to find in Paris these days. Cornflakes—exactly what she had been looking for. I heaved a sigh of delighted relief. Before I could say more, Basket, her big poodle, bounded into the room and frisked about me like an enormous white sheep. Gertrude Stein laughed at the joyful welcome Basket was giving me. I began feeling comfortable as we sat down. Basket, at the side of his mistress, looked ready at any moment to join the conversation.

I wish I could report that we discussed deep and weighty problems of art and literature. The truth is, we didn't. She wanted to hear about my home, my parents. At the tales of my numerous Army misadventures, she laughed richly and wholeheartedly. Instead of talking about her own work, she was much more interested in talking about mine—what I had done, and what I planned to do. When I confessed I hoped to be a writer, she nodded and answered, "Yes, if that's what you really want, then you will be."

But she warned me it would be difficult. She told me how discouraging it had been for her, how long she had worked before publishing anything—and then only to be severely criticized. It had taken years for readers to discover her books. Still, she kept on. Everything in living is a matter of finding out what you are, and she knew she was a writer.

We talked back and forth for almost an hour, then sat quietly. I felt the time had come to take my leave and thanked her, though not half as eloquently as I would have wished. Even so, she invited me to come back the following week, an invitation I gladly accepted.

That autumn, I visited her several more times. Basket was always on hand, always in high spirits. But I missed an even more famous member of the family circle: Gertrude Stein's lifelong friend and secretary, Alice B. Toklas. If there had been one single book that assured Gertrude Stein's reputation, it was her graceful and witty *Autobiography of Alice B. Toklas.* The title was a sly joke because she was merely pretending to be Alice, and was writing as much about herself as about her companion. However, the subject of the "autobiography" was busy elsewhere, and we never met.

With winter coming, the days had begun drawing in. She told me she felt weary, that she might go to the south of France and rest. She would try to stay in touch with me. But it was the last we were to see of each other.

I was in the midst of being discharged from the Army to attend the University of Paris, and further enmeshed in the red

WHAT'S AN <u>AUTOBIOGRAPHY</u>? IS IT THE STORY OF A CAR?

NO, SLUGGO — IT'S THE STORY OF A PERSON'S LIFE, WRITTEN BY THAT PERSON! I COULD WRITE MY OWN <u>AUTOBIOGRAPHY</u>, BUT IF I WROTE YOUR LIFE'S STORY, IT WOULD BE A <u>BIOGRAPHY</u>!

SOMEDAY, I'LL WRITE THE <u>AUTOBIOGRAPHY</u> OF ANNA P. AUNT!

OH, NO YOU WON'T, MARIANNE! YOU WRITE YOUR OWN AND LEAVE MINE TO ME!

LLOYD ALEXANDER

tape of getting military permission to marry a Parisian girl named Janine. In early spring, Janine sailed for the United States with other war brides, and I followed as soon as I could, deciding I'd much rather be home in Philadelphia with my wife than finish the term at the University. I sent a note to Gertrude Stein and, before leaving France, telephoned the Rue Christine apartment. There was no answer. At home, I learned that she died at the end of July in the American Hospital in Paris.

I remember her giving me a book during one of our afternoons, signing the flyleaf for me and adding, "May it be as good as he hopes." Indeed it was, but I realize now her gift was much more than that. Although eight years were to go by before her prediction came true and my own books began to be published, what she gave me was an understanding that art and literature don't magically appear on museum walls and library bookshelves. They're the work of real women and men who lived in the real world, as much as they live for us in the pages they write and the canvases they paint. All art is a kind of miracle, but the great books we read, the great pictures we admire—these are human miracles.

Sweeter than water or cream or ice. Sweeter than bells of roses. Sweeter than winter or summer or spring. Sweeter than pretty posies. Sweeter than anything is my queen and loving is her nature.

Loving and good and delighted and best is her little King and Sire whose devotion is entire who has but one desire to express the love which is hers to inspire.

—*Gertrude Stein*

Trina Schart Hyman,
Cricket *Editorial Board Meeting 1972*

I'm Not Sure If I'm Making This Up, But...

a conversation between Trina Schart Hyman and John Grandits about the early days of *Cricket*

Trina Schart Hyman was art director of Cricket *magazine from the first issue, September 1973, through the March 1979 issue. John Grandits was the designer of the magazine starting with the second issue, and was art director from the April 1979 issue through the September 1985 issue. In October 2002 they pulled out a pile of ancient* Cricket *magazines and talked about the old days.*

John: How did you get mixed up with Marianne and Blouke Carus in the first place?

Trina: I was doing illustrations for their textbook division. The Caruses came out here to Lyme, New Hampshire, to explain about the Open Court Readers. They were looking for an illustrator and maybe they had seen something of mine in a bookstore. They wanted to use fairy tales and folk tales to teach kids to read instead of Dick and Jane, and that was something I

John Grandits in January 1973

totally agreed with. So I agreed to do illustrations for their readers. I must have done twenty or thirty illustrations for them. Then Marianne called during the summer of 1971. She said that she and Blouke wanted to talk about a magazine idea. I had some trepidations about it. I'd never had any experience with magazine work at all. And they wanted me to be an art director. I didn't know what an art director did. I mean, I didn't know anything about art direction. I didn't even know any other working artist in the world. And I didn't know anything about production.

John: But you had done books already.

Trina: I had done books. I knew how to put a dummy together. I knew how to spec type. I had learned that in art school. I knew about typefaces. I knew about the printing process. I knew about color separation. There was no thought in those days of having a full-color magazine. It was going to be black-and-white at first. But I pushed for two colors—black and a second color. It needed some color.

John: Had you illustrated readers for other companies?

Trina: I had worked for Ginn and for Houghton Mifflin and for Bobbs-Merrill and for Addison-Wesley. It was horrible, punishing work. You put the same amount of effort and care and imagination into it—or I did anyway—but the editors were crazy people. You couldn't show navels, and in those days you couldn't show a black child, everyone had to be white. The only reason I worked for textbooks at all was because they paid very well.

It was good money, and I couldn't afford to turn down any job. And I figured it was good experience for me also. I've been illustrating professionally for forty-three years. I've illustrated over two hundred books. And there are only a few books that make a living for me. Those royalty checks come in twice a year, and that's what I live on. Three books out of two hundred is like going to a slot machine. But I made a vow right before I started to work for *Cricket,* that if I got into the profession and my books started to sell that I would never, ever work for textbooks again, no matter what, and that has been my goal, and you can put that on my tombstone: "She lived up to her vow. She never had to do textbook work again."

Anyhow, the Caruses compared to all the other textbook publishers seemed to me to be the most charming, reasonable, good-tempered, intelligent people I'd met so far.

John: They found all the rules involving textbook illustration as ludicrous as we did.

Trina: Right. So, I was tickled to work for the Open Court readers. It was a pleasure to do business with them. They respected whatever work I did, and they were very pleasant to work with.

So, when Marianne asked me if I would be the art director for a new children's magazine they wanted to publish, and I said that I knew absolutely nothing about being an art director, she very nicely said, We'll help. Why don't you come out to La Salle, Illinois. That's where the main office was. We've got a great library of children's books from all over the world. You can look at these books and you pick out what art you like. We'll find the artists for you, and you write to them.

I went out there and spent three or four days. It was great. Looking at pictures all day long and writing down the names of the illustrators I liked. The books were literally from all over: Swiss books, French books, German books, English books. I got a list of artists together, and the staff in La Salle found out addresses.

The most important thing to do next was to write a letter that would get all of these artists that I wanted into the magazine. The pay *Cricket* was offering was very little, so I had to think of some reason the illustrators would want to work for *Cricket*. So, I thought, What would make *me* want to work for this magazine? What would pull me in? I thought it would be tempting for the artists if they could do anything they wanted to do. If you've spent your whole life drawing bunnies and chickies and duckies and you love it, then you can draw bunnies, chickies, and duckies for us. But if you've always wanted to draw intimidating, surreal-looking monsters, you can do that. This magazine is an excuse to play and to find out stuff about yourself as an artist as well as to draw kids. So, it had to sound like fun to do. I sent out that first letter to my list of artists.

I don't have a copy of that letter here, but what I said at the end of the letter was, I would like to make this into a magazine for kids that is like the *New Yorker.* A magazine for children as much fun to look at, and as sophisticated, and as clever, and as funny, and as serious as the *New Yorker* is for grownups. I got an amazing response. I heard from people I never thought I would hear from. For instance, Garth Williams and Nancy Ekholm Burkert and Shirley Hughes. Artists in Europe as well as here. Enrico Arno and Paul Galdone, and Nonny Hogrogian—a lot of people said yes. Oh, the letters that came back were works of art themselves—they were fabulous. All of these letters, the whole *Cricket* file, all the letters that I ever wrote to the artists and all of the letters that they wrote back to me are at the Special Collections in the University of Connecticut. So anyone can get them and see them if they want to. You know the artists drew all over them. Erik Blegvad draws all over his envelopes—he makes a work of art out of the envelopes. There is some fabulous original art in this correspondence.

One of the letters that intrigued me the most and made me laugh the hardest was from Jan Adkins.

John: He writes a great letter.

Trina: Oh man, does he write a good letter, and it was all in that beautiful calligraphy of his.

John: Yes, he uses that Carolingian Round-hand.

Trina: One of our starting-up problems was a logo for the magazine. We had the title. Marianne Carus wanted to call it *Cricket,* and I thought the name was catchy. So we needed to have a logo like *Ms.* or the *New Yorker.* I had written to Jan Adkins because I saw his book on *Sandcastles.* Oh

man, I thought, this is the kind of guy we need for this magazine. He's full of information. He can draw. He can write. He can do anything and whoever heard of him? So I wrote to Jan and said, Would you be willing to do the logo for us in your beautiful calligraphy? And he did, and that was it. It's the *Cricket* logo that you see today.

John: At the first Editorial Advisory Board meeting at Starved Rock Lodge in Illinois, all those famous people Blouke and Marianne had gathered came to talk about *Cricket.*

Trina: I knew of Clifton Fadiman, who didn't? We all grew up with that name. I knew of Lloyd Alexander, but I had never met him. I was shouting with glee to meet this guy. Eleanor Cameron, I knew because I had illustrated a book of hers way back called *A Room Made of Windows.* I knew Virginia Haviland because she was a friend of one of my Boston editors. Sheila Egoff I didn't know. Paul Heins I knew because he was a Boston children's book person, the head of the *Horn Book.* Walter Scherf, the director of the International Youth Library in Munich, came in a Bavarian suit. He looked like a professor of German history and spoke with a really thick accent. Kaye Webb, very British, was built like a ship under full sail and with a big bosom and iron-gray hair sweeping back. She was the first person I ever knew to use a cell phone, some kind of personal phone that she carried around with her. Marcia Leonard was there, tall and beautiful, and she had long, brown hair down to her waist, and she was just as enigmatic as she was smart.

John: Clifton Fadiman was ostensibly the leader.

Trina: He led the meeting, but Marianne swiftly took over. You know she's been top dog right from the beginning. I remember saying to Blouke, you know I'm worried about Marianne with all these high-powered strong-minded guys around, like you, and Kip, and Walter. Blouke laughed and said, Don't worry about Marianne, she can hold her own. And he was right.

Before I left New Hampshire for the meeting, I had collected a little jar of real live crickets. I took them to Illinois.

At the meeting, at what I thought was an appropriate moment, I brought the jar out of my tote bag and put it in the middle of the table and opened it. All the crickets hopped out. I thought this would be a good launch for *Cricket* magazine. But I also wanted to put the point across that I thought we were all being a little serious about this magazine. It was supposed to be for children and not an intellectual, stuffy learning experience. If you are going to reach kids, you have to be a little goofy, because otherwise they're not going to hear you. There's got to be something to laugh at. And there has to be something to hold their interest throughout. All along, I had thought the way to do that was with a cartoon strip. Who doesn't love cartoons, right? This idea, as you might imagine, was not greeted with wild enthusiasm.

John: It could be that the Board had this idea that cartoons meant *Archie* or *Superman* comics. I bet that was hard to sell!

Trina: It *was* a hard sell, even when I mentioned *Little Nemo,* something that had a story line that was connected to the magazine and would keep the kids going through and want to read the next issue. There would be characters that they could identify with, characters that were like kids. Everybody was against it at first. Then I said, Well let me do a couple and show you what I mean. Let's just try it. So I'm not sure if I'm making this up or if it really happened, but I think I did the first couple of cartoons then and there.

John: Those characters, those bugs Cricket and Ladybug, appear in your work earlier.

Actually you were used to drawing little buggies.

Trina: I loved to draw buggies. Still do. Like any little kid I identify with little things. And since I was a little kid, I've believed that everything in the world has a story—it has a life and you can talk to it, even if it is a worm or a flea. I'm the kind of person who after it rains goes down the road and picks up all the worms and puts them back on the grass and says, "Have a good life." I was a natural for this cartoon strip, I guess. The one person who stood by me was Lloyd Alexander. He absolutely agreed that we needed some humor. We needed some light touch that was fun and visual. That's when I learned that Lloyd was also an artist and had always wanted to be an illustrator. He's a good cartoonist! So with Lloyd's support, eventually everyone bought the idea of a *Cricket* cartoon. It started out with Cricket and Ladybug, and I guess a younger cricket, Charlie. George, the worm, was there at the beginning. Sluggo, too. The cast of characters grew over the years. I kept adding. Also, Blouke wanted some way to explain the hard words—some way to define the words right there on the page. I hated that idea from a design standpoint.

John: Using the bugs in the margins to explain the words was a really nice touch. It especially worked well in the early issues because you also used them to continue the story line a bit. And you put in little jokes and remarks. Pretty soon the kids were going through the magazine to read the cartoons first. Then they'd read all the vocabulary words in case they were saying anything funny.

Trina: These first cartoons are very clumsy.

John: The characters have grown a lot throughout the years.

Trina: I didn't know anything about headline type, so every single title in this first issue was hand lettered.

John: And some of it was very complicated, so you must have gone nuts?

Trina: No, I loved it. You know me, I love to do lettering. But the big criticism with this pilot issue was that it was just too homemade-looking. It was too funky and hippie-looking because of all the hand lettering, and that's when you came in.

John: I was hired right after the pilot issue to be the designer for the Open Court textbook division. The first week I arrived, this complaint came up, and so Marianne wanted me to take over the design for

Cricket. I guess to get rid of the homemade look. I had a Bauhaus design school background, and so my reaction to the first issue was a raised eyebrow. It was so loose.

Trina: You were incredibly disapproving. But you have to tell about the first time you came here with the Caruses. Come on.

John: It was my first couple of months on the job. Blouke and Marianne wanted to come out to Lyme, New Hampshire, from New York, and they asked me if I would come along. We flew from New York to Boston into a wild snowstorm. The flight to Manchester was canceled, and Lyme, New Hampshire, was 140 miles away. We decided we could get to Lyme that night; we had a hotel reservation there. So, we rented a car and started driving. It was a nightmare trip.

The farther north we went, the worse the storm got. We arrived in Lyme in the middle of the night and went to the Lyme inn. It was shut up for the night, of course. So Blouke and I made snowballs and pelted all the windows. Finally, the people who owned the Inn came down in their nightgowns and let us in. For a city kid like me —the drive into the hinterlands, and the deserted town, an old inn, and the nightgowns—it was just too Charles Dickens.

Trina: And the next morning you made

all these condescending remarks about the pilot issue, about how there was no use of type whatsoever, and the white space was nonexistent. What a riot!

John: I was trying to figure out how I was going to work in this style. Finally, I thought if I could steer it closer to the design of William Morris and the Arts and Crafts Movement, I'd be O.K. But really, it's your own art direction style. And I continued to use it after you left.

Trina: Wally Tripp is in the first issue. He was another mainstay.

John: Let's talk a little about the craft of matching up the illustrator to the story. How did you do that?

Trina: Well, that was the most fun part of the job. To me an artist's work says a lot about the artist as a person. The more you get to know one, the more you could put a story with an illustrator. There were certain illustrators who had specialties. There are animal and nature illustrators like Jim Arnosky. Or for fantasy animals there was Wally Tripp. And Eva Hülsmann could do anything realistic.

John: Tell the story about Jim Arnosky with his portfolio. Jim sent you some drawings, and they were all mass-market cartoon drawings with Day-Glo colors. They were horrible, and you wrote him a note saying, Don't send me this horrible stuff. This is terrible. Don't send me this junk.

Trina: He wrote back and said, I thought this is what people wanted. It's easy enough for you fat cat art directors sitting behind your big desks with your cigars to judge honest artists like myself trying to earn a living. And it went on and on. It was like the Artist Communist Manifesto. He was down in Pennsylvania, living in the Poconos in a log cabin with no heat and no running water. They had just had their first baby. So, I wrote back and said, Well I don't know what kind of image you have in your mind, but I'm not fat and I live on a farm and I don't make much more money than you do probably. I'm trying to earn a living, too. So get real. Send me what you do that you don't make money with. He sent me all his nature drawings, and they were beautiful. For the first job he did for *Cricket* he earned about $300.00. And I said this is how much we owe you, but I'm not going to send you the check unless you promise to put running water in the house. And he did.

John: Jan Adkins was a genius with everything, but back then he had trouble with the human figure.

Trina: Yeah, I talked to Jan about it, and his figures improved. And they continue to improve from what I can see of his recent work. That's the joy of working with creative people. Any artist wants and needs constructive criticism, myself included, to this day. If somebody makes a comment about my work that I know is right, I learn from it.

John: Well, it has to be constructive. And it can't be mean. It has to come from someone you respect. The artist has to be able to see the truth in it at some level. So you can't just write to somebody and say give it up and become a longshoreman. You've got to say, Here's where you can improve.

Trina: The artist has to be ready to hear it, too. One of the best pieces of criticism I ever received in my life was from Garth Williams. He was always one of my heroes. I met him through being art director for *Cricket.* I got in touch with him, and he did do work for *Cricket.* He was living in Mexico at the time and he came here to visit his daughter, who lived in the area. He came over for an afternoon, but then he decided he would stay for a week. I was working on *Snow White* at the time. He stood and looked over my shoulder one day while I was working and said, "You know this is so beautiful! But there's one thing that I don't see present in any of your work. You need to define your light source. Where's the light coming from? If you show that, it will not only create mood but it'll define the forms of your figures."

Man. It was like a big door opened for me, and I thought, God, you know he's right! It's something I never thought about. Everything always was flat, treated equally.

Garth did new illustrations for "Chester Cricket's Pigeon Ride" and "Chester Cricket and the Terrible Crash" in *Cricket*. Oh I was so excited. They're beautiful drawings.

John: Look at this. In about the third issue you've got a Hilary Knight drawing.

Trina: Yes, I wrote to Hilary because I wanted to *be* Hilary Knight. *Eloise* was published when I was in high school. Here's a guy illustrating children's books that are crossover books. They are sophisticated, they're witty, they're funny. They are also gorgeous children's books. And he's just delightfully acerbic. He has a wonderful sense of fantasy, and Hilary can really, really draw.

John: And in so many styles! He does theater posters. But then he can draw bunnies in costume. He can draw the Eloise type of a realistic child.

Trina: So many wonderful artists did such amazing stuff. Sometimes they worked for *Cricket* only once, and I never heard from them again. Or they were European, and we lost track. At that time American art directors did not like to work with artists in foreign countries because it was chancy.

John: It *was* chancy, and there were a lot of other problems, too. There are so many great Italian artists, but if the Italian mail service went on strike, they'd just dump all the mail in the river.

Trina: This was before the days of FedEx or the electronic communication of faxes and e-mails.

John: Friso Henstra from the Netherlands was always brilliant. He had been a political cartoonist in Amsterdam, and he also sculpted. He had a studio on a barge in one of the Amsterdam canals where he did sculpture.

Trina: And David McPhail—I heard of him through a friend in Boston. He needed work and he was a genius as far as I was concerned. He can draw like Rembrandt. He was also an extremely handsome young man, but he was not dependable.

John: Now, here's an example of how a

TRINA SCHART HYMAN AND JOHN GRANDITS

*Cover illustration for February 1982, conté dust and conté pencil by Chris Van Allsburg. Cricket's cover was black-and-white. A color version of this illustration appears in Van Allsburg's **The Wreck of the Zephyr** (1983)*

Cricket cover turned into a book. This cover features a flying sailboat. The next year Chris Van Allsburg developed it into a book. How did you find him?

Trina: He was a friend of David Macaulay.

John: They both taught up at Rhode Island School of Design. Chuck Mikolaycak was also able to take a cover he did for *Cricket* and use the technique for a book. He was fooling around with a traditional form of Polish folk art—paper cutting. And he did this Easter Monday cover.

Trina: Then he did a book about Babushka.

John: He was worried about how much work a book would be—hours and hours of using an X-Acto knife and all those little, tiny pieces of paper floating around. I guess it was worth it.

Trina: Quentin Blake was one of our English illustrators.

John: He illustrated all those Roald Dahl books, and he's famous in Britain.

Trina: But then, nobody knew of him on this side of the water.

Shortly after the pilot issue came out, in order to introduce *Cricket* to the New York publishers and to drum up enthusiasm for the magazine from both authors and illustrators, critics and agents, the Caruses threw a big party in New York City at the St. Moritz Hotel. Everybody was there: Clifton Fadiman, Isaac Bashevis Singer, Sammy Levenson, John Ciardi, all of them. They all gave little speeches and said, Come on, we need to get kids involved in reading. We need to get kids interested in literature. There were hundreds and hundreds of people packed into that sky garden roof. It was wonderful food. Everybody got a chance to meet everybody and networked. It's where we first met Marylin Hafner. What a trip! I met a lot of people at that party. It was really elegant, fabulous. Some of the artists hadn't eaten for three weeks, and all of a sudden they were confronted with . . .

John: . . . shrimp! Tons of it!

Trina: Tons of shrimp and smoked salmon! It was very beautifully done. And it worked! It worked gangbusters.

Marvin Friedman came to that party in New York, and that's how I got to know Marvin and as far as I'm concerned he's one of the finest illustrators this country has ever produced. After the party a bunch of us went out to dinner.

John: We went to the late, great Russian Tea Room. There were at least a dozen of us there. We sat for hours and ate and drank and talked. That's when it occurred to us that a lot of these people had never met each other before. Many of them had been admiring each other's work but never talked. Some said they never really got together with other illustrators at all.

Trina: It was so much fun. I have to tell you this. In the middle of this eating and drinking party at the Russian Tea Room, I had one of those out-of-body experiences. I actually left my body and I was looking down at this table full of all these people whose work I had admired all my life. And there I was—little me. We were all eating and drinking and having a good time together, and I thought, I can die now. Because this is what I wanted to do my whole life. These were all my friends. And we were all working together to create something. And it was just wonderful.

Then, because we were using so many artists from England and some from the Continent, it was a bright idea to throw a similar party in London—a party to launch an English edition of *Cricket*. The Caruses very kindly agreed to foot the bill for that, and Dilys Evans and I put it together. Dilys was an English transplant, so she knew London, and we got help from Kaye Webb, the editor at Puffin. It was an afternoon tea at a lovely hotel. We had a little orchestra like they do in those English movies. All these English artists came. It's where I met Malcolm Bird and Alan Dart, Fritz Wegner, Faith Jaques, and Victor and Glenys Ambrus.

Fritz Wegner and Faith Jaques danced a beautiful waltz, and then they did a tango. It was just fabulous. Shirley Hughes brought Quentin Blake, who drank gin the whole time and swirled his muffler.

John: I learned that Quentin Blake is ambidextrous and draws with both hands at once.

Trina: Yep. Both hands at once. With a pen in both hands. Works on the same drawing. Is that cool?!

John: It's so great. I can't even understand how Leo and Diane Dillon both work on the same painting.

Trina: That I can understand better because they take turns doing different things.

I believe that in educating kids you can learn anything you need to know about the world, including math and science, through art.

John: That's a good argument.

Trina: I've always believed this. I think that art is as important if not more important than many other subjects. It's equally as important as literature for instance. While I was art director at *Cricket,* it was part of my self-important pompous mission to test this out. I wanted to bring all kinds of visual art to kids. Expose them to all kinds. Not just cutesy, sweet children's book illustration, even if it was very well done and technically proficient, but more exciting art and real fine art, as well.

Art should make you ask questions, and it should make you think, and it should make you figure stuff out. Everything. Just the way literature does. Just the way music does. The way science does. It should make you question. Not just accept the norm. As I've gotten older, I've learned that everybody in the world has an opinion about art. Unfortunately, nobody *knows* anything about it. They all have an opinion. Someone will say, Oh, I can't stand this, without even questioning why. I know that my work, my book illustration, really upsets some people. Why that is, I don't know. Maybe it strikes some kind of chord from their childhood. Maybe they looked at an Arthur Rackham book and got all upset and got a spanking, I don't know. You get some of the weirdest comments like, The art is too emotional. And people get all upset because it's too emotional. Well, yeah, that's life. So, my biggest challenge as art director for *Cricket* was to try and keep true to my own goal: to bring art to kids with this magazine.

John: Which is interesting because when I came on board I always liked art, but I didn't examine it very closely. When I started designing the magazine with you being the art director, I had to really start learning about illustration and drawing and art. I had to learn how to become an art director. And so . . .

Trina: Right, it was an education for you, too.

John: You learn to think about art. You have to learn how to look at art.

Trina: It's like learning to read music or learning to listen to music. Marianne's musical god is Mozart. She would have put anything in the magazine relating to Mozart. We all have favorites, that's true.

John: André Carus and I would have conversations about what makes something art, and is art communication, or is art expression, is art technique. We came around to believe that every artist has a

language, has a way of speaking, if you will. And it's our job, the viewer's job, to learn that language if you want to hear what that artist has to say.

Trina: In those days I wasn't together enough or articulate enough to make a concerted fight for this point of view. I just didn't have the confidence.

John: But your actions were consistent, and so, what ended up being in the magazine really is a great step toward that goal.

Trina: Visually, we made a pretty nice magazine.

I wanted to mention the development of the *Cricket* cast of bugs and other characters. They grew like Topsy, in a very organic way. We started out with Cricket and then he had to have a pal, and that was Ladybug. Their personalities were very clear to me because it's the two halves of my very own self. I'm half nice guy and half nudge—a crazed power-mad ladybug. I guess all the characters are parts of people I knew. And it was really, really a lot of fun creating that whole little world. The earlier ones were quite primitive. They were in their infancy. They had to develop just like real people. Along with the characters, the whole landscape evolved. Come on, they went on balloon trips and they met a toad and his mom and a big giant spider. And I introduced Charlie and on and on.

At some point I started sending the bugs on an adventure or an expedition every summer. So there was a lot of story-telling and a huge amount of writing for me. Toward the end of my doing this, after fifteen years, I got really, really tired. I wanted to expand, but I couldn't. I was limited to the spaces that the bugs had available to them. If I had the whole issue to do just a Cricket and Ladybug story, I could have done it. What I wanted to become was a real comic strip artist. But it's also tiring having to think of fresh episodes every month. It got to be a real push for me toward the end. And then I started having fantasies of ending their lives by having a giant foot come down and crush them all. I thought, it's time to stop, so I handed it over to Jean Gralley. Although she was doing very little illustration at the time, I knew she had a good cartoon sense. She could draw and most important she had a good sense of humor.

The cartoon was a lot of fun up to a point. And then it got to be work.

John: It became the model for the other magazines. The format works pretty well. Marylin Hafner does one for *Ladybug*.

Omar Rayyan does one in *Spider*. Brian Floca draws, and I write one for *Click*. Larry Gonick does a strip for *Muse*.

Trina: Looking back on everything, it was quite an experience. But the best thing is now, today, when adults who have kids of their own come up and say, I loved *Cricket* so much that I saved every single copy for my own kids. And it's like wow, O.K., that's something that made an impression.

John: Consider the impact. We had a huge circulation. I don't think we ever made much money, but for a while we were print-ing 300,000 copies per month. Most of the time, we were printing closer to 100,000. Even so, every month that many kids get a copy of *Cricket*. Compare that to a trade picture book. If you printed 5 or 6,000 copies, especially in the 1970s, that was a big print run.

Trina: There's another important thing about being the art director of *Cricket*. I got to launch a good number of illustrators into the children's book field. Some sent their portfolios to me as young unknown artists, sometimes right out of art school, and now these are people who are big in the field. That and the children who loved *Cricket* so much made it all worthwhile.

John Grandits has been employed as an art director, designer, or freelance writer for *Muse, Click,* Cricket Books, Crown Books for Children, and Lothrop, Lee & Shepard. He was art director of *Cricket* magazine from 1979 to 1985.

Trina Schart Hyman is a widely loved and respected illustrator of over one hundred children's books. Her many awards include the Caldecott Medal for *Saint George and the Dragon;* Caldecott Honors for *Little Red Riding Hood, A Child's Calendar,* and *Hershel and the Hanukkah Goblins;* and Boston Globe–Horn Book Awards for *King Stork* and *The Fortune-Tellers.* As *Cricket*'s first art director (1971–1979), she created the characters of Cricket, Ladybug, and the gang. She has served on the *Cricket* Editorial Board since 1988.

A Chorus of Crickets
Finding Our Work and Finding You

BALDING

INTELLIGENT FOREHEAD

BIG NOSE

SQUINTY EYES

SCRAGGLY MOUSTACHE

DIMPLES

DOUBLE CHIN

Jan Adkins, a triple self-portrait, from the May 1977 Cricket

"That would be a good trick: to die at 90 with a boy's heart!"
—CARL SANDBURG

**by
Jan Adkins**

WE DIDN'T KNOW what we were doing, exactly. We were swept into the excitement of starting *Cricket,* and it made us happy, even giddy. We knew that we were trying something new, but none of us knew how to make it work. We wanted to create a magazine kids would wait for every month. "Is it here yet?" We wanted to make it so surprising and interesting that they would eat it up with their reading eyes the way they gobbled up doughnuts or French fries. "Is it here yet? Is the new *Cricket* in the mailbox?"

All this happened thirty years ago. Almost all of us were young, at the beginning of our working lives. We didn't know in which direction our work should go. We suspected, though, that the best work had a lot to do with writing and illustrating for kids.

Then we went to the first *Cricket* picnic. It was in Lyme, New Hampshire, where the first art director, Trina Hyman, lived. We met the other Crickets. There, on Trina's front porch, we knew what would make us happy, in which direction we could go, and who our friends would be on the long, strange, happy journey. And you were with us!

All of us knew we loved kids. Not at all in the usual grown-up way. "Aren't children just the cutest things?" No! We knew kids were smart and thought about everything. Kids knew what was the good stuff and what was just more oatmeal. We loved the kids who lived inside us. All of the people on that porch had managed to stay children in their hearts—even after they had children of their own and cars and houses. Even after they met the sadness and worry that hides the kid in many grownups. All of us loved and protected the kids inside us, and we loved you. We still do, and it's been a long, long time.

Of all our times together, the picnics at Trina's were the sunniest and craziest. Remembering them now is like seeing a carnival at night on the next hill—all flashing lights and whirling and music. We talked and strolled and rolled in the hay barn and told stories. We laughed more than anyone else in Lyme, New Hampshire. And we ate! Mountains of food! A curious thing: people who write and illustrate usually love to cook. We crowded into the kitchen to make brownies, coleslaw (my specialty), hamburgers, macaroni and cheese, bread, green salad, sliced tomatoes with scallions and vinegar. Those who didn't cook crowded in with us and talked and told us, "not so much mayonnaise," and "more pepper," and we told them to go back to the porch. But they didn't. And we didn't mind.

We played music and sang. We danced—even without music. We began to learn about one another: who was good at drawing horses, who was great at crazy poems, who wrote wonderful tales. We shared our little problems and our frustrations. "Don't you just hate it when your pencil drawing gets all smudgy? What do you do about that?" We met people whose work had made us wonder how anyone could be so good, and we told them so. "I love the way you draw!" "I love the way you write!" We felt, with a great surge of our hearts, that we would know these people forever. Another curious thing: we were right.

Trina was a great art director and a great hostess. She was small, dark, pretty, and wore thick glasses. Her house was airy and fun. Her art and art from friends hung on all the walls. She had painted some of her doors with flowers and lyrics from songs.

John Grandits (he has been a designer and art director for most of the *Cricket* magazines) was a scrawny, odd-looking bird with long hair in a ponytail, glasses, and a fedora hat. Come to think of it, he still is. He became one of my best friends in the world, and we have talked about all the people at those parties for all these years.

Sweet, quiet Wally Tripp—who drew the best and funniest animals—lived nearby and brought his family. His wife was a skillful seamstress, who had made Wally a bright blue frock coat and knee britches in the style that was fashionable around 1776. He looked elegant in that outfit! It was like having Benjamin Franklin or John Adams walking around our picnic.

Most of us visited Trina when it wasn't picnic season, just to talk with her. She always helped us with advice on our illustrations, showing us some of her tricks, suggesting how we might get better. I hope we did. She is still my dear friend and yours, too.

I remember another magical *Cricket* time, a few years later when the magazine was doing well, lots of kids had subscriptions, and it was becoming a favorite with librarians and teachers. We had a celebration in New York City. We were all dressed up and on our best behavior because the celebration was held at the fancy St. Moritz, overlooking Central Park. Even though we didn't roll in the hayloft, we laughed more than anyone in Manhattan. We told stories, of course, talked about our work, and we talked about you.

After the St. Moritz, a lot of us walked to the famous Russian Tea Room for dinner. The famous writer of tales, Isaac Bashevis Singer, was there with his wife. He was a jolly man whose face wrinkled all over when he smiled and chuckled. He was close to eighty then, and he talked to John Grandits and me as if we were his sons. "Boys," he said, "my wife wants me to be quiet and sensible. I tell her I will, but I won't. It's a little lie, but it makes her feel better." We felt very close to him, though it was strange to tell stories and laugh with one of the best writers in the entire world just as you would with your uncle or your best friend.

Isaac taught us all a lot. He trusted children with his tales. He knew that you would listen for the real story behind the story, the meaning behind the words. He called us "boys," but we knew he was a boy, too. Like Carl Sandburg, close to eighty, he still had a boy's heart.

After the dinner and the good-byes, John and I stood on the street with our dear Marianne Carus, the smart, beautiful woman who started *Cricket* and brought us all together. We were all in love with her. Still are. "I know what we need," she said. John and I nodded at one another: she always knew what we needed. "We need a ride!" Marianne summoned one of the horse-drawn carriages that wait around Fifty-sixth Street for people who are celebrating. The three of us scrambled into the graceful, open carriage, and the big, quiet horse pulled us into the bus and taxi-cab traffic. We clop-clopped into Central Park on a dark, warm evening when everything seemed possible and the world felt wonderful.

I love history. I was telling John and Marianne how New York must have looked a hundred years before when the only traffic on the street was horses. It was beautiful but dirty, too. The iron wheels of carriages and freight wagons and horse trolleys ground the horse droppings into dust that stuck between the street's bricks and cobblestones. When it rained, the hems of women's long skirts were coated with this gray, horse dust. The driver of our carriage was from Jamaica and had a wonderful musical accent. He turned around on his high seat and asked, "How you know 'dis, mon? Were you really here in those old days?"

The ride was too short. We would have gone on until morning if the horse could have managed it. The lamps of Central Park glided past the carriage, and the horse's hoofs clop-clopped. I remember thinking, "This is one of those signposts that stick up from the rest of your life. It's a special moment I will be able to see from a long distance in time." I can see it, still, over almost a quarter of a century.

I know you don't remember all this, but you were there with us.

Jan Adkins is a frequent contributor to *Cricket, Click,* and other magazines. His books *The Art and Industry of Sandcastles* and *The Craft of Sail: A Primer of Sailing* were National Book Award nominees.

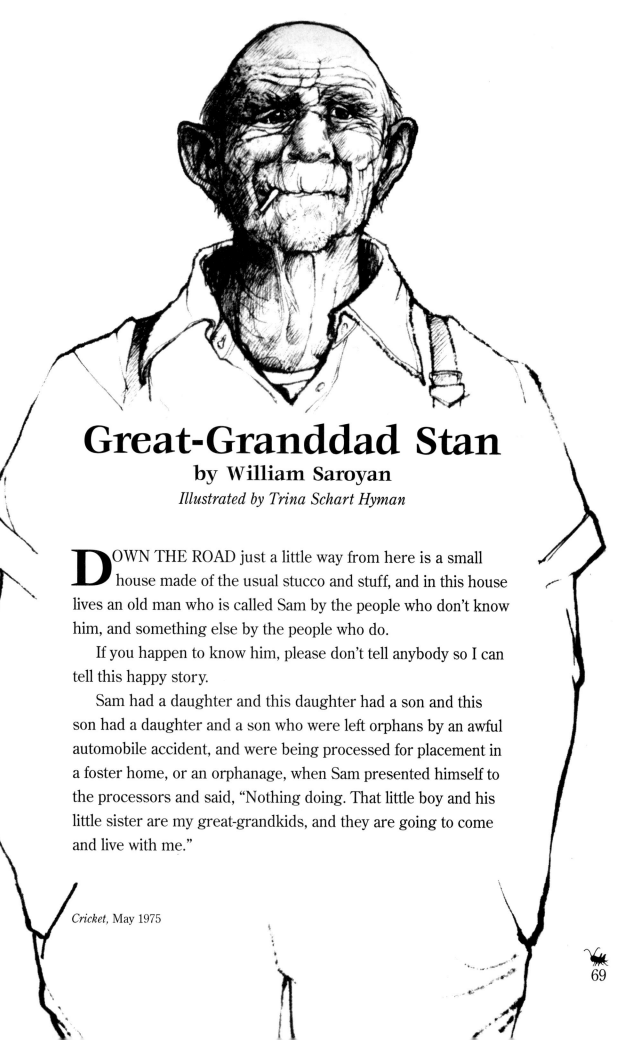

Great-Granddad Stan

by William Saroyan

Illustrated by Trina Schart Hyman

DOWN THE ROAD just a little way from here is a small house made of the usual stucco and stuff, and in this house lives an old man who is called Sam by the people who don't know him, and something else by the people who do.

If you happen to know him, please don't tell anybody so I can tell this happy story.

Sam had a daughter and this daughter had a son and this son had a daughter and a son who were left orphans by an awful automobile accident, and were being processed for placement in a foster home, or an orphanage, when Sam presented himself to the processors and said, "Nothing doing. That little boy and his little sister are my great-grandkids, and they are going to come and live with me."

Cricket, May 1975

And so three or four years ago that's exactly what happened.

The boy was then seven years old, and his name was Dan. His sister then was six years old, and her name was Ann.

Dan and Ann—it was an accident sad and simple that took away their father and mother, and another accident pure and simple that named them Dan and Ann.

One way or another you've got to give a boy a boy's name and a girl a girl's name, although there are very nice people who struggle through life with a name that seems to be reserved for a member of the opposite sex—that means a boy has a girl's name, like Evelyn, and a girl has a boy's name, like Leslie.

Dan was a very serious-minded boy from the word "go," and when he started living with his great-granddad in the little house made of stucco and stuff down the road, he was more serious than ever.

He just stood right where he happened to be and you could tell he was thinking.

"What's on your mind there, Dan?" his grand-dad asked him that first day, and Dan without batting an eye came right back with, "Nothing. I was just thinking."

"Good," the old man said. "You just keep that up, and before you know it, you'll be president of this whole country."

"Don't want to be," Dan said.

"You can say that at the proper time," Dan's granddad said. "Fun, that's the ticket, in the time of boyhood."

"Don't want the ticket," Dan said.

WILLIAM SAROYAN

His sister Ann, having patiently listened, now said, "Let *me* have it, then."

"A woman president," the old man said. "What is the human race coming to? Intelligence, mayhap? Well, whatever it is coming to, Ann, fun is the ticket for *girlhood* as well as for boyhood. Let him be president who will, be he boy or be she girl. President Ann. I rather like the ring of that, Ann, if I do say so myself."

"I like it, too," Ann said. "Where do I sit?"

"Right there across from where your brother sits, of course."

"Not for *lunch,*" Ann said, "for being president."

"It's the same place," the old man said. "You've got to eat sometime. President or plumber, you've got to sit down and take a meal."

"I don't want to," Dan said, and the old man said, "Not you, Daniel out of the Lions' Den, and someday I want you to tell me how you got out of there. What did you tell the lions to keep them from eating you? Sit down, sit down. And you, too, Madam President."

"Am I the first?" Ann said.

"First, second, third, fourth, last, and forever," the old man said.

"What are we having?" Dan said.

"Lion, that's what we're having," the old man said.

"These look like plain ordinary hamburgers to me," Dan said.

"Look again," the old man said. "Hamburgers they are, and plain they may be, but that meat in there, that's lion meat."

"Can I ask a question?" Ann said.

"No, you can't," Dan said, "because I'm trying to think."

"Can I ask *you* a question, Great-Granddad?" Ann said.

"Well, first," the old man said, "let's get forms of address a little simplified. You're Ann, your big brother's Dan, and I'm not Great Granddad or anything like that. I'm Stan."

"Really?" Ann said. "Great-Granddad, surely you can't expect me, a mere girl of six going on seven, to address you as Stan. I can't even think of doing that. You are my father's mother's father; how can you expect me to call you Stan? Dan, isn't there a baseball player who is called Stan something or other?"

"Stan the Man they call him," Dan said. "I saw him on TV."

"Go wash your mouth," Ann said. "You know perfectly well Great-Granddad does not want the word TV said in this house."

"Oh, he can say it once in a while," the old man said, "but what I would rather he didn't do was get hypnotized by it. Did I ever tell you about the month I got hypnotized by the TV in the parlor and nearly lost my life? Well, it's the truth, but I won't tell it just now because there is a time and a place for everything, and this is the time for chomping down on our hamburgers made out of lion meat, or steers who imagined that they were lions for all we know, and for getting forms of address straightened out in this family and established once and for all. You're Dan; you're Ann. Who am I?"

"Great-Granddad," Ann said. "That's who you are, Great-Granddad."

"Well, that's one way of looking at it," the old man said. "But this household is democratic, and so what is your vote, Dan? Wouldn't you rather call me Stan instead of Great-Granddad?"

WILLIAM SAROYAN

"No, sir," Dan said. "Great-Granddad is who you are, and that's how you ought to be addressed."

"As president," Ann said, "let me make it official. I pronounce you great, and I pronounce you granddad. Go and fight no more."

"O.K.," the old man said. "But I wasn't really fighting, I was only trying to be like you two."

"Oh, look who's talking," Dan said. "You know you can't be like us, so what do you want to *try* for?"

"It was a mad idea at that," the old man said. "I'm exactly eighty years old, and it'll be a year before either of you will be eight. Well, let's get along and make the most of our good luck."

William Saroyan was a playwright, short-story writer, novelist, and essayist. He earned the Pulitzer Prize in drama and the New York Drama Critics Circle Award for *The Time of Your Life*.

In the Beginning

by Marcia Leonard

I T WAS AN AD in the *Boston Globe,* in July of 1972, that introduced me to *Cricket* magazine. "Wanted," read the ad. "Assistant Editor for new children's literature magazine. $12,000 plus. Solid knowledge of children's literature and publishing experience essential. 1½ hours from Chicago Loop." This was intriguing. A new children's *literature* magazine? There hadn't been one since *St. Nicholas* folded. With my newly minted degree in children's literature, I had the "solid knowledge" required, but the "publishing experience" might have been a stretch. I could only point to the summer school Publishing Procedures course that I was currently attending at Radcliffe. One and a half hours from the Loop? I had grown up in Urbana, Illinois, and I knew my geography. Allowing for rush-hour traffic, that could mean an office in a tony, northern suburb along Lake Michigan or perhaps in one of the charming Victorian-era towns along the Fox River! I sent off my résumé immediately.

Several weeks later, I found myself in La Salle, Illinois, headquarters for Open Court, the textbook publisher that was *Cricket*'s parent company. I was there for an interview with Marianne Carus, *Cricket*'s editor-in-chief, and her husband, Blouke, Open Court's publisher. But before our meeting, I drove around a bit to get a feel for the place. La Salle turned out to be a small, backwater town with an economy based on farming, light industry, and trucking. It was in the middle of nowhere and surrounded by cornfields—one and a half hours from Chicago's Loop only if

Marcia Leonard in 1972

you made the journey early on a Sunday morning and drove eighty miles an hour! I was completely discouraged. This was not the life I wanted. I would meet with the Caruses to be polite—and to satisfy my curiosity about the magazine they planned to publish —but there was no way I would take the job they were offering. Two hours in their company changed my mind.

The Caruses were completely committed to the idea of producing a literary magazine for young readers, with work by the best authors and illustrators in the business. They had already assembled an impressive international editorial board, and they had convinced Trina Schart Hyman, a brilliant illustrator, to be their art director. *Cricket* would be launched with a pilot issue in January 1973 and would start publication the following September. If I signed on now, I could be in on the beginning of an exciting new venture! Given my experience—or lack of it, really—they offered me the position of editorial assistant and asked me to commit to two years with the company. I took the job and promised one year. I figured it was a tossup whether the magazine— or I—would survive beyond that, but at least I'd have an interesting job experience to add to my résumé when I moved East.

The *Cricket* office was on the second floor of an old building that housed Open Court's production department, directly over the print shop, with machines that clacked and whirred all day long. The in-house staff was small: Marianne, her part-time secretary, and me. (Trina, the clever thing, had taken the job on the condition that she could work from her home in New Hampshire.) My first task was to proofread the typeset copy for the pilot issue. Several Open Court textbook editors had already given it the O.K., but I managed to prove my worth by finding a typo, "baloons" instead of "balloons" in a tall tale by Sid Fleischman. (I didn't tell anyone that I was a terrible speller and unreliable proofreader and only found the mistake by reading the entire magazine backwards.)

My next job was to sift through the huge piles of unsolicited stories and poems that had arrived the moment *Cricket*'s publication was announced. For the most part, these manuscripts represented the worst, not the best, of children's literature, and many had clearly made the rounds of several other publishers. But every once in a great while, a small gem would appear, cause for great rejoicing in the office, and we could send out an acceptance letter instead of one of our standard rejections. Thirty years later, I can still recite that letter word for word!

Gradually, Marianne trained me to do other tasks. I corresponded with authors, artists, and agents; reviewed sales copy and promotion pieces; negotiated with publishers for permission to reprint material from existing books; and answered queries from librarians and booksellers. I was The Staff, so I did a little of everything! I also participated in the first *Cricket* Board meeting at the lodge at Starved Rock State Park on the bluffs of the Illinois River.

The lodge was built in the 1930s by the Civilian Conservation Corps. It has an enormous log-and-stone great room with a soaring ceiling and two massive fireplaces. Very intimidating—but not half as intimidating as meeting Trina and the members of the Board. I was twenty-three, a hippie chick barely out of school. These people were international figures in children's books. Lloyd Alexander had won a Newbery Medal! The collective experience and knowledge they brought to our meetings was amazing, but I quickly found that they were very human, very quirky, and funny—though not always intentionally so. They were also opinionated. That is, they all had strong views about the content, structure, design, and philosophy of the magazine, and they were more than willing to share them. But they were willing to listen to other people's ideas, too. Even mine.

The pilot issue of *Cricket* came out in January 1973. Trina had painted a great cover: children—and a giant troll—being read to by a cricket. And we started getting complimentary letters from publishers, librarians, teachers, reading specialists, and parents. Established authors took notice, and the caliber of manuscripts we received took a giant step up. Best of all, the magazine found its way into children's hands, and we got fan mail, much of it directed to Trina's bug characters: nice guy Cricket, bossy diva Ladybug, villainous Ugly Bird, and slow-but-steady Sluggo, a snail with an amazingly capacious shell. Kids had taken *Cricket* to heart.

So . . . I had a great job, but I was not happy living in La Salle and left town almost every weekend. The problem was, even though I was an Illinois girl born and bred, I didn't fit in. I wasn't married, I wasn't a local, and I didn't have any connections in the community. I was also breaking ground within the company. I was the first woman they'd hired as a professional staff member— and the first feminist. This required a certain attitude adjustment on the part of some of the men who worked for Open Court. But I had Marianne's support, and eventually other female editors joined the staff, so I was no longer a curiosity.

Feminism played a part in the magazine, too. Marianne had carefully chosen selections for the pilot that reflected ethnic and gender diversity, but we were having a hard time finding stories with strong female characters for future issues. Almost all of the manuscripts we received had male characters. Even the animals were males! We combed the library for reprint material, and Marianne wrote to authors specifically requesting stories about girls, but it took quite a while for children's literature to catch up with the rest of society.

Soon after the pilot was released, *Cricket* added a new staff member: John Grandits. He was a great liaison between Trina and the production department, and he and I worked together well. He had strong opinions about literature; I had strong opinions about design. I think in all the time we were at *Cricket,* we only had one big disagreement. I haven't a clue now what it was about, but we both got huffy and stopped talking to each other until the rest of the staff ganged up on us and told us to behave. Best of all for me, John had a subversive streak, a great sense of humor, and he and his wife, Joanne, were outsiders, too. This was the beginning of what, over time, became a real community, a group of young staff members who were truly friends as well as colleagues and who remain friends to this day.

A big event in 1974 was a children's literature conference cosponsored by Open Court and *Cricket* and held in late summer in Tarrytown, New York. Both Board members and staff attended the conference. The mornings were devoted to demonstrations of the Open Court method of teaching reading, and the afternoons featured speeches by noted children's authors. I remember two in particular: Lloyd Alexander's witty, self-deprecating description of how he came to be an author and to write the Prydain series, and Virginia Hamilton's explanation of the genesis of her characters in *The Planet of Junior Brown* and *M. C. Higgins, the Great.* Heady stuff!

Cricket was underway. In September the pilot was rereleased as volume 1, number 1, and the following month the first brand-new issue was published. It was a shock. We'd lived with the pilot for a year, and now here was something completely different! The magazine had a cover by Walter Lorraine instead of Trina, and even the second color was different: Halloween orange instead of grass green. Of course we'd been on a regular production schedule for months, and I'd seen text and art in all stages of development. But seeing each new magazine in printed form was a novelty and a pleasure I never got tired of. It was physical proof of all our hard work.

My year anniversary came and went. The magazine survived, and so did I. In fact, I was promoted to assistant editor and given a raise, and Marianne started teaching me to line edit. Basically she would turn me loose on a manuscript, usually by a novice author, and then we'd sit side by side and go through the changes I'd made. She'd listen while I explained what I'd done, she'd offer suggestions, then we'd hammer out any disagreements. It was a very instructive process, and it wasn't until much later that I learned how few editors took the time and effort to train their staff in this way. She also turned over the craft articles to me and had me winnow the children's correspondence for the "Letterbox" and their stories, poems, and drawings for the popular "Cricket League" competitions before the final selections were made for publication.

Cricket grew. It had been launched as a September-to-May, nine-issue-a-year publication, to coincide with the school calendar. But parents quickly let us know that summer was *the* most important time for their kids to receive the magazine, so, beginning in September 1975, we regularly published twelve issues per year.

To my great surprise, I ended up staying with *Cricket* for six years, moving up to associate editor and then managing editor. There were always fresh challenges, so the job continued to be interesting, but I couldn't have lasted all those years in La Salle if it hadn't been for the camaraderie of the in-house staff, particularly John Grandits, Charnan Simon, Susan Sinnott, and Tom Kazunas, and the fun of working (long distance) with Trina and Dilys Evans. Thirty years after the pilot issue appeared, *Cricket* is still going strong and has, in fact, given birth to seven other children's magazines: *Babybug, Ladybug, Spider, Cicada, Muse, Ask,* and *Click.* I'm proud that I was in on the beginnings of a magazine that has given reading pleasure to so many children—including my own daughter—and I trust it will still be around for another thirty years. Happy anniversary, *Cricket!*

Marcia Leonard is the author of over ninety books for young readers, including *Pumpkin Magic* and *Haunted House,* both of which are illustrated by Hilary Knight.

A Portrait of the Editor as a Young Cricket by Charnan Simon

MEMORY #1: SPRING 1974. It's my senior year at Carleton College, and I'm baby-sitting for a favorite professor. The kids bring me something called *Cricket* magazine to read aloud. The cover shows a weird grasshopper lady reading to a couple of surrealistic butterfly kids. What *is* this? I look inside. The first story is a translation of a contemporary Russian children's story. There's a Flemish folk tale and an Irish tall tale and a Chinese anecdote and something funny by Sam Levenson about a bunch of brothers going for a hike in New York City. There are poems by John Ciardi and Elizabeth Coatsworth and Walter de la Mare and Norma Farber and Lee Bennett Hopkins; illustrations by Maurice Sendak and Hilary Knight and Enrico Arno and Jim Arnosky and Marylin Hafner and that fabulous cover by Friso Henstra, a Dutch artist. The margins are busy with a nice-guy cartoon cricket and his totally silly ladybug friend. Clearly, this is not your father's children's magazine.

Charnan Simon in 1975

MEMORY #2: FALL 1974. I'm an editorial assistant in the Children's Book Division at Little, Brown & Company in Boston. I meet Trina Schart Hyman, who is illustrating *Snow White* and who also happens to be *Cricket*'s art director and the person responsible for those buggy margins. I don't say a word. When she leaves, I order two subscriptions of *Cricket*—one for myself and one for my pediatrician father to put in his waiting room. The kids in Walla Walla deserve a treat.

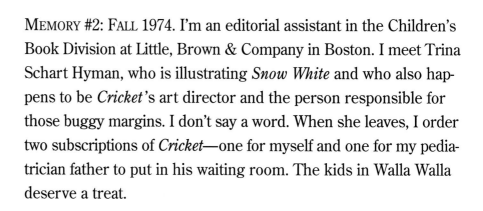

MEMORY #3: SPRING 1975. *Cricket* is advertising for an associate editor. I tell my Little, Brown editors, Casey Cameron and John Keller, that I want the job. Casey writes me the best recommendation I have ever read, mostly full of gross exaggerations and maybe an outright lie or two, and tells me not to let her down. I send in a résumé and wait.

MEMORY #4: Marianne Carus—*Cricket*'s editor, do I really have to introduce her?—calls me in Boston. She sounds so charming! Warm and friendly and funny, and with the nicest possible accent. It's after six, and she only has a minute—Marianne always only has a minute—because she's on her way to a tennis match (remember when you still had time for tennis, Marianne?), but she's received my résumé and Casey's letter and wonders if I would be interested in flying out to La Salle, Illinois, for an interview.

MEMORY #5: The Greyhound bus is passing through endless miles of Illinois cornfields between Chicago and La Salle, and I am growing suspicious about the *Cricket* ad. This doesn't look like "outskirts of Chicago" to me. We pull into La Salle and I am—appalled. I remember my college boyfriend's disbelief when I told him where I was going and what I was doing: He used to work on the Illinois River and maintains that "What La Salle has is barges and bars. What it *doesn't* have is a children's magazine." I get off the bus and find the Hotel Kaskaskia, where I am to meet Marianne and Blouke Carus. On the veranda are black fiberglass chairs shaped like cupped hands with gold fingernail polish. At least I can relax about this interview. There is *no way* I would ever live in La Salle, Illinois.

MEMORY #6: I got the job! This is the best thing that has ever happened! Even though I tanked on the interview and couldn't remember a single title when Marianne asked about my personal favorite children's books (did I ever read any?), something clicked, and they offered me the job. And I accepted! It isn't hard to see how Blouke and Marianne got this impossibly literary and astonishing children's magazine off the ground in our age of television and Marshall McLuhan—they are rather impossibly literary and astonishing people themselves. Also completely oblivious to the magnitude of the task they've taken on . . .

MEMORY #7: Fall 1975. As *Cricket*'s new assistant editor, I am sitting in a conference room at Starved Rock Lodge for my first Editorial Board meeting. There are Big Names everywhere, and I am totally intimidated. "Now don't be shy!" Marianne admonishes. "We want to hear from you!" Right. The surprising thing is that Marianne really *does* want to hear from me—as does everyone else in the room. They are all so gracious and so totally lacking in ego—the only thing these phenomenally talented people seem to care about is coming up with creative solutions to the problem of how to make—and keep—*Cricket* the best of all possible children's magazines.

MEMORY #8: LATE FALL 1975. The Board meeting is over, and we are all back at work. I try to subdue my rapidly rising hysteria as I look at the pile of manuscripts Marianne has given me to edit. Ruskin Bond? Mary Calhoun? Myra Cohn Livingston? Does she really think a kid like me has anything to say to illustrious authors like these? And of course she doesn't, not really, not at first. Marianne has many talents, but part of her genius is knowing how to train and polish young editors. A huge part of this training is simply reading and absorbing. It is impossible to read *Cricket* authors and not learn a great deal about how language could—and should—be used. From dabbling in a little tentative copyediting to making confident substantive textual suggestions, I come into my own as an editor. The old Walter de la Mare caveat about "Only the rarest kind of best in anything can be good enough for the young" is gospel at *Cricket*—in the early days and forever after. I am lucky enough to learn from the masters during my years in La Salle, and for that I will forgive the town everything.

MEMORY #9: WINTER 1975. My first issue of *Cricket* goes to press! Marcia Leonard and I alternate shepherding monthly issues through the various production stages, and the December 1975 issue is the first one I've been in charge of from start to finish. The first best thing is that "my" issue has a Trina Schart Hyman cover—I'm swoony with pride and good fortune. Then there's the gift of Isaac Bashevis Singer's "A Parakeet Named Dreidel" and Norma Farber's sweetly jubilant poem, "Ladybug's Christmas." I adore Shirley Hughes's illustrations for Gunilla Norris's lovely story about a Swedish child's "Wish for Dunking Day"—I will always need tissues to read this one. But it's more than wishing that has made this *Cricket*—well, all *Cricket*s—such a marvel. In our tacky little offices above the print shop, we staffers have worked with the best of the best authors and artists everywhere in the world to bring something truly new and exciting to the world of children's reading. We are mostly too young, too inexperienced, and too dumb to know that *Cricket* can't possibly succeed. So when Marianne says, "Hey, kids, let's put on a magazine!" we just slip on our tap shoes and say, "Why not?"

MEMORY #10: Kathleen Stevens, Jim Arnosky, Eric Kimmel, Arnold Adoff, Jan Brett, Dennis Lee, Marylin Hafner, Rachel

Isadore, Rosemary Wells, Johanna Hurwitz, Steven Kellogg, Ed Young, Seymour Simon, Leo and Diane Dillon, Tomie dePaola, Harry Allard, Jean Van Leeuwen, David Wiesner, Wally Tripp, Jane Yolen, Marjorie Sharmat—who could name all the authors and artists with whom we have the honor of working during *Cricket*'s first years, people in the earlier stages of their brilliant careers. Some come to us via the unsolicited manuscript pile or an art portfolio sent to Trina. Others we find through the New York and Boston children's book publishing network—we preview their first or second books and love them so much, we know we need to adapt the stories for our magazine. I like to think we all belong to a mutual admiration society—certainly my admiration for these authors and illustrators is boundless. As for our more celebrated contributors—I don't ever plan to get over feeling awed by the likes of Lloyd Alexander and Joan Aiken and Barbara Cooney.

MEMORY #11: 1978. Talk about feeling awed. Marianne and I are in New York doing the rounds of book publishers, and tonight we are having dinner with *Cricket* Board member Isaac Bashevis Singer and his charming wife, Alma. I don't even pretend to take part in the conversation. It's quite enough to listen to Marianne and Mr. Singer talk about art and literature—and to hear Mrs. Singer admonish her Nobel Laureate husband to eat, eat! Marianne asks Mr. Singer if he has seen "The Tin Drum," which had just opened, and the great man shakes his head "no," commenting firmly that "Movies are for women." Do I take this sitting down? You bet I do.

MEMORY #12: Reading letters from our subscribers is a hoot. Kids really do say the darndest things. Also the most touching, hilarious, insightful, and off-the-wall things. I love this part of my job.

O.K., time to stop. Those early years at *Cricket* were rich and full and weird beyond belief, and there are just too many memories. We were a bunch of visionaries stuck in a little, Illinois river town, collaborating on that deadliest of all deadly sounding publications— a literary magazine for children. Amazingly enough, and with a lot of help from our friends, I think we pulled it off. We gave kids a monthly magazine that was as good to look at as it was to read —a true treasure. And personally? I came away with a lifetime of friends, a wealth of knowledge about children's books, a bunch of original artwork still hanging on my walls (why didn't I collect more?), and even a husband—Tom Kazunas, *Cricket*'s first production manager. Thank you, *Cricket*—that's not a bad haul.

Charnan Simon was employed as a *Cricket* editor from 1975 to 1985. Since leaving *Cricket* she has published more than fifty books for young readers.

The Birth of *Cricket*

by Eleanor Cameron

Eleanor Cameron at a library appearance in the 1970s

for The Pacific Grove Tribune *and* Pebble Beach Green Sheet *(California) on 5 December 1975*

IT WAS AT the end of a talk on fantasy I had given in Philadelphia that a man by the name of Blouke Carus came up to me and asked if I would be interested in being in on the start of a new children's magazine by consenting to become a member of its Editorial Board.

We had no time to talk then, so he gave me his card, from which I learned that he is president of the Open Court Publishing Company.

Later I learned that it was because of the emphasis I had put on excellence in children's literature in my book of critical essays, *The Green and Burning Tree,* and the need for parents to know what their children are reading and to make every effort to put only the best into their children's hands that Blouke and his wife, Marianne, had decided to ask me to join the Editorial Board.

First of all, when we began corresponding, they brought up *St. Nicholas* and asked if I remembered it. Did I not! How many of us here on the Peninsula must remember with the greatest affection the days when we would run home from school knowing that a new issue of *St. Nicholas* would be there waiting for us!

And whether we could be persuaded to do anything else than devour the pages of that beloved magazine at one sitting would be a question, for we desired only to be let alone!

In *St. Nicholas*'s pages, edited by Mary Mapes Dodge, some of us met for the first time the writing of Rudyard Kipling, who began *The Jungle Books* especially for it, and there the earliest poems of Edna St. Vincent Millay appeared on the contributor's pages, poems sent in in her teens.

And by the time we finally met again at an Open Court textbook conference in Lake Bluff, Illinois, they had asked Clifton Fadiman to become the magazine's senior editor.

Marianne Carus, as editor-in-chief, had gone through the agonizing throes of trying to discover just the right name for the magazine. But, for this meeting, Marianne had come up with yet another name: *Cricket.* There was no great enthusiasm for it, but Clifton Fadiman, the Caruses, their staff, and I gradually found ourselves at this meeting referring to the magazine by one name only, out of all the possible names on our list. "You and Kip keep calling it *Cricket,*" Marianne exclaimed to Fadiman and me. And so we had been, and so it came to be—*Cricket.*

So we could begin. By the time the Caruses had called us to come to the first Board meeting at Starved Rock Lodge near Utica, Illinois, Marianne, the editor-in-chief, had combed through a mountain of her favorite children's stories and poems, of which she has a vast knowledge.

She had visited Kip Fadiman and me out here in California to talk over details and had communicated various reactions to all the other Board members and asked for their critique. She had then put together the chosen material for a pilot issue.

What struck me most forcibly about the first Board meeting was the fun we had. We worked—yes—in spite of the fact that we were meeting in a resort lodge set in one of the most beautiful sections of Illinois, high on wooded ground that looks out over the thickly forested valley where the Illinois River flows.

We listened with absorption, first to Marianne Carus and then to Clifton Fadiman, as they gave their send-off talks, which stated in memorable terms their convictions of exactly what *Cricket* must be for children and the ideals we would keep in mind as we decided on each piece of material sent us.

Another thing that struck me was how well, despite our diverse personalities, we all got along. And there was no holding back in the criticism of each other's ideas.

And so it would go, praise and criticism and suspended judgments alternating, with no hurt feelings—and no inflated egos, for that matter—to be dealt with tenderly in later sessions. We knew that each of us would have to suffer the pricking of cherished notions, or the analyzing of them into nothingness—or usefulness—yet each came up ready to offer still another.

No prima donnas emerged, for which we were all thankful, because we *wanted* to stick together, and we knew that everyone had only a single goal in mind: the success of the magazine. We tried to be as honest with ourselves and with the others on the Board as we possibly could.

Following that session of September 1972, the pilot issue of *Cricket* was sent out in January 1973 all over the United States.

Early in June of 1973 a party was given by the Caruses, the *Cricket* Launching Party, in the Sky Room of the St. Moritz Hotel in New York. To it came poets, editors, writers, artists, publishers, agents, critics, reviewers from all those hives of publishing activity that center in that seething city. Never have I attended a more exciting gathering.

No sooner had I turned from greeting Ann Durell, director

and editor of children's books at Dutton, than I faced Jean Karl, editor of children's books at Atheneum, and then Margaret McElderry of McElderry Books at the same house, and from her turned to Emilie McLeod, editor of children's books at the Atlantic Monthly Press, and next to Jim Giblin, children's editor at the Seabury Press.

Having spoken to them, I saw Jean Craighead George and pressed my way over to her to congratulate her on her Newbery Award for *Julie of the Wolves,* then twisted round to tell Eleanor Estes (of the well-loved Moffat family books) that I thought it high time she received an award for overall excellence in her contribution to children's literature.

Later I went out onto the balcony overlooking New York to talk with John Ciardi about the demise of *Saturday Review* and its incorporation into Norman Cousins's *World* and to ask him when he was going to send in some poems for *Cricket.*

And right in the middle of the party, we were all quiet while Marianne Carus, Clifton Fadiman, Lloyd Alexander, Kaye Webb, and Isaac Singer got up on a platform and told us all they hoped for *Cricket* and what they feel about childhood.

Since that unforgettable party, *Cricket* has received 130,000 subscriptions. Certainly there could be no more eloquent tribute to the idea that parents in this country *are* concerned about what their children read, about moral and aesthetic values, and are determined to settle, not for the third rate that can be so easily picked up on the newsstand and in the supermarket, but for the best.

Eleanor Cameron is the author of the popular Mushroom Planet and Julia Redfern series. Her novel *A Room Made of Windows* earned the Boston Globe–Horn Book Award, and she won the National Book Award for *The Court of the Stone Children.* Her excellent critical essays on children's literature are collected in *The Green and Burning Tree* and *The Seed and the Vision.* She served on the *Cricket* Editorial Board from 1973 to 1996 and passed away in 1997.

Love to Everybuggy

by
Tomie dePaola

WHEN I HEAR or see the word *Cricket,* I don't automatically think of Jiminy or the cricket on the hearth or those clicker-things Catholic nuns wielded (in my childhood) in church to get all the children to stand, sit, stand, kneel as an ensemble. No, I automatically think of Trina Schart Hyman. Trina was art director for *Cricket* when I first met her. Of course, I knew *who* she was from her beautiful books, and even though we lived a scant twenty-five miles from each other in New Hampshire, we had never met.

Trina and I were on the same speaking program in Vermont. Our mutual friend Caroline Ward thought we'd be a good mix. So, the night before, I walked into a restaurant in Rutland, Vermont, to join Trina and her friend, Dilys Evans, for dinner.

To be corny, I could say the rest is history, but hysterical would be a better word.

It wasn't too long after that first meeting that Trina asked me to do a cover for *Cricket* magazine. I remembered how as a child I would look forward every month to my own special magazine subscription issue to arrive, so I could see what artist would do the cover! *Children's Playmate* was the magazine, and I even had a favorite artist. Her name was Fern Bisel Peat. I loved her work. Maybe some child would feel the same way about me!

Trina was a great art director. It was always—"whatever moves you—whatever you want to do."

Doing a cover has more freedom than illustrating a book. No words to be faithful to—just a concept.

So, I joined the ranks of some very fine "cover" artists for *Cricket*.

And of course, my friendship with Trina grew. We even went out on a small lecture circuit with the Trina/Tomie Show. Often we'd wear each other's nametag.

Of course, I'd be remiss if I left out one of the best perks of being a *Cricket* artist—Trina's annual *Cricket* party at her house in Lyme, New Hampshire. The parties each lasted *two* days! Truman Capote's historic Black-and-White Party at the Plaza had nothing on Trina's *Cricket* Party!

Fond, funny, fabulous memories and all because of a little bug!

As Cricket would say, "Love to everybuggy!"

Tomie dePaola has illustrated more than two hundred children's books, almost half of which he authored. He is that rare author who has earned both a Caldecott Honor (for *Strega Nona*) and a Newbery Honor (for *26 Fairmount Avenue*).

McBroom Meets *Cricket*

Sid Fleischman in 1976

**by
Sid
Fleischman**

WHEN IT COMES to story ideas, authors are happily acci-dent-prone. A passing stranger may trigger an entire novel (it has just happened to me). Josh McBroom, the hero of ten tall tales, was a chance encounter. He even got himself born into the wrong book.

While writing a novel, *Chancy and the Grand Rascal,* I needed a liar's contest. I developed a short tale—a few sentences long—about a nameless farmer bragging about his amazingly rich farm.

I finished up the scene and moved on. Had I not felt a certain unease, as if someone were looking over my shoulder, McBroom would never have met *Cricket.*

I began to wonder what would happen if I ripped him out and ran that truth-spouting farmer through the typewriter again (the computer hadn't yet been invented). Out he came, now with a name, a wife, and eleven children. He lived on a fabulous one-acre farm so rich the McBrooms could plant and grow two or three crops a day. The tale had grown to fifteen typed pages.

Once in print, McBroom unleashed heaps of fan mail and still does. (When kids asked for a sequel, I would reply that I don't write sequels.) I felt it was almost impossible to maintain the magic of a first story. On the other hand—

On the other hand, the first McBroom tale had been so much fun to write, why not indulge myself? With fingers crossed (it's very hard to type that way), I pursued the McBroom saga. He and those kids of his held up like old pros. I was amazed.

At about the same time, Marianne Carus was creating a literary amazement of her own—*Cricket* magazine. A charming letter turned up in my mailbox inviting McBroom into the first issue. Would I agree? Of course. I learned then, and in subsequent years, that it's quite impossible to say no to Marianne.

And that's the absolute truth.

Sid Fleischman has written more than fifty books for readers of all ages. He won the Newbery Medal for *The Whipping Boy,* the Boston Globe–Horn Book Award for *Humbug Mountain,* and the Paul A. Witty Short Story Award for "The Scarebird." His autobiography, which looks back to his early days as a magician, is called *The Abracadabra Kid: A Writer's Life.*

McBROOM THE RAINMAKER

by Sid Fleischman

Illustrated by Quentin Blake

I DISLIKE TO tell you this, but some folks have no regard for the truth. A stranger claims he was riding a mule past our wonderful one-acre farm and was attacked by woodpeckers.

Well, there's no truth to that. No, indeed! Those weren't woodpeckers. They were common prairie mosquitoes.

Small ones.

Why, skeeters grow so large out here that everybody uses chicken wire for mosquito netting. But I'm not going to say an unkind word about those zing-zanging, hot-tempered, needle-nosed creatures. They rescued our farm from ruin. That was during the Big Drought we had last year.

Dry? Merciful powers! Our young'uns found some polliwogs and had to teach them to swim. It hadn't rained in so long those tadpoles had never seen water.

That's the sworn truth—certain as my name's Josh McBroom. Why, I'd as soon grab a skunk by the tail as tell a falsehood.

Now, I'd best creep up on the Big Drought the way it crept up on us. I remember we did our spring plowing as usual, and the skeeters hatched out, as usual. The bloodsucking rapscallions could be mighty pesky, but we'd learned to distract them.

Cricket, September 1973

"Will*jill*hester*chester*peter*polly*tim*tom*mary*larry*andlittle-
clarinda!*" I called out. "I hear the whine of gallinippers. Better
put in a patch of beets."

Once the beets were up, the thirsty skeeters stuck in their
long beaks like straws. Didn't they feast, though! They drained
out the red juice, the beets turned white, and we harvested them
as turnips.

The first sign of a dry spell coming was when our clocks
began running slow. I don't mean the store-bought kind—no one
can predict the weather with a tin timepiece. We grew our own
clocks on the farm.

Vegetable clocks.

Now, I'll admit that may be hard to believe, but not if you
understand the remarkable nature of our topsoil. Rich? Glory be!
Anything would grow in it—lickety-bang. Three or four crops a
day until the confounded Big Dry came along.

Of course, we didn't grow clocks with gears and springs and

a name on the dial. Came close once, though. I dropped my dollar pocket watch one day, and before I could find it, the thing had put down roots and grown into a three-dollar alarm clock. But it never kept accurate time after that.

It was our young'uns who discovered they could tell time by vegetable. They planted a cucumber seed, and once the vine leaped out of the ground, it traveled along steady as a clock.

"An inch a second," Will said. "Kind of like a second hand."

"Blossoms come out on the minute," Jill said. "Kind of like a minute hand."

They tried other vegetable timepieces, but pole beans had a way of running a mite fast and squash a mite slow.

As I say, those homegrown clocks began running down. I remember my dear wife, Melissa, was boiling three-and-a-half-minute eggs for breakfast. Little Clarinda planted a cucumber seed, and before it grew three blossoms and thirty inches, those eggs were hard-boiled.

"Mercy!" I declared. "Topsoil must be drying out."

Well, the days turned drier and drier. No doubt about it—our wonderful topsoil was losing some of its get-up-and-go. Why, it took almost a whole day to raise a crop of corn. The young'uns had planted a plum tree, but all it would grow was prunes. Dogs would fight over a dry bone—for the moisture in it.

"Will*jill*hester*chester*peter*polly*tim*tom*mary*larry*andlittle-*clarinda!*" I called. "Keep your eyes peeled for rain."

They took turns in the tree house scanning the skies, and one night Chester said, "Pa, what if it doesn't rain by Fourth of July? How'll we shoot off firecrackers?"

"Be patient, my lambs," I said. We used to grow our own firecrackers, too. Don't let me forget to tell you about it. "Why, it's a long spell to Fourth of July."

My, wasn't the next morning a scorcher! The sun came out so hot that our hens laid fried eggs. But no, that wasn't the Big Dry. The young'uns planted watermelons to cool off and beets to keep the mosquitoes away.

"Look!" Polly exclaimed, pointing to the watermelons. "Pa, they're rising off the ground!"

Rising? They began to float in the air like balloons! We could hardly believe our eyes. And gracious me! When we cut those melons open, it turned out they were full of hot air.

Well, I was getting a mite worried myself. Our beets were growing smaller and smaller, and the skeeters were growing larger and larger. Many a time, before dawn, a rapping at the windows would wake us out of a sound sleep. It was those confounded, needle-nosed gallinippers pecking away, demanding breakfast.

Than it came—the Big Dry.

Mercy! Our cow began giving powdered milk. We pumped

MCBROOM THE RAINMAKER

away on our water pump, but all it brought up was dry steam. The oldest boys went fishing and caught six dried catfish.

"Not a rain cloud in sight, Pa," Mary called from the tree house.

"Watch out for gallinippers!" Larry shouted, as a mosquito made a dive at him. The earth was so parched, we couldn't raise a crop of beets and the varmints were getting downright ornery. Then, as I stood there, I felt my shoes getting tighter and tighter.

"Thunderation!" I exclaimed. "Our topsoil's so dry it's gone in reverse. It's *shrinking* things."

Didn't I lay awake most of the night! Our wonderful one-acre farm might shrink to a square foot. And all night long the skeeters rattled the windows and hammered at the door. Big? The *smallest* ones must have weighed three pounds. In the moonlight I saw them chase a yellow-billed cuckoo.

Didn't that make me sit up in a hurry! An idea struck me. Glory be! I'd break that drought.

First thing in the morning I took Will and Chester to town with me and rented three wagons and a birdcage. We drove straight home, and I called everyone together.

SID FLEISCHMAN

"Shovels, my lambs! Heap these wagons full of topsoil!"

But Larry and little Clarinda were still worried about Fourth of July. "We won't be able to grow fireworks, Pa!"

"You have my word," I declared firmly.

Before long we were on our way. I drove the first wagon, with the young'uns following along behind in the other two. It might be a longish trip, and we had loaded up with picnic hampers of food. We also brought along rolls of chicken wire and our raincoats.

"Where are we going, Pa?" Jill called from the wagon behind.

"Hunting."

"Hunting?" Tom said.

"Exactly, my lambs. We're going to track down a rain cloud and wet down this topsoil."

"But how, Pa?" asked Tim.

I lifted the birdcage from under the wagon seat. "Presto," I said, and whipped off the cover. "Look at that lost-looking, scared-looking, long-tailed creature. Found it hiding from the skeeters under a milk pail this morning. It's a genuine rain crow, my lambs."

"A rain crow?" Mary said. "It doesn't look like a crow at all."

"Correct and exactly," I said, smiling. "It looks like a yellow-billed cuckoo, and that's what it is. But don't folks call 'em rain

crows? Why, that bird can smell a downpour coming sixty miles away. Rattles its throat and begins to squawk. All we got to do is follow that squawk."

But you never heard such a quiet bird! We traveled miles and miles across the prairie, this way and the other, and not a rattle out of that rain crow.

The Big Dry had done its mischief everywhere. We didn't see a dog without his tongue dragging, and it took two of them to bark at us once. A farmer told us he hadn't been able to grow anything all year but baked potatoes!

Of course, we slept under chicken wire—covered the horses, too. My, what a racket the gallinippers made!

Day after day we hauled our three loads of topsoil across the prairie, but that rain crow didn't so much as clear its throat.

The young'uns were getting impatient. "Speak up, rain crow," Chester muttered desperately.

"Rattle," Hester pleaded.

"Squawk," said Peter.

"Please," said Mary. "Just a little peep would help."

Not a cloud appeared in the sky. I'll confess I was getting a mite discouraged. And the Fourth of July not another two weeks off!

We curled up under chicken wire that night, as usual, and the big skeeters kept banging into it so you could hardly sleep. Rattled like a hailstorm. And suddenly, at daybreak, I rose up laughing.

"Hear that?"

The young'uns crowded around the rain crow. We hadn't been able to hear its voice rattle for the mosquitoes. Now it turned in its cage, gazed off to the northwest, opened its yellow beak, and let out a real, ear-busting rain cry.

"*K-kawk! K-kawk! K-kawk!*"

"Put on your raincoats, my lambs!" I said, and we rushed to the wagons.

Sid Fleischman

"K-*kawk! K-kawk! K-kawk!*"

Didn't we raise dust! That bird faced northwest like a dog on point. There was a rain cloud out there, and before long Jill gave a shout.

"I see it!"

And the others chimed in one after the other. "Me, too!"

"K-*kawk! K-kawk! K-kawk!*"

We headed directly for that lone cloud, the young'uns yelling, the horses snorting, and the bird squawking.

Glory be! The first raindrops spattered as large as quarters. And my, didn't the young'uns frolic in that cloudburst! They lifted their faces and opened their mouths and drank right out of the sky. They splashed about and felt mud between their toes for the first time in ages. We all forgot to put on our raincoats and got wet as fish.

Our dried-up topsoil soaked up raindrops like a sponge. It was a joy to behold! But if we stayed longer, we'd get stuck in the mud.

"Back in the wagons!" I shouted. "Home, my lambs, and not a moment to lose."

Well, home was right where we left it.

I got a pinch of onion seeds and went from wagon to wagon, sowing a few seeds in each load of moist earth. I didn't want to crowd those onions.

Now, that rich topsoil of ours had been idle a long time—it was rarin' to go. Before I could run back to the house, the greens were up. By the time I could get down my shotgun, the tops had grown four or five feet tall—onions are terrible slow growers. Before I could load my shotgun, the bulbs were finally busting up through the soil.

We stood at the windows watching. Those onion roots were having a great feast. The wagons heaved and cracked as the onions swelled and lifted themselves—they were already the size of pumpkins. But that wasn't near big enough. Soon they were larger'n washtubs and began to shoulder the smaller ones off the wagons.

Suddenly we heard a distant roaring in the air. Those zing-zanging, hot-tempered, bloodsucking prairie mosquitoes were returning from town with their stingers freshly sharpened. The Big Dry hadn't done their dispositions any good—their tempers were at a boil.

"You going to shoot them down, Pa?" Will asked.

"Too many for that," I answered.

"How big do those onions have to grow?" Chester asked.

"How big are they now?"

"A little smaller'n a cowshed."

"That's big enough." I nodded, lifting the window just enough to poke the shotgun through.

Well, the gallinippers spied the onions—I had planted red onions, you know—and came swarming over our farm. I let go at the bulbs with a double charge of buckshot and slammed the window.

"Handkerchiefs, everyone!" I called out. The odor of fresh-cut onion shot through the air, under the door, and through the cracks. Cry? In no time our handkerchiefs were wet as dishrags.

Well! You never saw such surprised gallinippers. They zing-zanged every which way, most of them backwards. And weep? Their eyes began to flow like sprinkling cans. Onion tears! The roof began to leak. Mud puddles formed everywhere. Before long the downpour was equal to any cloudburst I ever saw. Near flooded our farm!

The skeeters kept their distance after that. But they'd been mighty helpful.

With our farm freshly watered we grew tons of great onions—three or four crops a day. Gave them away to farmers all over the county.

The newspaper ran a picture of the whole family—the rain crow, too.

McBROOM THE RAINMAKER BREAKS BIG DROUGHT

The young'uns had a splendid Fourth of July. Grew all the fireworks they wanted. They'd dash about with bean shooters—shooting radish seeds. You know how fast radishes come up. In our rich topsoil they grew quicker'n the eye. The seeds hardly touched the ground before they took root and swelled up and exploded. They'd go off like strings of firecrackers.

And, mercy, what a racket! Didn't I say I'd rather catch a skunk by the tail than tell a fib? Well, at nightfall a scared cat ran up a tree, and I went up a ladder to get it down. Reached in the branches and caught it by the tail.

I'd be lying if I didn't admit the truth. It was a skunk.

Cricket Is 30! Congratulations!

**by
Eve Bunting**

I WISH I COULD remember more detail about my first sale to *Cricket*. It was back in the 1970s when *Cricket* was a fledgling . . . a *Cricketette* perhaps? I do remember my elation on making such a prestigious sale. I came into my writing group brandishing the acceptance of my story, proud as could be.

That first story, "A Fish for Finn," had as protagonist Finn McCool, my favorite giant . . . Irish of course. I actually did a picture book about Finn and his arch enemy Culcullan, the Scottish giant. When I speak to children, I let them know that Finn McCool wasn't the smartest giant in the world, but he was gentle, kind, and compassionate. And so he was in "A Fish for Finn," saving the life of the magic fish and being rewarded. What a guy!

Working with Marianne on that story and subsequent ones was a joy. *Cricket* may be thirty years old, but Marianne isn't thirty years older since my first sale to her. I want to wish her and *Cricket,* which has since given birth to several offspring, many, many more years together. I knew from the beginning that a top-quality children's magazine would be a wonderful success, and of course, I was right. I am honored to have been a small part of it.

Eve Bunting is one of the best-known creators of books for young readers. She is the author of the Caldecott Medal–winning *Smoky Night* and many other award-winning books.

A Fish for Finn

by Eve Bunting

Illustrated by Enrico Arno

INN McCOOL was the only giant in all Ireland, and a terrible good one he was, too. He lived in the town of Dunmill with his wife, Oonagh, and the people thereabouts thought very well of him.

When it was time for a man to put new thatch on his roof, he knew who to call on for help. Big as Finn was, he could stand on the ground and do the thatching with no need of a ladder.

If a horse needed shoeing, Finn worked with the blacksmith, lifting the beast clear off the ground so the work could be done with no fuss or bother.

When the fishing boats set out of a windless morning, Finn waded waist deep in the Irish sea, pushing two before him and pulling two behind, tied to his belt. The sorrow of it was that he could never go fishing with the rest of them, for there wasn't a boat built that could carry him. And when the salmon ran fat in

Cricket, May 1974

the deep River Boyne, all the men of Dunmill angled and trolled from the green grassy banks, all except Finn McCool. Finn stayed home or came to watch, for his hands were too big to hold a rod, and the rod he could hold was too big for the fish. It was a sad circumstance altogether, and he longed and he longed for a fish of his own.

One morning, very early, Oonagh heard a knocking at her front door. Finn was still snoring in the bed beside her, his two big feet sticking clear out of the bedroom window. When Finn built their house, he had measured himself standing up, for he knew he'd have to fit. But he'd forgotten entirely that he'd need to lie down. Finn did things like that. But then, as the people of the town always said, a man can't have everything. "Finn's as good a big fellow as ever wore a hat," they said, "and sure if his brains don't match his size, what matter? We'll take care of him."

Rat-tat-tat. Oonagh heard the knocking on her door again. She slipped out of bed carefully, not to waken Finn. Michael Mor, the village baker, stood on the step.

"God bless all here," he said, taking off his cap and making a little bow. "I've come for himself, but I can hear he's sleeping."

Oonagh smiled. "Aye. He has a fine pair of lungs in him. You could hear him in Cork if you'd a mind to it."

Michael Mor could hardly stand still. "A giant salmon's been spotted in the river!" he squeaked with excitement. "The biggest fish seen by man since the minds of any of us can remember."

"You do say!"

Michael Mor nodded. "He has a hooked snout and a humped back and he's six foot if he's an inch. We none of us made to catch him, for sure there wasn't a man there with a line fit to hold him. No, nor six of us with the strength to pull him in." He stopped for breath. "Anyways, we were thinking, the fish by rights should

106

belong to Finn. He's our only giant, and a good one he is. This is one salmon he could take with his own line and hook."

They looked at each other, and Oonagh smiled. "A fish of his own! I'm thanking you, Michael Mor."

They listened and heard the silence. Oonagh looked at the bedroom window. The snoring had stopped, and the two big feet were gone.

"Where is this fish?" Finn stood behind Oonagh. He was dressed and he carried his fishing pole made from the topmost

branch of a sycamore tree. His line was a mooring rope, the line that had never taken a fish. "Where is this salmon?"

"He's headed upstream and he's headed fast," Michael Mor shouted. "But sure with the legs you have on you, Finn, you could be in Ballyblae before him and awaiting his pleasure."

"I'm off!" Finn set his fishing hat on his head. "I'm obliged to you, Michael. Wife, get a good fire going. There'll be fish for supper."

Then he was gone. Two big steps took him down the hill. Two more took him through the town of Dunmill, the thunder of his feet cracking the whitewash on the cottages. He stepped over a bridge, over a windmill, over a mountain where sheep grazed, and saw before him the roofs of Ballyblae.

There he stopped where the Boyne ran clear and deep, the pebbles on the bottom brown and speckled as thrush eggs. He took from his pocket a round red cheese and a hook the size of a ship's anchor. The shadow of him spread dark on the water, and he remembered what the fishermen made him do when he went with them. He lay the length of himself on the riverbank and stuck the round red cheese on the end of the hook. Then he dropped his line and let the current have it. The cheese bobbed like a football.

Finn put his hat beneath his head and lay still, waiting. The sky and the fields and the river were empty. Except . . . except for a shadow that came sliding and gliding along the bottom of the Boyne.

Finn held his breath. In that instant he saw the fish, and it was bigger than he had known a fish could be. He saw the silver sheen of it and the big hooked snout of it and the eyes like two glass bowls of currant jelly. He saw that the eyes were on the round red cheese and that the mouth was open and ready. The salmon bit and Finn leaped up, pulling the line from the water. The fish was not on the hook. Neither was the round red cheese.

EVE BUNTING

"You stole it, so you did," Finn roared. "You stole my round
red cheese!" He took the hook from the line and blundered into
the river, holding it in his hand. "I thought I'd caught me a fish of
my own, but you tricked me, so you did." He hacked at the river
with the hook, laying about himself like a thresher with a scythe.
"Begorrah, I'll get you, if I have to empty the river to do it!"

He saw a flash of silver between his feet, and he brought the
hook down and felt it catch on something soft and firm, and he
lifted the hook from the water and saw the fish speared on the

barb. The river streamed from the silver sides, and the salmon flashed and thrashed so that the Boyne itself seemed to scatter and scream.

Finn raised the hook high in the air. "I've got you. The first fish of my own, and a right looking one you are."

The fish hung motionless, a shining kite on a windless day.

Finn brought it down and took it in his hands, and they studied each other face to face. Finn saw where the hook went into the fish's neck, and he was sorry. "Stay still," he said. "I had no mind to hurt you, though isn't that the silly thing to be saying, and me making to take you home for my supper? I'll have this wicked thing out of you in a minute. There's nothing in my heart says you have to be suffering." He held the fish in one hand and worked at the hook with the other.

The eyes of the big salmon grew dull and cloudy.

"Are you dead already?" Finn asked, and he felt a terrible sorrow, for he was a good and gentle man, and this was the first living creature he had ever in his life harmed. "There's a difference, I'm thinking, to salmon on a plate and salmon in the river. Sure if I was a fishing man, I'd lose my appetite for the stuff entirely."

He had to twist the hook to free it, and he had to tug, and it came loose with a jerk, the end of it catching itself in Finn's own thumb.

"Ow!" He leaped in the air at the sharpness of the pain.

A FISH FOR FINN

"Pull it out, man. Pull it out."

Finn was so surprised that he stopped yelping and jumping. "You can *speak?*"

"Aye," the salmon said. "And you'd better take that thing from your thumb, for it's a desperate weapon altogether. And I'm the one that knows it!"

Finn looked at the fish and saw the wound in its neck, and he looked at his thumb and saw the bright blood oozing around the hook. "Ow, ow!" He danced a little pain jig.

"Take it out, man!" The salmon's voice was impatient.

"But sure I have no free hand."

"That's true. You'd better put me back in the Boyne, for I'm thinking now you have need of that hand for more than holding me."

Finn dropped the salmon and saw the river open and cover it with the comfort of its waters. He sat on the riverbank and worked on the barb in his thumb and whimpered a bit, for though he was bigger than anybody else, he wasn't any braver. He twisted and jerked, and the barb came free.

"Suck your thumb now," the salmon called from the river. "It'll be all right so."

Finn put his thumb in his mouth and felt the pleasure of his own warmth on the hurt, and all at once he knew things he'd never known before. He knew how birds flew and how fishes swam and how men thought and what kept the stars in the sky and the names of every one of them from the smallest to the largest. He was dizzy with knowledge. He took his thumb from his mouth, and the world steadied.

The salmon swam in widening arcs. "I should be telling you that I'm not only the biggest salmon in the world, I'm also the smartest salmon in the world," he said.

EVE BUNTING

Finn shook his head. There was no way he could understand the things that were happening.

"You see, Finn McCool, you live with friends, and there's nobody yet has sought to harm you. Me, now, the bigger I got, the more men tried to catch me. So I got smarter. Too smart for them."

"I caught you," Finn said.

"Aye!" The fish curved in two wings of creamy water. "But I've never met up with a giant before, swinging a hook like a madman. It's a wonder you didn't scare the senses right out of me."

"I'm regretting that, salmon."

"I know you are. You put the barb in my neck, but the eyes of you and the hands of you were full of sorrow, after. And remember, giant, you were smart enough to catch me but not smart enough to keep me. You could as easily have put me on the bank as back in the river. I'd be in your pocket this minute and ready for the pan." The fish sighed. "You're a good man, Finn, but I'm thinking your brains leave a lot wanting. And that won't do. Big isn't enough, for the day may come when you meet up with an enemy who's bigger than you and smarter than you, too. So I'm bequeathing a gift to you. That thumb of yours, the one where our two bloods mixed, will be your wisdom thumb from this day on. When you have a need to know where the wind comes from or what makes the river run or the name of every king in Ireland since time began, suck on your thumb. The wisdom's there and waiting."

Finn looked at his big ugly thumb with the gash across the breadth of it. "You do say!"

"Good-bye to you then, Finn McCool. Thanks for the cheese. And don't be worrying yourself about my sore neck. I heal fast."

Finn watched as the waters opened for the big salmon and closed behind him. "Now why did I put him back in the river?"

he asked himself. "I'm a gormless creature, so I am!" He put his thumb in his mouth to ease the hurt, and he knew about the fish and about himself. Smart he was not and never had been, but he cared about people and about creatures. He had known when he saw the fish face to face, that he couldn't kill it, or any living thing. He had known that giants are few, be they fish or man, and rare enough to be left alone. These things he understood with his heart, not his mind. It was almost enough.

Finn shouldered his rod, tucked his thumb in his belt for the day he might need it, and stepped over the mountain where the sheep grazed, over the windmill, over the bridge, through the town of Dunmill, and up the hill, home.

EVE BUNTING

How Did Mary Poppins Find Me? by P. L. Travers

WHERE DO IDEAS come from? Have you any idea where you get an idea? So many people—many of them children—have asked me where I got the idea for Mary Poppins. They want to know whether she is taken from somebody in real life, or whether she is just invented. But how could she be taken from somebody in real life? Did *you* ever know anybody who slid *up* the banisters? On the other hand, who could have "just invented" somebody who slides up banisters and flies from place to place with no other means of propulsion than a parrot-headed umbrella?

These are tricky questions, and I never knew how to answer them till Hendrik Willem van Loon, who wrote and drew so many things for children, came hurrying to my rescue. "No one thought her up," he told me. "She's an idea that came looking for *you!*" And as he was speaking, the idea of three dancing elephants apparently came looking for him, for he drew them for me on the back of an envelope.

But why me? I wanted to know. Why didn't she happen to somebody else? And then I remembered that a boy of sixteen had once asked me to promise him never to become clever. Well, it was a strange request but one I could readily agree to—though of course I wanted to know what he meant. "I've just been reading *Mary Poppins* again," he told me, "and it could only have been written by a special sort of lunatic!"

Well, in a way I understood. To think things up you have to be clever. But to sit still and let them happen to you clearly needs something else. Maybe a kind of listening. Perhaps Lewis Carroll sat still and listened and the idea of Alice in Wonderland came by and tapped him on the shoulder. Perhaps the world is full of ideas, all of them looking for the right person. If so, all you have to do—in addition to being a lunatic—is simply to sit quite still and listen and one of them may happen to you.

Art by Mary Shepard from the book Mary Poppins Comes Back

Cricket, December 1973

P. L. Travers was the creator of the Mary Poppins series. Stories about her life and work are collected in the recently published book *A Lively Oracle: A Centennial Celebration of P. L. Travers.*

A Hike in New York City
By Sam Levenson

Illustrated by
Hilary Knight

Many years ago I used to be on TV and radio. One show I worked on was called This Is Show Business. *We introduced many fine performers on this show, and one of the best of them was a young comedian named Sam Levenson, who is now famous. He and I became great friends, partly because we had both been high school teachers when we were younger, and partly because our childhoods were very much alike. It's for that last reason I enjoyed reading "A Hike in New York City." I hope you will too.*
—Clifton Fadiman

AT LEAST ONCE each summer we kids went off on a hike, but never without strong opposition from Mama. When it came to the open road, Mama had a closed mind.

Her method of discouraging us from venturing into the unknown was to make the entire project appear ridiculous:

"You're going on a what?"

"We're going on a hike."

"What's a hike?" Mama would ask.

When we started to explain it, the whole idea did in fact become ridiculous.

"We go walking, Ma."

"Walking? For that you have to leave home? What's the matter with walking right here? You walk; I'll watch."

Cricket, May 1974

"You don't understand, Ma. We take lunch along."

"I'll give you lunch here, and you can march right around the table," and she would start singing a march, clapping her hands rhythmically.

"Ma, we climb mountains in the woods."

She couldn't understand why it was so much more enjoyable to fall off a mountain than off a fire escape.

"And how about the wild animals in the woods?"

"Wild animals? What kind of wild animals?"

"A bear, for instance. A bear could eat you up."

"Ma. Bears don't eat little children."

"O.K. So he won't eat you, but he could take a bite and spit out! I'm telling you now, if a wild animal eats you up don't come running to me. And who's going with you?"

"Well, there's Georgie—"

"Georgie! Not him! He's a real wild animal!" She then went on to list all the conditions for the trip. "And remember one thing, don't tear your pants, and remember one thing, don't eat wild berries and bring me home the cramps, and remember one thing, don't tell me tomorrow morning that you're too tired to go to school, and remember one thing, wear rubbers, a sweater, warm underwear, and an umbrella, and a hat, and remember one thing, if you should get lost in the jungle, call up so I'll know you're all right. And don't dare come home without color in your cheeks. I wish I was young and free like you. Take soap."

Since the consent was specifically granted for the next day only, that night none of us slept. There was always a chance that it might rain. Brother Albert stayed at the crystal set all night like a ship's radio operator with his earphones on, listening to weather bulletins and repeating them aloud for the rest of us. "It's clearing in Nebraska. Hot air masses coming up from the Gulf. They say it's good for planting alfalfa. Storm warning off the coast of Newfoundland. It's drizzling in Montreal."

At 6 A.M. we were ready for Operation Hike, rain or shine, but we had to wait for Papa to get up. We didn't need his permission, but we did need his blanket.

Into the valley of Central Park marched the six hundred, bowed down with knapsacks, flashlights, a Cracker-Jack box compass-mirror (so you could tell not only where you were lost but who was lost), a thermos bottle (semiautomatic—you had to fill it but it emptied by itself), and an ax. Onward! Forward! Upward! Philip was always the leader. He was the one to get lost first. Jerry was the lookout. He would yell, "Look out!" and fall off the cliff. None of us knew how long we were supposed to march. We went on because we didn't know what to do if we stopped. One brave coward finally spoke up. "I can't go on anymore. The heat is killing me. Let's start the fire here."

No hike was complete without Georgie and his Uncle Bernie's World War I bugle. This kid had lungs like a vacuum cleaner. With him outside the walls of Jericho, they could have sent the rest of the army home. He used to stand on a hill and let go a blast that had the Staten Island ferries running into each other.

Lunch, naturally, had been packed in a shoe box—sandwiches, fruit, cheese, and napkins all squashed together neatly. The lid would open by itself every twenty minutes for air.

It happened every time, the Miracle of the Sandwiches. One

kid always got a "brilliant idea." "Hey. I got a brilliant idea. I'm tired of my mother's sandwiches. Let's everybody trade sandwiches." All the kids exchanged sandwiches, and miraculously we all ended up with salami.

Albert was the true nature lover. "You know, you can learn a lot about human nature from the ants," he always said as he lifted up rock after rock to study his favorite insects. And he was right. While he was studying the ants, someone swiped his apple.

We came home with color in our cheeks—green. To make sure we could go again, we didn't forget Mama. We brought her a bouquet. She took one whiff and broke out in red blotches. Papa yelled but didn't lay a hand on us. He was afraid it was catching.

Sam Levenson was best known for his quotable sayings and witticisms, which are collected in a number of popular books. From 1959 to 1964 he hosted *The Sam Levenson Show* on television. He died in August 1980.

Dreadful Consequences of Absent-Mindedness

by Michael Ende

Translated from the German by Doris Orgel
Illustrated by Eric von Schmidt

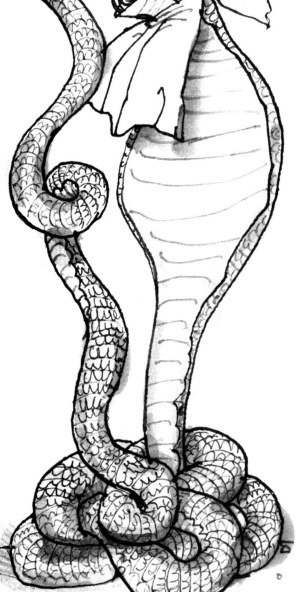

There was a cobra, real, not fake
(Known also as the "eyeglass-snake")
Who, owing to an absent mind,
Left her eyeglasses behind.
Then almost nil became her sight.
"Still," did the dauntless reptile hiss,
"Voracious is my appetite,
And my dinner I can't miss."
So she began to writhe and bend,
And, seeking food, found—her own end,
Which first she merely nibbled at,
Then gulped it down. "How delicate,
Yet, odd," thought she, and ate a little
More. And more, and more. Around the middle
She felt an unaccustomed dread
Which did not stop her as it ought
To have. She ate herself from tail to head.
"How dark it's out—no, in," she thought.
Her last, did this thought prove to be.
All that was left now, lit'rally,
Of the eyeglass-snake, forlorn,
Was to herself herself to mourn.

Cricket, October 1982

Michael Ende was a popular German author who wrote many award-winning books, including *The Neverending Story.*

Doris Orgel has written and translated many books for readers of all ages. She won a Sydney Taylor Book Award for her novel *The Devil in Vienna.*

Cricket Opens a Door

by James Cross Giblin

WHETHER I SPEAK to a gathering of aspiring adult writers or to students in a middle-school English class, the questions that come from the audience are remarkably similar. "Where do you get your ideas?" is one, and "How did you first get published?" is another. I have a simple, one-word answer for the second: *Cricket.* Some of those present inevitably look puzzled, so I go on to tell how it came about.

Back in 1977, New York City faced one of its frequent budget crises, and the public library was particularly hard hit. Its hours were reduced and its program funding cut. A group of children's writers responded to the library's plight by planning a book about the city and its attractions, all proceeds from which would go to the library's children's rooms. Invitations to contribute a piece to the book, titled *The New York Kids' Catalog,* went out to hundreds of children's book professionals, and I received one of them. The contributors would not be paid for their efforts, but would have the satisfaction of giving to a good cause.

At that time I was known primarily as the editor-in-chief of Clarion Books. But I'd also written two travel pieces about a trip I'd taken to China, and some articles for adults on how to write for young people. I hadn't written anything for children myself, though. Frankly, I was hesitant to take the plunge because I knew from my editorial work how hard it was. A writer for children has to see the world through the eyes of a child without ever being childish. But now that I'd been invited to contribute something to the *Catalog,* I decided to accept the challenge.

Following the time-honored advice of writing about something you know, I chose as my topic the Flatiron Building, one of New York's earliest skyscrapers. It was just a few blocks from my apartment, and I'd long been curious about its history. I had fun researching and writing the piece, and the editors of the *Catalog* accepted it without asking for any changes. Their positive response encouraged me to show the piece to other publications. Although Doubleday had exclusive book rights to the material, the contributors were free to submit their manuscripts to magazine editors for possible advance publication. With this in mind, I decided to send my article to Marianne Carus, editor of *Cricket.*

If I'd expected another easy acceptance, that hope was dashed when Marianne returned the manuscript a few weeks later. In the letter that accompanied it, she wrote, "It is a good piece, but mainly and especially for New York kids. . . . If those kids are not familiar with the Flatiron Building, they could go and see it—other kids could not." She went on, "I don't think that children in other places would really care about this piece unless you could change it somewhat and include more general information about skyscrapers (it's a fascinating subject and one we haven't had in *Cricket*). For example, more about the architectural history of skyscrapers and about the men who first designed and built them. Why did they change from stone to steel? How did sky-scrapers change the cities they were built in? Which ones are the most interesting (not only in New York) or the fanciest or the tallest? I don't know if you'd be willing to do that much research in architecture, etc.," she continued, "but if you're interested, per-haps we could discuss this further. . . ."

Of course I was interested. Like all good editors, Marianne had fired my imagination and helped me to see all sorts of new possi-bilities in the material. I wrote her a note saying I appreciated her comments and suggestions and would be happy to broaden the scope of the piece. Then I began the additional research, fitting it in around the demands of my full-time job.

The revision took more than six months and involved visits not just to skyscrapers in New York, but to tall buildings in Boston, Cleveland, Chicago, and other cities. I read several histories of skyscrapers, and articles about the impact—often negative—that they have on the environment. Then I compressed all the infor-mation I'd gathered into a manuscript of just over 2,000 words. Now my work was done except for the title. I could call the piece simply "Skyscrapers," but I wanted something more intriguing, more lyrical. After experimenting with several variations, I finally settled on "Buildings That Scrape the Sky."

At last, on a snowy day in January 1978, I was ready to send the revision to Marianne. In a cover letter, I wrote, "As you'll see from the enclosed manuscript, I haven't forgotten your suggestion of last June that I broaden the article on the Flatiron Building into a more general piece on skyscrapers." I took it to the post office before going to work at Clarion and said a silent prayer as I slipped the Manila envelope down the mail chute. And then I waited—and waited—in that state of suspended animation that all writers experience while their work is being evaluated. When I'd submitted the manuscript to the magazine originally, I'd gotten a postcard acknowledging its receipt. It struck me as odd that none came this time, but I put it down to an oversight. I was still waiting for word in early March when I met at Clarion with Marcia Leonard, *Cricket*'s associate editor, to discuss future books on our list that the magazine might be interested in excerpting.

All during our conversation I longed to ask Marcia about my article, but I held back. As an editor I'd received countless phone calls from anxious authors, eager for word on their submissions, and I knew how annoying such inquiries could be. But just before Marcia left, I couldn't hold back any longer. "Do you know if Marianne got the revision of my skyscraper article?" I asked.

Marcia looked startled. "No," she said, "I'm sure she didn't." She promised to check on its status when she got back to Illinois; in the meantime, she suggested I send another copy to Marianne.

I did so the following day, and a few days after that an acknowledgment card arrived from *Cricket* along with a note from Marianne.

This time around, I didn't have to wait nearly so long for a reaction. In early April, a letter from *Cricket* was in my mailbox when I got home from work. I was immediately hopeful because the envelope was slim; that meant it contained only a letter, not the returned manuscript. Still I was hesitant to read it, fearing it might be a rejection. Only when I'd climbed the stairs to my third-floor apartment and sat down in my favorite chair did I finally tear open the envelope. I could feel a smile spread over my face as I read Marianne's words. "Good news for you!" she began. "'Buildings That Scrape the Sky' is a very nice article on the subject, much better and more comprehensive than the short piece you sent a while ago. I'm so pleased and thought I should tell you immediately that I am happy to accept it for publication in

Cricket." Marianne went on to say that the piece might have to be shortened a bit here and there, and that I'd receive a copy of the edited version for my approval in six to eight weeks. But at that point all I could think about was one thing—the article had been accepted!

The edited manuscript arrived on schedule two months later. It came with a covering letter from Charnan Simon, the associate editor to whom the piece had been assigned. "I had to shorten the text somewhat to fit our tight space limitations," Charnan wrote, "and I tried to simplify the language where I felt our younger readers might have trouble, but in general your style and organization suit us just fine. There is one major change I ought to explain," she continued. "Marianne and I both think the ending as you have it is a bit negative—even though you're right to point out the safety hazards and possible drawbacks to skyscrapers, we don't like the idea of ending the piece on a downbeat. So, we've deleted the last paragraph and changed the second to the last as marked. What do you think?"

I'd never been completely satisfied with the ending, so I was open to the idea of changing it. After several back-and-forth exchanges, we reached a compromise.

"Does all this seem like nitpicking?" Charnan wrote when she sent me the final version. "I can't help thinking of Ezra Pound's invocation to God to set him up in a tobacco shop, or anything except this damned profession of writing, where one has to use one's brains all the time."

If it was nitpicking, I was grateful for it, and I expressed my gratitude in a note to Charnan and Marianne. "Thanks to you both for being so concerned about making the final paragraph as clear and effective a conclusion to the piece as possible. I appreciate it." What I didn't say, because I didn't know it then, was that the experience had taught me a lesson about the value of revising something until it was right. This lesson would stand me in good stead with all of my future writing.

"Buildings That Scrape the Sky" appeared in the April 1979 issue of *Cricket,* almost exactly a year after the manuscript was accepted for publication. Trina, the art director, had gone all out with the piece, persuading David Macaulay to do the striking line drawings that illustrated it. I couldn't have been more pleased with the way the total package looked in the pages of the magazine. The check for $440 that arrived on publication was gratifying, too, especially since it was the first income I'd received from my children's writing. (The article also turned out to be my first published work for children. Because of production problems, *The New York Kids' Catalog,* which contained the piece on the Flatiron Building, was delayed until the fall of 1979.)

My interest in skyscrapers did not end with the publication of the article. The research I'd done for it made me want to explore the topic in even greater depth, and I did so in my second book for young people titled, naturally enough, *The Skyscraper Book* (Thomas Y. Crowell/HarperCollins, 1981). It has been followed in the years since by more than twenty other nonfiction books for children and young adults, several of which have been excerpted in *Cricket.* But none of these publications has meant quite as much to me as that first sale to the magazine back in April 1978. It truly opened the door to a new career.

I'm just one of many writers who has made his debut in the pages of *Cricket* during its first thirty years. If all of them could share their experiences, I'm sure they would be similar to mine, from the initial excitement of acceptance to the deep satisfaction at seeing their fledgling efforts in print. Now it'll be interesting to see what new talents *Cricket* discovers and supports in its next thirty years as it continues to promote the best in writing for children.

James Cross Giblin's most recent honor is the Robert F. Sibert Award—the award for best nonfiction book for younger readers—which he received for *The Life and Death of Adolf Hitler* in 2003. In recognition of his body of work, he was given the Washington Post–Children's Book Guild Award for Nonfiction in 1996.

Please remember that this article was written in 1979 when no one imagined that the World Trade Center towers would become a target for terrorists.

EVERY DAY THOUSANDS of tourists from all over the world line up in the blue-carpeted lobby of the World Trade Center in New York City. They are waiting to board express elevators that will whisk them up to the enclosed observation deck on the 107th floor of one of the Center's twin silver towers.

On calm days, visitors can take escalators from the 107th floor up to the open promenade above the 110th floor. At an altitude of 1,377 feet, this promenade is the world's highest outdoor observation platform. From it, great structures like the Brooklyn Bridge appear to be only two feet long, and cars in the streets look like tiny toys. Visitors feel the thrill and sense of power that people must have felt whenever they stood on high places and surveyed the world around them. But only in the last 100 years or so have we had the technology to

Buildings That Scrape the Sky

by **James Cross Giblin**

Illustrated by David Macaulay

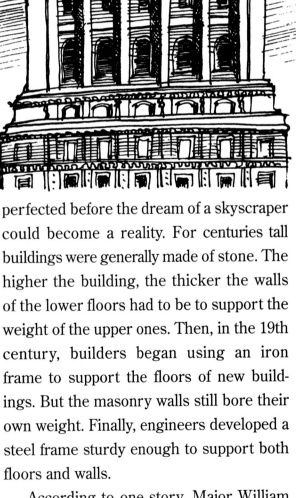

construct buildings of 25, 50, or 100 and more stories—the buildings known as skyscrapers.

One invention that helped make tall buildings possible was the passenger elevator. Elisha Otis created a sensation when he demonstrated a steam-powered elevator at the Crystal Palace Exhibition in New York in 1853. Before then, few buildings were more than five or six stories tall, because people could not comfortably climb stairs that went higher.

New construction methods also had to be perfected before the dream of a skyscraper could become a reality. For centuries tall buildings were generally made of stone. The higher the building, the thicker the walls of the lower floors had to be to support the weight of the upper ones. Then, in the 19th century, builders began using an iron frame to support the floors of new buildings. But the masonry walls still bore their own weight. Finally, engineers developed a steel frame sturdy enough to support both floors and walls.

According to one story, Major William

129

Le Baron Jenney, a Chicago engineer and architect, first realized how strong a steel frame could be when he got angry at the squawkings of the family parrot. He slammed a heavy book down on the parrot's steel wire cage and was surprised when the wires neither bent nor cracked. Whether that story is true or not, Jenney was the first architect to use a steel frame in the construction of a tall building, and the 12-story Home Insurance Company Building he designed in Chicago in 1884 paved the way for skyscrapers all across the United States.

There was a strong economic need for the tall new office buildings. After the Civil War, the United States had grown rapidly, and recent immigrants and people from rural areas crowded into the cities to fill the jobs opening up in factories and offices. As the demand for land in city centers rose, so did prices. Naturally, landlords wanted to have as many floors and as much rentable space as possible in their new buildings.

Although many people think of New York as the home of the skyscraper, Chicago actually led the way. After a great fire destroyed most of central Chicago in 1871, business leaders wanted to rebuild the city in the most modern, attractive, and profitable style possible. In the 1880s and 1890s,

JAMES CROSS GIBLIN

one skyscraper after another went up in downtown Chicago.

Probably the most talented and most famous of the young architects during this time was Louis Sullivan, who had come to work in Chicago after studying at the Massachusetts Institute of Technology and in Paris. Sullivan, a rebellious, poetic Irishman, believed in what was known as "organic architecture." He thought the form of a building should reflect its function and should harmonize with its environment.

"What is the chief feature of an office building?" Sullivan asked in an article he wrote in 1896. "At once we answer, it is lofty. It must be tall, every inch of it tall . . . it must be a proud and soaring thing, rising in sheer exultation from top to bottom without a single dissenting line."

Eastern architects like Richard Morris Hunt and Charles McKim disagreed with Sullivan. They believed that skyscrapers should borrow designs from the Greeks, the Romans, and the Gothic cathedrals of Western Europe.

Financial backers of the new skyscrapers seemed to agree. The more Greek columns or Gothic arches a skyscraper boasted, the more they thought it would impress people with its magnificence. For the skyscraper had quickly become a symbol of wealth and success for the firms that built and owned them.

The 20-story Flatiron Building—built in 1902 and nicknamed because its triangular shape reminded many people of the flatirons used to press clothes—was the first skyscraper in New York City. More soon followed, and in 1913, the Woolworth Building, erected by the owner of the successful chain of dime stores, reached the unprecedented height of 60 stories or 792 feet. With its strong vertical lines leading to a Gothic tower at the top, the Woolworth Building combined many of Louis Sullivan's ideas with past architectural styles, and journalists called it the "Cathedral of Commerce."

Not everyone admired skyscrapers, though. City planners had already begun to criticize the tall buildings for creating sunless streets and traffic jams, and in 1916 New York City enacted the first Building Code Resolution. This Resolution gave the city legal control over the height and floor plans of new buildings, as well as the right to establish health and fire prevention standards for them. Other cities soon followed with resolutions of their own.

To provide adequate light and air for buildings and streets, many of the new laws required that the exterior walls of tall buildings be set back above certain heights. This led to the steplike profiles of many office buildings and apartment houses built during the 1920s and 1930s.

By 1929, American cities boasted 377 skyscrapers of more than 20 stories, and 188 were in New York City. Of those 188, 15 were over 500 feet tall. The tallest of all, the Chrysler Building, rose to a height of 77 stories or 1,046 feet. Its tower was decorated with metal designs inspired not by Gothic churches, but by the hubcaps on Chrysler automobiles.

The Great Depression that hit the United States in late 1929 put a stop to many new skyscrapers. But plans were too far along to halt construction for what would be for many years the tallest building in the world—the 102-story Empire State Building in New York City. Completed in 1931, its stepped-back tower rises 1,250 feet, and on a very clear day, visitors on its highest observation deck can see an area with a circumference of nearly 200 miles.

There was a fresh surge of skyscraper construction in the late 1940s. The Depression and World War II were both over, business was thriving, additional office space was needed, and steel and other building materials were available once more.

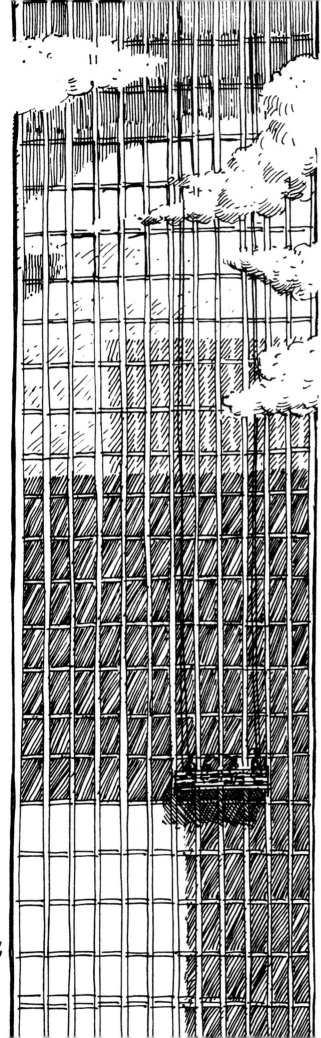

No longer were skyscrapers a purely American phenomenon. In the cities of England, Europe, and Asia, skyscrapers rose for the first time from the bombed-out rubble of the old city centers. But the United States was still the leader. The stepped-back style of the 1920s and '30s gave way to the single slab rising from an open plaza, as in the Seagram Building erected in New York in 1958.

Skyscrapers assumed bold new shapes, from circles to triangles to octagons. Outer walls of tinted glass often replaced the concrete surfaces of earlier buildings, and sometimes the steel structure was deliberately exposed as part of the design. Rarely was a postwar building ornamented with Gothic or Renaissance details like the skyscrapers of the past.

The Empire State Building remained the world's tallest until the twin towers of the World Trade Center opened in 1972. But the Trade Center's triumph was short. A mere two years later, in 1974, the 110-story Sears Tower was completed in Chicago. It reached a height of 1,454 feet—nearly 100 feet higher than the World Trade Center. The skyscraper had started its worldwide journey in Chicago in the 1880s, and returned in triumph with the Sears Tower.

What of the future? Will skyscrapers go even higher? It's possible—technologically. Engineers are prepared to build taller structures, braced with stiff exterior walls to prevent swaying in high winds. Elevator manufacturers are confident their vehicles can carry passengers up to at least 180 floors.

Architect Paolo Soleri has designed and made models of future cities that would be contained in a few giant air-conditioned buildings two or three miles high. Around these great towers the land would remain in its natural, undeveloped state.

Meanwhile, critics argue against erecting more skyscrapers by pointing out serious hazards in today's tall buildings. Deadly smoke and flames can quickly sweep up through the elevator shafts, air-conditioning ducts, and mail chutes in a skyscraper with an inadequate sprinkler system. Tall buildings distort the winds, causing downdrafts that can blow pedestrians off their feet. Those who work or live in high-rise buildings are more vulnerable to muggers and thieves, who can escape easily via the many elevators and stairs. Ecologists point out that a cluster of tall buildings in a city often overburdens the public transportation and parking lot capacities.

Skyscrapers are also lavish consumers —and wasters—of electric power. In one recent year, the addition of 17 million square feet of skyscraper office space in New York City raised the peak daily demand for electricity by 120,000 kilowatts, enough to supply the entire city of Albany, New York.

Skyscrapers put a severe strain on a city's sanitation facilities, too. If fully occupied, the World Trade Center would generate 2¼ million gallons of raw sewage each day—as much as a city the size of Stamford, Connecticut, which has a population of more than 109,000.

Skyscrapers can also interfere with television reception, block bird flyways, obstruct air traffic, and sometimes stand out as ugly objects in the city landscape. Lewis Mumford, a well-known commentator on our modern industrial civilization, has said, "Skyscrapers have always been put up for reasons of advertisement and publicity. They are not economically sound or efficient."

And yet, throughout history, people have built tall structures—from the towers of medieval castles, to the lofty spires of Gothic churches, to the commercial skyscrapers of the last 100 years. And in the future, despite all problems, skyscrapers will most probably continue to be raised higher and higher into the sky.

Cover for September 1978, **"Cricket's Birthday Party,"**
illustration by Trina Schart Hyman, ink and watercolor

*Cover for August 1976, illustration by Hilary Knight, watercolor and pencil
with metallic gold ink overprinting*

ABOVE: Cover for November 1979, **"The Circus Is Coming!"** *illustration by Hilary Knight, watercolor and pencil*

The circus poster on the back of this cover includes an in-house joke for staff artist Trina Schart Hyman and art director John Grandits: two of the acts advertised are "La Trina, Temptress of the Trapeze" and "Grandits the Great, alone in a cage with a giant gorilla"!

RIGHT: Cover for January 1988, **"Knight's Arabian Cricket,"** *illustration by Hilary Knight, watercolor, colored pencil, and tempera*

Cricket
the magazine for children

volume 1 number 9   may, 1974

Cover for May 1974,
illustration by Friso Henstra, oil

Cover for May 1983, "The May Basket,"
illustration by Tomie dePaola, pencil and waterproof ink

Cover for May 1975,
illustration by Irene Haas, watercolor

Cover for June 1979, **"Cricket Woman,"**
illustration by Leo and Diane Dillon, watercolor and pastel

Cover for June 1982, "Lucy Meets the Faun,"
illustration by Lisbeth Zwerger, watercolor

Cover for June 1983, **"Maui: Then and Today,"** *illustration by Charles Mikolaycak, colored pencils and watercolor on diazo print from pencil drawing*

143

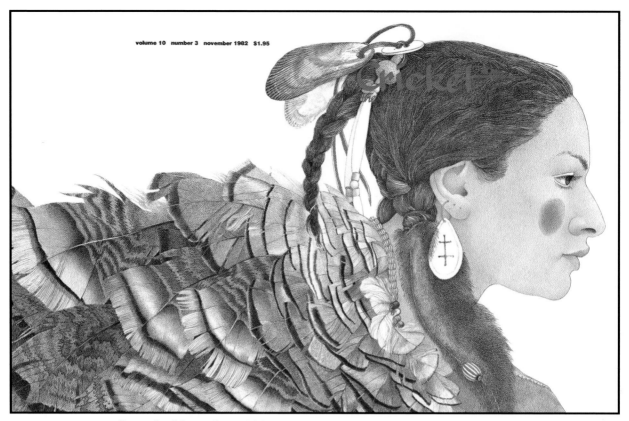

Cover for November 1982, "Wampanoag: A Coat of Feathers,"
illustration by Nancy Eckholm Burkert, colored ink

Cover for October 1988, illustration by Sue Truesdell, watercolor

Cover for October 1990, **"Autumnal Air,"** *illustration by Troy Howell, acrylic*

Cover for February 1989, "We ♥ G. W.," illustration by Marylin Hafner (with apologies to Emanuel Leutze), gouache and pen and ink

Cover for August 1989, **"Danny 'New Corn' Ryder,"**
illustration by Mary Beth Schwark, oil

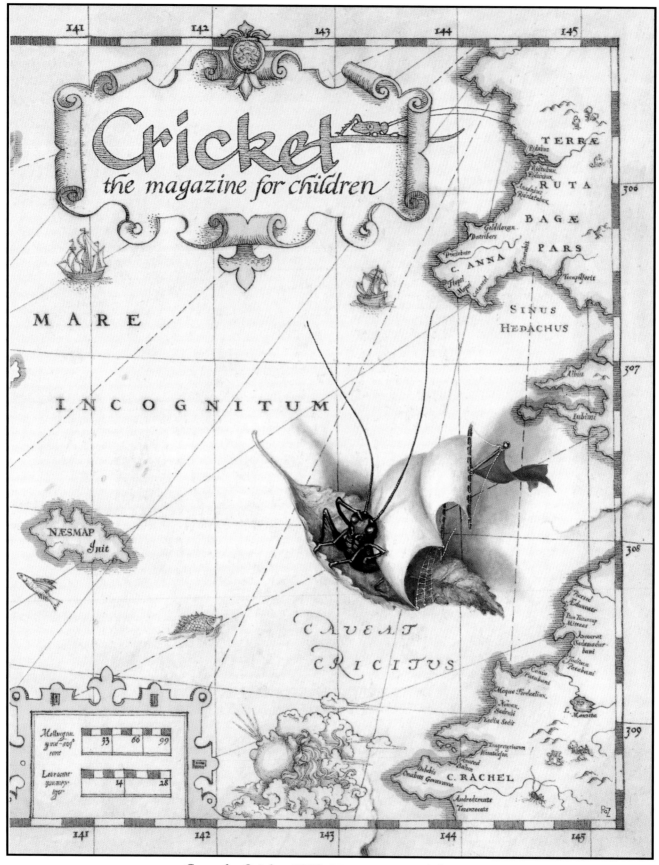

Cover for October 1992, **"Beware, O Cricket,"**
illustration by Paul O. Zelinsky, pen and ink, watercolor, and oil

*Inspired by the 500th anniversary of Columbus's voyage, Zelinsky's map is
full of puns. The cricket was to beware of a not-quite-sleeping cat on the back cover.*

Cover for April 1987, **"Hula Cricket (Gryllus honolulucus),"**
illustration by Paul O. Zelinsky, ink, pencil, and watercolor

Cover for September 2000,
"Chang E Flees to the Moon,"
illustration by Brett Helquist, oil and acrylic

Cover for February 2001,
illustration by Ann Strugnell,
watercolor

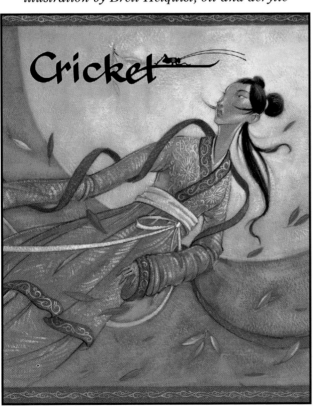

Cover for March 1979, **"The Giant Cricket Expedition,"**
illustration by David Wiesner, watercolor

"Do Anything You Want to Do"

by
David Wiesner

CRICKET MAGAZINE will always have a special place in my life. Many of the people associated with *Cricket* became life-long friends, and the pieces I did for *Cricket* became pivotal events in my artistic career.

Cricket was the door I first walked through to join the world of children's books. After art school I might have entered the illustration world without a real focus were it not for a moment of great serendipity. At the end of my senior year at the Rhode Island School of Design, Trina Schart Hyman came to speak about being a children's book illustrator. She stayed a second day to look at student portfolios. I was on my way out of the Illustration Building when one of my teachers said, "Aren't you going to talk to Trina?" I wasn't. I was considering children's books, but for some now-mysterious reason, I was also considering things like science fiction and fantasy book jackets and editorial magazine illustration. Thankfully, I did show her my work. At the time, of course,

Trina was the art director for *Cricket*. We had a great talk, and as we finished looking at my portfolio, she said, "How would you like to do a cover for *Cricket*?" I believe my reaction was something like "Huh?" I thought this must have been some kind of a cruel art joke. But she wasn't kidding, and I did the cover, and I never thought about editorial or science fiction illustration again. This was a risky and generous offer on Trina's part, and one that was so exciting and challenging that it pointed me down the path to picture books without any wasteful detours.

As it turned out, my cover came through Trina's hands just as her assistant art director, Dilys Evans, was creating an agency to represent children's book illustrators. Dilys called me to see if I would like to be part of her portfolio. Twenty-four years later we are still working together, in what has been my most gratifying, and fun, professional relationship.

That cover, "The Giant Cricket Expedition," was for the March 1979 issue, the first in the new, larger format. The second cover I did for *Cricket*, "Air Raid," was the March 1989 issue, exactly ten years after the first. This has created a wonderful set of bookends for my first decade in the field.

As with the first cover, I was presented with the most desirable art direction possible—do anything you want to do. This time it was Ron McCutchan making the offer. Ron also let me know that because this was the March issue, there would be stories about St. Patrick's Day and about frogs—the link between them being greenness, I think.

St. Patrick's Day didn't strike a chord—but frogs, they had potential. I got out my sketchbook and a pencil. Frogs were great fun to draw—soft, round, lumpy, and really goofy-looking. But what could I do with them?

I drew one on a lily pad. That shape . . . the round blob with the saucerlike bottom . . . suddenly, old movies were running through my head: *Forbidden Planet* and *The Day the Earth Stood Still.* Together the frog and lily pad looked like a 1950s B-movie flying saucer! As I drew, I saw that the frogs and toads weren't actually flying. It was the lily pad that had the power of flight, like a magic carpet from *The Arabian Nights.*

For the *Cricket* cover, I showed a group of frogs rising up out of a swamp, heading off to who knows what mischief. I liked the picture a lot and I began to like the frogs and toads themselves. They had distinct personalities, and I wanted to know what happened before and after this scene. When I sat down to draw and find out what happened, well, *Tuesday* happened.

That cover grew to become my book *Tuesday,* which won the 1992 Caldecott Medal. It is a satisfying feeling to know that *Tuesday* exists because of a phone call from *Cricket.* The world is a better place because Marianne and Blouke Carus created the *Cricket* universe. I am delighted to have had the opportunity to use that world as a canvas.

David Wiesner earned Caldecott Medals for *The Three Pigs* and *Tuesday* as well as Caldecott Honors for *Sector 7* and *Free Fall.*

Cover illustration for March 1989, **"Air Raid,"** *watercolor by David Wiesner*

Old Cricket and the Hanukkah Goblins

by Eric A. Kimmel

ONE OF THE most rewarding parts about writing for children is the way your stories touch people's lives through several generations. *Hershel and the Hanukkah Goblins* was published as a picture book in 1989. Over the years I've run into children, then teenagers, and now young adults who tell me it's their favorite story. If I last long enough, I fully expect to encounter middle-aged people and eventually elderly people who will tell me how they've shared that story with their children and grandchildren as part of their family tradition for the holiday season.

That's not bad for a story that nobody wanted. People are shocked when I tell them that because Hershel and his goblin pals have become such a part of the Hanukkah landscape. But it's true. I couldn't give that story away. I know. I tried.

Hershel and the Hanukkah Goblins grew out of a Russian tale, "Ivanko, the Bear's Son." One of the challenges that Ivanko faces is fooling a goblin who lives in a lake. I liked that goblin a lot. To tell the truth, I liked him so much that I used him again in another story, *The Magic Dreidels*. That tale, however, lay several years in the future. For now, in 1984, an idea began hatching. Why not write a different kind of Hanukkah story? Perhaps one with a goblin in it? Maybe more than one?

To tell the truth, I never thought Hanukkah stories were especially interesting. They fell into two categories: "How We Celebrate Hanukkah" and "The Heroic Maccabees." I wanted to create a Hanukkah story that would be different; one that hadn't been told before.

My model was Charles Dickens's *A Christmas Carol*. The musty creepiness of Dickens's classic is more appropriate to Halloween than Christmas. That's what makes it so intriguing. Scrooge and his ghostly visitors form a black hole in the midst of the accustomed holiday hoopla. Contrast, tension, irony—it works!

Another point to consider is how Dickens creates an all-inclusive secular holiday out of a Christian festival. Jesus, Mary, Joseph, angels, shepherds, wise men never appear. No one attends church. Tiny Tim's words, "God bless us, every one," are as close as the story comes to the religious roots of Christmas. It is as much a story for people who aren't Christians as it is for people who are.

That's what I set out to do. I wanted to write a Hanukkah story for Jewish children so they could have at least one interesting tale to share with their classmates during the holiday season. I also wanted it to be a story that non-Jewish children could enjoy without having to know much about Hanukkah or the Jewish religion.

I quickly jettisoned the heroic Maccabees and their miraculous jar of oil. Like Dickens, I assumed my audience already knew something about the holiday. If they didn't, there were plenty of other books around to give them that information. I replaced Ivanko, the Russian hero, with Hershel Ostropolier, one of my favorite characters from Jewish folklore. Hershel personifies the marginal man, trying to survive from day to day with nothing but his wits. He's more sarcastic than heroic in the traditional tales. That was about to change.

If one goblin is good, eight is better. I pitted Hershel against increasingly menacing foes, a goblin for each night with the most dangerous, the king, saved for last. I had fun imagining the different goblins that Hershel might face. When I was done, I had a long manuscript. Too long! That wasn't the only problem. It was too weird. Way too weird! I sent the story to several editors, and they all politely turned it down because they didn't know what to do with it. No one had ever seen a Hanukkah story that looked more like a Halloween story.

Different editors gave me different hints: shorten it; define Hershel's character; do more with the villagers; bring in Hershel's family. I tried to follow these ideas. However, none of them felt right. They slowed the story down and diffused its focus. I didn't want villagers. I didn't want Hershel's wife and kids. I wanted goblins. Scary, creepy, menacing goblins.

After eight months of trying, I gave up. Here was another good idea that never went anywhere. I have lots of those. I shoved the story in the file where I save failed efforts. There it might have stayed, and nobody in the world would know anything at all about Hershel and his goblins. However, in March 1985, I received a telephone call from my friend Marianne Carus, the editor of *Cricket* magazine. Marianne had been my best friend and supporter throughout my writing career.

She asked if I could help with a problem. She needed a Hanukkah story for the December 1985 issue, and she needed it fast.

ERIC A. KIMMEL

The issue's deadline was approaching. Did I know a good Hanukkah story or remember a family tradition associated with the holiday that she could use?

I told Marianne that I didn't know any good Hanukkah stories and didn't think there were any. I didn't have any special family traditions, either. I did, however, have this peculiar tale buried in my files that she was welcome to use if she liked it. I promised to mail it that day. If it didn't work out, I would have at least a few weeks to try to come up with another story.

To my amazement, Marianne liked the story. However, there was a problem. "It's too long," she said. "Much too long. We have an absolute limit of 1,800 words. Some of those goblins have to go."

So go they did. "On the following nights, other goblins came..." Or went, because that's where I made the cut. What were the missing goblins like? One was a large cat. Another had one eye, one arm, and one leg. He challenged Hershel to a race around the synagogue. Hershel won, because he never moved. He waited until the goblin rounded the last corner, then said, "What took you so long?"

I forget what the third goblin did.

When the December issue came out, I was astonished to see that Trina Hyman had done the pictures. I never dared hope that an artist of Trina's stature would ever illustrate one of my stories. It was a dream come true. I was even more astonished when John Briggs, editor of Holiday House, wrote to ask if I'd consider doing the story as a picture book. Holiday House would like to publish it, with Trina as the illustrator.

And then, a month or two later, my editor at Holiday House, Margery Cuyler, asked if I knew any good animal stories. She was looking for a clever animal story for one of her favorite artists to illustrate. That artist was also one of my favorite artists—Janet Stevens.

I thought long and hard. What was the best animal story I knew? The answer was easy: *Anansi and the Moss-Covered Rock.*

You know the rest. *Hershel and the Hanukkah Goblins* went on to become a Caldecott Honor Book. *Anansi and the Moss-Covered Rock* was the first of four Anansi stories that Janet Stevens and I have done together.

Within three years, I had left my regular job to become a full-time writer. All my dreams of a writing career had come true. I owe it all, every bit, to my friend Marianne, Old Cricket, and his pals.

Eric A. Kimmel, author of the Caldecott Honor book *Hershel and the Hanukkah Goblins,* has won Sydney Taylor Picture Book Awards for *The Chanukkah Guest* and *Gershon's Monster: A Story for the Jewish New Year.*

Hershel and the Hanukkah Goblins

by Eric A. Kimmel ✶ *Illustrated by Trina Schart Hyman*

IT WAS THE first night of Hanukkah. Hershel of Ostropol was walking down the road. He was tired and hungry. Nonetheless, his step was light. Soon he would reach the next village, where bright candles, merry songs, and platters piled high with tasty potato latkes awaited him.

But when he arrived, the village was silent and dark. Not a single Hanukkah candle was to be seen.

"Isn't tonight the first night of Hanukkah?" Hershel asked the villagers.

"We don't have Hanukkah, Hershel," one of them answered sadly.

"No Hanukkah? How can that possibly be?"

"It's because of the goblins. They haunt the old synagogue at the top of the hill. They hate Hanukkah. Whenever we try to light a menorah, the goblins blow out the candles. They break our dreidels. They throw the potato latkes on the floor. Those wicked goblins make our lives miserable all year long, but on Hanukkah it's really bad."

Hershel knew he must help the village people. "I'm not afraid of goblins," he said. "Tell me how to get rid of them."

Cricket, December 1985

"It's not as easy as you think," the rabbi warned. "You must stay in the old synagogue where the goblins live. There you must light the Hanukkah candles eight nights in a row. On the eighth night, the King of the Goblins must light them himself. That is the only way to break their power."

"I'm not afraid, Rabbi," Hershel said. "If I can't outwit a few goblins, then my name isn't Hershel of Ostropol."

The villagers wished Hershel good luck. They had no potato latkes to give him, so they packed several hard-boiled eggs for him to eat, along with a big jar of pickles. The rabbi gave Hershel a brass menorah, a package of candles, and a box of matches. Then the villagers said good-bye. Nobody expected to see Hershel again.

It was long past sundown by the time Hershel climbed to the top of the hill where the old synagogue stood. The crumbling building was gloomy and dark. Rusty hinges squealed as Hershel opened the door. He stepped inside. Starlight shining through the broken windowpanes cast eerie shadows on the walls. Hershel shuddered. Well could he believe that goblins lived here!

Hershel put two candles in the menorah and set it on the window sill. He struck

a match and lit the shammes candle. He said the blessings and was about to light the other candle when he heard a voice.

"Hey! What are you doing?"

Hershel turned around. Here was a goblin no bigger than a horsefly, with a long, pointy tail and two little bats' wings, hovering in the air.

"I'm lighting Hanukkah candles," Hershel said. "Tonight is the first night of Hanukkah."

"Oh no, it's not! We don't allow Hanukkah. Not around here."

"Is that so?" said Hershel. "Who's going to stop me? A little pipsqueak like you?"

"I may be little, but I'm strong," said the goblin.

"Really? Can you crush rocks in your hand?" asked Hershel.

The goblin laughed. "Crush rocks? You're joking. Nobody's that strong!"

"I am! Watch!" Hershel took a hard-boiled egg from his pocket and squeezed it until the yolk and the white ran through his fingers. "That's how hard I'm going to squeeze you if you try to stop me from lighting this candle."

The little goblin's eyes opened wide, for in the dim light the egg looked exactly like a rock. The little goblin shook with fear. "You leave me alone," he squeaked.

"Gladly," said Hershel, "if you let me light my candle in peace."

"All right," said the goblin. "One night won't make a difference. But you better not be here tomorrow. Big, scary goblins are coming—much bigger than me! If they catch you lighting Hanukkah candles, you'll be sorry!"

"We'll see about that," Hershel said to himself. He lit the first candle.

On the second night, another goblin appeared. This one was big and fat and waddled like a goose.

Hershel was finishing his dinner of pickles and hard-boiled eggs. "Have some pickles," he said to the goblin.

"Pickles?"

"Here, catch!" Hershel tossed him a sour pickle. The goblin caught it in his mouth and swallowed it.

"*Mmmm!* Pickles are good!"

"Do you like them? I have plenty in this jar. Take all you want."

The greedy goblin grabbed as many pickles as his claws could hold, but when he tried to pull his fist out of the jar, he couldn't. He was holding too many pickles for his hand to fit through.

"I'm stuck!" the goblin shouted. "You put a spell on this jar to hold me fast!"

"That's right," Hershel said, laughing.

"And it's a very powerful spell. You came here tonight to stop me from lighting Hanukkah candles. Now you must stand here with your hand in that jar and watch while I light them all. How do you like that?"

"No! No!" the goblin screamed. "I hate Hanukkah!"

"Too bad. You'll have to get used to it." Hershel said the blessings and lit the candles—slowly. Then he sang all his favorite Hanukkah songs. The goblin wailed and carried on so that Hershel finally decided to let him go.

"Shall I tell you how to break the spell?"

"Yes! Yes! I can't stand it anymore!"

"Let go of the pickles. Your greed is the only spell holding you prisoner."

The goblin let go of the pickles. His hand slipped out of the jar easily. How that goblin raged! Here he had stood with his hand in the pickle jar while Hershel lit Hanukkah candles under his nose. The furious goblin stamped his foot so hard that he shattered into a million pieces. The wind blew them away.

On the following nights other goblins came. One had six heads. One had three eyes. All were terrible and fierce. They growled and roared and changed themselves into horrible shapes. They tried to stop Hershel from lighting Hanukkah candles. But Hershel fooled them all.

Finally it was the seventh night. Eight tiny candles flickered on the window sill.

ERIC A. KIMMEL

Hershel sat back to enjoy their light. Where were the goblins? Had they finally given up?

Hershel felt very sleepy. His eyes closed. Suddenly, he sat up. He heard a horrible sound—a voice that spoke with the cracking of bones.

"Happy Hanukkah, Hershel of Ostropol."

"Who is it? Who's there?"

"Don't you know who I am, Hershel? Weren't you expecting . . . THE KING OF THE GOBLINS?" The voice rose to a hurricane roar. It ripped the shingles from the synagogue roof and shattered the windows. The Hanukkah candles reeled in the savage blast, but they did not go out.

"You're too early!" Hershel shrieked. "You're not supposed to come until tomorrow!"

The great wind died down. "Don't worry, Hershel. I am far away, but I have the power to see you and speak to you. Enjoy this Hanukkah evening, my friend. It will be your last! Tomorrow night I will come for you. You fooled my slaves, the other goblins. Let's see if you can fool me."

Poor Hershel! What was he to do? The King of the Goblins was on his way and no power on earth could stop him. Unless . . . unless . . . Hershel had an idea. He knew he had to try. It was the only way to save himself—and Hanukkah.

It was the last night of Hanukkah. Hershel set the candles in the menorah. But instead of placing it on the window sill, he put the menorah and the box of matches on a small table near the door. Then he sat down to wait.

Night fell. It grew dark as pitch inside

the gloomy old synagogue. Outside, the whole world lay cold and silent.

Suddenly a great gust ripped the synagogue door from its hinges. The whole building shook. A fearsome voice spoke.

"HERSHEL OF OSTROPOL!"

"Did I hear something?"

"IT IS I, THE KING OF THE GOBLINS!"

Hershel laughed. "Don't be silly. You're one of the boys from the village. You're trying to scare me."

"I AM NOT A BOY! I AM THE KING OF THE GOBLINS!"

"I'll believe it when I see it. Show yourself to me."

"BEHOLD! I STAND BEFORE YOU! DO YOU BELIEVE ME NOW?"

Hershel tried not to look. Even in the darkness he could see the outline of a monstrous shape filling the doorway, a figure too horrible to describe. He pretended not to care.

"It's too dark. I can't see anything. A candlestick and some matches are by the doorway. Why don't you light a few candles? Then I'll see what you really are."

"INDEED YOU SHALL!"

A match flared. The shammes candle caught the flame. Hershel's blood turned to water at the awful sight before him, but he did not lose courage. "Master of the world," he silently prayed. "Thou who created the heavens and the earth and the spirits of the air, stand by me now." Then he addressed the goblin. "It's still too dark. What are you afraid of? There are plenty of candles. Why not light them all?"

A hideous hand took the shammes candle and lit the others one by one. Hershel felt himself growing faint, but he forced himself to look. His eyes grew wider and wider as each candle caught the flame. Six . . . seven . . . eight. The King of the Goblins stood before him.

ERIC A. KIMMEL

"NOW, HERSHEL, DO YOU KNOW WHO I AM?"

" I know you're not Queen Esther."

"VERY FUNNY! ENJOY THE JOKE! IT WILL BE YOUR LAST!"

"That's what you think. Begone, or I'll take a stick to you!"

"HOW DARE YOU SPEAK TO THE KING OF THE GOBLINS THAT WAY!"

"I'll speak to you any way I please. You have no power. Your spell is broken. See! The menorah is lit. You thought those were ordinary candles you were lighting. They weren't. They were Hanukkah candles! And you lit them yourself!"

The King of the Goblins roared with fury. The earth trembled. A mighty wind arose. It ripped off the synagogue roof, blew down the walls, and splintered the great timbers, scattering them like matchsticks. Around the menorah the whirlwind howled,

but the candles never flickered. They burned with clear, steady flames. The King of the Goblins had no power over them. The spirit of Hanukkah had triumphed.

The great wind vanished as suddenly as it had risen. Hershel rubbed his eyes. The night was as still as before, even though the synagogue was gone. Walls, floor, roof —even the foundation stones had vanished. But the menorah remained, standing tall upon the little table where Hershel had placed it.

Hershel waited until the last candle burned down. Then he started back down the road that led to the village. I'd better hurry, he thought. I don't want to miss the last night of Hanukkah.

But there was no reason to worry. In every widow there stood a menorah with nine gleaming candles to light the way.

The whole village was waiting for him.

ERIC A. KIMMEL

Sendak Sent Me to *Cricket*

SENDAK SENT ME to *Cricket*.

In those days, when we'd ask him where to go to show our work he'd say, "Go everywhere," so we went everywhere claiming Maurice Sendak had sent us. But in this case he really did come to me in class to tell me about *Cricket* magazine. They had an art director named Trina Schart Hyman, he said. She was open to new illustrators. I should send her samples.

So that's how I got my very first *Cricket* jobs while still a student at Parsons School of Design. No, just kidding. It wasn't that easy.

First, I had to package my best student work (crosshatch studies, spheres and cones, you know, "impressive" stuff). Then I had to send it to Trina with a letter mentioning you-know-who. Lastly, I had to wipe the enormous egg off my face because in no time this art director threw it all back at me

by Jean Gralley

with a blistering note. "If you want to illustrate for children, I want to see a CAR, a GRANDMOTHER, a LION—CHILDREN, for Godsakes!" It ended with an expletive and something about "not darkening her door again" until I do.

After catching my breath, I took out a large, white poster board and began a cartoon of me in the lobby of my Brooklyn apartment building, opening my mailbox in the wall. Out balloons this enormous front end of a limousine, followed by a grandmother in the front seat and a cat in shades behind the wheel, followed by a lion and two kids in the backseat, excitedly waving an envelope and yelling, "Letter from Trina!" With this wild congregation around my cartoon character, the letter is read aloud, word for word. Faces fall. One wails, "What do we do now?" I signed the board "Try, try again" and mailed it off. The response was immediate again ("That's the spirit! That's what I like to see!"), and with it came promises of work, which Trina did send for years.

And that's how I became a *Cricket* artist.

It was great fun being a *Cricket* artist. Trina, Dilys Evans, and Marcia Leonard made it fun. Art assignments were sent with funny notes and artwork was received with appreciation (and, if requested, constructive criticism). Newcomers like me found our work in the pages of the magazine alongside that of masters like Victor Ambrus and Quentin Blake. This is still true of *Cricket*. But when I was just starting out, I marveled at this big, egalitarian stew.

That would be a good way to describe the parties, too.

Every summer invitations went out to the "*Cricket* Artist Picnic and Debauch": "COME SEE Wally Tripp in his striped pajamas! HEAR Jim Arnosky tell of his live experience with a skunk! WATCH Tomie dePaola tap-dance on an empty tin of caviar!" *Cricket* artists—rich and poor, pro and beginner, famous and not-yet-famous—came from all over to rub shoulders and mix it up on Trina's New Hampshire farm. For two days there was Frisbee-tossing and singing and shenanigans and exotic and strange eats (I remember an avocado-and-peach-yogurt pie) and lots and lots of talking.

Artists not only found work and camaraderie at *Cricket,* they found good advice. From Sendak I learned how deep an art form book illustration can be; from Trina I learned which editors to see, which to avoid, and that dipping a pen in gin will keep the ink from beading on acetate.

And I wasn't the only one. Trina did not suffer fools gladly, but she was also uncommonly generous to new artists, especially her *Cricket* artists. She was a mentor for many, and I'm lucky to have been one of them.

So now I'm staff artist of *Cricket,* a position Trina assumed after stepping down as art director and then passed along to me. Over the years we had developed a "cartoon friendship"; I'd send her cartoons about my adventures and travels, about questions I had, and she sent letters and cartoons back. I guess when it came time to think of someone to continue the cartoon "Cricket and the Gang" adventures, she thought of me. I couldn't believe my luck. We had a ceremony at headquarters in Peru, Illinois, at which Trina dubbed me new staff artist with a "magic wand" and handed over the three rapidographs with which she penned the series. Wand and pens are still in my studio, along with a photo of me, younger than I am now and obviously swimming in happiness.

The *Cricket* "cast of characters" has been my charge for fifteen years; that's 180 stories in Scooby-Doo years. I inherited the bunch from Trina, who invented them all. Their little personalities rang so true and presented such opportune combinations that they themselves always suggested story lines with hardly a dry spell. I didn't try to change the characters, but they have changed, as they naturally would. Trina's Crystal was girly but tomboyish, while mine became something of a squealy, Barbie-loving cricket. I created Tater, the potatobug/kid with a penchant for French fries and (often flawed) inventions, and Elvis, the once-prehistoric praying mantis. I have had a secret love for Zoot, the aunts, for George and Tail (two ends of the the same worm), and for Ugly Bird, who has been everyone's favorite "love-to-hate" character. He, in particular, generates much wonderful mail. Letters consistently come in for him, lecturing him about what he should do about his dandruff, about his spelling, how he should stop menacing "the Gang" and how he should/could find a girlfriend. Some of the writers who scolded also took pains to staple rubber worms or a bag of bird seed to their letters, tender offerings "to get him through the winter" or to encourage him to "try to not eat the Gang." This has been one of my very favorite parts of the job, the mail and e-mail that's come from *Cricket* readers all over the world.

Now it's time for me to turn over the pleasure of this position to the very capable and funny Carolyn Conahan, dub her with the magic wand, and wish her good fun with Cricket and the Gang.

After fifteen years as staff artist, I'm still proud to be part of this magazine. It's still a place where the best literature for kids can be found, where the famous and yet-to-be-famous rub shoulders in its pages, where artists and writers can get their first publishing credit, and where new stories can become acclaimed books. (Paul Fleischman's "Weslandia" was a *Cricket* story before it became an award-winning picture book—I know, because I was the first to illustrate it!)

Over the years I've been to many conferences and sat down with many book artists to swap stories. It's amazing how many got their first breaks in *Cricket* magazine and had stories to tell about the encouragement they found there. I'm glad to have been one of them. Thanks, *Cricket*!

Jean Gralley served as *Cricket* staff artist from 1988 to 2003, during which time she won the Ezra Jack Keats and Don Freeman Fellowships for book illustration. She has been an on-air commentator for National Public Radio and, lately, has been writing and illustrating picture books, such as *Hogula: Dread Pig of Night*.

A Quiet Revolution by Marylin Hafner

1973—It's a wintry afternoon in New York, and Mr. Clifton Fadiman is speaking at a Society of Children's Book Writers meeting in the old Biltmore Hotel. His favorite children's book, he says, is by Russell Hoban. *A Mouse and His Child* is dedicated to H. B. Cushman. I decide to miss my 4 P.M. train to Connecticut so that I can tell Mr. Fadiman that Harvey Cushman is my late husband and that the toy mouse Russ borrowed had been part of our collection of German windup toys.

As I leave to catch the next train, Mr. Fadiman says he is on the staff of a new children's magazine. "This magazine will be unique," he says. He already knows that I am an illustrator, so he gives me the name and address of the art director.

I sent some drawings and tear sheets to Trina and got a poem to illustrate for the third issue of *Cricket* magazine.

My stars realigned themselves!

All of us who got invited to the sensational party the Carus family gave at the St. Moritz Hotel in New York to introduce *Cricket* to the publishing world knew that we had landed on the Moon!

Marianne Carus's dream was becoming a reality. I had been working for magazines for twenty-six years—and had half a dozen books published by 1973. But I'd never felt part of a family of writers, editors, and artists before. We were so inspired by one another! The freedom we were allowed to design the pages of this beautiful little magazine took precedence over other assignments.

And so *Cricket* started a quiet revolution in magazines for children. A publication that combined quality and creativity in its good writing and witty, beautiful graphics made *all* of us part of Marianne's dream.

Thirty years have flown by. Now there is a crowd of *Cricket* descendants. This family of magazines is a testament to the vision, hard work, and faith of Marianne Carus and her loyal associates. I feel so privileged to have been on this journey with her.

In 1973 children everywhere were lucky to find *Cricket,* their *own* magazine. Now in 2003, *their* children—who have a long list of Carus publications to entertain, teach, and delight them—are even luckier.

Thank you, Marianne!

Marylin Hafner is the creator of the Molly and Emmett cartoon strip in *Ladybug* magazine. Among the books she has illustrated are *A Carnival of Animals* by Sid Fleischman, *Science Fair Bunnies* by Kathryn Lasky, and *The Missing Tooth* by Joanna Cole.

MEET YOUR ARTIST... MARYLIN HAFNER!

I'VE BEEN DRAWING ever since my father, who was an artist, too, nailed a blackboard to my bedroom wall. I sold my first artwork to my sister for seventy-five cents, but as it was done on that blackboard, her purchase had a certain quality of impermanence! But I also drew on any other available flat surface—including, I blush to admit, those lovely blank pages at the beginning and end of my books.

This all happened in the days before TV. We went to the movies a lot, and saw plays, circuses, and puppet shows, too—and afterward I would rush home to draw the scenes as I remembered them. I also spent a major portion of my childhood stumbling around in my mother's old red chiffon evening dress and high-heeled satin shoes with cut-steel buckles!

I started drawing professionally while still in art school and I kept working when I married (another artist!) and had three daughters. I fit my assignments into the spaces of the day (or night) when I wasn't baking bread or driving someone to the dentist. When I needed to draw dogs or cats or kids, there they were (stumbling around in *my* old high-heeled shoes!).

I still like to dress up in costumes and I love to dance at parties. I love music, eating, and walking on the beach. But drawing is the most fun of all.

I'd like to find a way to draw at the edge of the sea and never have to go indoors at all.   *Cricket,* October 1981

MOM RUINED THESE OLD BOOKS!

My Life with *Cricket*

by Shulamith Levey Oppenheim

MY RELATIONSHIP WITH *Cricket* stretches back more than twenty years.

I cannot recall which of my writer friends suggested that I submit a story to the magazine, but today, so many years later, I salute her (or him!) and offer thanks for what a gift I was given, for what a joyous affiliation it has been for me.

My literary contact during those years was mainly with Marianne Carus—letters and phone calls. Both were always caring, thoughtful, perceptive. We discovered that we shared many interests—travel, history, family, etc. But despite such connections, I knew that Marianne would accept only the material she felt was absolutely what she and her editors deemed best for the magazine. Needless to say, not every story I submitted was accepted!

Then, sometime in the 1980s, my husband was lecturing at the University of Bologna during the week of the Bologna Book Fair.

This was my chance! Off I went to the behemoth of a conference center, and there I finally met Marianne. In an instant I understood why my relationship with *Cricket* had been, was, and is to this day, such a splendid one. Marianne was exactly as I knew her to be—gracious, highly civilized and cultured, warm-hearted, accessible, so intelligent.

Now we have the Cricket Magazine Group—and now when I submit a manuscript I'm never quite sure for which publication it is destined. But no matter. The critique is always on the highest literary and ethical levels, and, no matter whether or not it is accepted, I learn from the evaluations and come away feeling that I am able to hone my craft a bit more, that I am the richer for having Marianne and her colleagues take the time to read and think about a piece I have written.

My years with *Cricket* have enriched my life. I can't say more!

Shulamith Levey Oppenheim has written many delightful children's books. *Iblis,* her retelling of a ninth-century Islamic version of the Biblical fall from grace, was an American Library Association Notable Book.

The Day I Rescued Albert Einstein's Compass

by Shulamith Levey Oppenheim

Illustrated by John Fulweiler

IF YOU ARE lucky, something special will happen to you in your life that you will never forget. Something so special, you know it could have happened only to you. For me, it was the day I rescued Albert Einstein's compass.

It was Sunday morning. As I came downstairs I heard someone playing the violin. The living room doors were slightly ajar. My mother and father were waiting for me.

My father said to me, "Do you remember, Theo, about five years ago, when you were seven years old and you met our dear friend Herr Professor Einstein? I told you then that he was the most famous man alive."

"Yes, I do, Papa," I said. "And I asked you why he was the most famous man alive, and you said because he is a great physicist who has made important discoveries." I looked at my father. "Is he *here,* Papa?"

My father nodded. "Yes, he is here. He is playing the violin."

Suddenly the doors to the living room flew open, and a deep voice said with a chuckle, "The last time I was here, your father assured you that I did not bite. And as your father and I have been close friends for many years, he knows that I still do not bite." And he chuckled even louder.

Cricket, June 2000

I looked up. There was the thick, black mustache and the large head with gray-black hair bushing out all around. There were the eyes, dark and merry. He hadn't changed, although he seemed much less formidable than he had five years ago. Perhaps because I was older now.

Herr Einstein laid his violin at the side of the piano. "Now, young man, let us get immediately to business. Your parents tell me that you have a sailboat. I, too, have loved sailing all my life. Will you take me out in your boat? It is a most beautiful day."

I looked at my parents. Take the most famous man alive sailing in my sailboat! My neck and cheeks felt hot. My mother looked very pleased. "Our guest is an experienced sailor, and so are you. We think it would be lovely for the two of you to go out on the lake. It will be something you'll always remember."

And the most famous man alive put his hand on my shoulder. "Then let us be off."

We walked down the hill from the house toward a line of giant blue spruces that edged the lake. "Is there always so much birdsong here, Theo?" my new friend asked. "It is *wunderbar,* wonderful, to have the air filled with such music."

So there was another thing we had in common! I was delighted that he was interested in birds. I was a keen bird watcher, and my parents had given me a very fine pair of binoculars for my last birthday. "It's spring," I said, "and the birds are laying their eggs in the nests they've built in the blue spruces. They're happy. Do you have birds where you live?"

"No, no, not now." He smiled, rather sadly I thought. "Not now. I live in the city. But when I was a boy and went sailing on a lake near my home, there were birds everywhere."

Just then our pier came into view. We could see my bright green boat with its jaunty green-and-white-striped sail rocking gently on the water. "What have you named your boat?" Herr Einstein asked.

"Fleet Felix," I answered proudly.

Herr Professor Einstein approved. "I like that. Or perhaps even *Felix the Fleet.*"

We put on the orange life jackets I kept in a giant tin drum by the end of the pier. Then I stepped into the boat. My crew of one untied the rope, coiled it up, and came aboard. He took over the tiller, and I held the sheet.

We were off! There was an easy breeze. We followed the shoreline. The clouds were pink cotton puffs, and the sky was as blue as my mother's eyes.

I decided that this was a perfect time to ask my question. I'd been thinking about it

SHULAMITH LEVEY OPPENHEIM

ever since I walked into the living room. I took a deep breath.

"Yes?" asked Herr Professor Einstein.

Of course, he would know I was going to ask a question. He was the most famous man alive!

I asked my question slowly. "Why did you want to be a physicist?"

He didn't answer my question. Instead, he put his hand into his pocket. "It has fallen through a hole in the lining!" And he threw back his great head and laughed and laughed. What? The greatest man alive had a hole in his pocket! I was glad it made him laugh, but I didn't quite understand.

"Excuse me, Herr Professor, but what has fallen through a hole in your pocket?" I asked politely.

"The answer to your question. That is what has fallen through the hole! *Himmel!* Heavens! I think it is somewhere under the pocket now . . . one minute, one minute, I must tear the lining . . . a little more . . . a little more . . . There! Now I shall fish it out, only it won't be a fish but . . ." By this time, I was laughing, too. He drew out his hand. Between his fingers was a compass!

"Now I'll tell you a story," said my friend softly.

I looked up at the sky. Two red-tailed hawks were riding the warm air currents—

the thermals. *Fleet Felix* was catching the breeze perfectly. My friend's voice was very low.

"When I was five years old, I was quite ill. I had to stay in bed for many days. My father gave me this compass." He peered at me. "You know what a compass is for, of course?" I nodded. "Good." He continued, "It was the first compass I had ever seen. There was the needle, under glass, all alone, pointing north no matter which way I turned the compass. To a five-year-old boy, it seemed like magic. Only it wasn't magic at all. Of course you know why."

I took a deep breath. "Because the needle is magnetic, and there is a magnet at the North Pole that attracts the needle."

My sailing partner raised his bushy eyebrows. "*Nearly* correct. There are two magnetic poles, north and south. So far away. And there, on the palm of my hand, was my compass, always pointing north! For me, it was the greatest mystery I could imagine. And so I decided, then and there, that I would learn all about the forces in the universe that we cannot see. For I certainly could not . . ."

At that moment a large motorboat zoomed past us, stirring up the water into high waves. One of them hit *Fleet Felix* smack against the side, knocking the compass from the professor's hand, right into the water!

He stared at his empty palm. "The compass, Theo. It is gone! Overboard?" Suddenly there was so much sadness in his eyes. "I should hate to lose it. And I cannot swim very well . . . and my eyesight is not good . . ." His voice trailed off, and he was looking far into space.

But *I* could swim! In a split second I dropped anchor into the water to keep the boat in place. I pulled off my life jacket. The waves had quieted down now. The compass would float. If I were lucky.

I jumped into the water.

My parents were sure I'd been a fish before I was a boy. Now was my chance to prove it! First, I swam round and round the boat. Then I dove under, searching beneath the hull once, twice, three times, staying under as long as my breath held.

Then I started swimming farther away from the boat. Under and under and round and round. No compass. I had to find it! Herr Professor Einstein might be the most famous man alive right now, but he was once five years old, and his father had given him a compass that he had treasured all these years. I thought about the splendid binoculars my parents had given me and how I would feel if I lost them.

I made another dive under the boat. As I came up for air, I felt something ever so gently hit my cheek. It was the compass, bobbing alongside *Fleet Felix,* just waiting to be rescued! Clutching it in my left hand, I grabbed hold of the boat with my right. Professor Einstein's eyes were closed.

"Pardon me," I called to him. "Pardon me, here is your compass!" And I clambered aboard.

He opened his eyes. "So," he said with a smile, "this is why I became a physicist," continuing just as if nothing had happened. "As you know, a physicist studies the forces in nature that we cannot know directly, only we know they are there from what we observe, like the compass needle or . . . ," he paused.

"Or gravity?" I offered, a bit tentatively.

"Bravo, young man. Or gravity. All these forces keep our planet running quite smoothly most of the time. And thank you, dear Theo. For me, you are the most famous boy alive!"

His eyes were merry again. I was still trying to catch my breath, but I had to ask another question. "Would you say it is because of the compass that you are now the most famous man alive?"

He sat very still. "The compass was my first mystery, and all my life I have worked to solve mysteries." He put the compass in his pocket—the one with the hole in it.

SHULAMITH LEVEY OPPENHEIM

"And I am *not* the most famous man alive, no matter what your dear father says. But you are surely the bravest and kindest boy I know."

When we reached home, my parents asked me why we were both wet and why *I* was soaking.

"We had an adventure," answered my friend, "one I don't think either of us will ever forget."

That night I wondered what my father and mother would say if they knew that the most famous man alive had a hole in his pocket . . . and couldn't swim very well. I don't think I shall ever tell them!

My husband, Felix, was a young boy when he met Albert Einstein. The great physicist had come to visit, and Felix's father introduced the professor as "the most famous man alive." Einstein had been given a compass by his own father when he was five and sick in bed. He also loved to sail and play the violin. The rest of the story is fiction.

When my husband, Felix, grew up and we

Albert Einstein (right) with the author and her husband on their wedding day

were married, Albert Einstein was our best man. During the ceremony, my wedding ring dropped through a hole in Einstein's pocket. He stared straight ahead without blinking, without moving a muscle, while my brother fished it out!

Albert Einstein was truly a man beyond time and space, yet very much of this world. His backyard was a haven for birds. He would sit in the garden for hours while his stepdaughter, Margot, talked to them. He rode his bicycle to the Institute for Advanced Study in Princeton, New Jersey, where he taught. He loved to hear and tell jokes, sometimes laughing so hard in the telling that we never heard the punch line! He had a small dog, Chico, who, he assured everyone, was the source of all his knowledge.

Albert Einstein gave us an overarching explanation for the working of the hidden forces in the universe. He joined time and space together. His theory of relativity revolutionized physics and made him the most famous man alive. His theory enabled the scientists who came after him to make discoveries and interpret their experiments in ways that they otherwise could not have done.
—S.L.O.

Cricket Crosses the Atlantic

by Ann Thwaite

AS A BIOGRAPHER, I'm used to trying to reconstruct a remote past. Frances Hodgson Burnett was born in 1849, A. A. Milne in 1882. *Cricket* was born in 1973, and I should be able to remember exactly how it all began, but I find myself looking at the material evidence, just as I do when writing my biographies.

The first item is the pilot issue, dated January 1973, inscribed, "To Ann Thwaite. Best wishes, Blouke Carus." Inside the copy is a note from Blouke to my husband, who was coeditor of *Encounter* magazine, "Please give this copy to your wife." It is dated 27 March 1973. The magazine, with its neat shape and sharp spine and its wonderful Trina Schart Hyman cover, looks much as it did for the next five or six years. There was just one color overlay in each issue. The pilot had lime green, and readers, who were asked to illustrate a Jellicle Cat (following T. S. Eliot's "Song of the Jellicles"), were told they could "use any color as long as it's black." T. S. Eliot in a children's magazine—with Cricket himself explaining that "terpsichorean" means dancing—that was exciting! The whole thing was extremely exciting and quite unlike any children's magazine we'd seen before.

The nearest thing to it we had in England was *Puffin Post,* and I see that Kaye Webb, its famous editor, was one of the distinguished guests at the "auspicious and extraordinary occasion"

Ann Thwaite in the 1960s

What is this magazine about?
Cover illustration for April 1980,
"Cricket Match," *ink and acrylic*
by David Macaulay

when *Cricket* was launched on 6 June 1973. I have my invitation as evidence that it was on the Sky Garden Roof of the St. Moritz Hotel at 50 Central Park South, New York. I wasn't able to accept, but six months later there was an even more exciting invitation for me personally. I was in New Zealand when I wrote in my diary, "I've thought a lot about Marianne Carus's offer. Thought of titles for the magazine: *Tops, Fairground, Roundabout.* Sent a cable." The offer was that I should be involved as "Contributing Editor" in a British edition of the new magazine. The title was a problem because in England the word "cricket" does not suggest a lively insect, but rather the summer game with men in white clothes on a green field—one of them running up to bowl, another poised with his bat in front of three stumps. In the end the British edition was simply called *Cricket and Company,* not an entirely satisfactory solution. It was years later, in December 1992, at a "think tank" on Lake Bluff, that I had the pleasure of choosing the name for one of *Cricket*'s younger siblings: my suggestion of *Spider* won the vote over such other possibilities as *Dragonfly* and *Bumblebee.*

The first issue of *Cricket and Company, Cricket*'s British edition, was published in October 1974, following a pilot issue that summer. My own children were young at the time, and I encouraged them and their friends to write letters and competition entries until the real ones started coming. Most of the magazine was the same as the American issue, but we had our own "Letterbox" and competitions, and John Rowe Townsend and I encouraged all the best English writers and illustrators to contribute to both magazines. There were soon huge numbers of drawings and poems and letters flooding into the millhouse where I live. I've enjoyed looking

182

ANN THWAITE

back at some of the entries. The children round the margins of this page are some of our readers nearly thirty years ago, some of them very young, of course, as it was long before the days of *Ladybug* and *Spider.* The drawings were entries for our competition "What Are *You* Like?" Do they look so different from the way children look today? They are certainly not Victorians. It's odd to think that those children are now all in their thirties, some of them undoubtedly with children of their own, skipping, dancing, skating, playing the cello, the guitar, and the recorder. The separate British edition, sadly, did not last for long, only until Halloween in 1975, with a marvelous Jan Pienkowski cover. My regular monthly visits to the English printers in Suffolk ceased.

Cricket continued to have a wonderfully international flavor, with readers all over the world. I've continued all these years to be a member of the Editorial Board, an honor I've much appreciated. I've watched with admiration the *Cricket* family flourish and expand.

Cricket was originally designed for "children who love to read." Fortunately, thirty years later, in an age of DVD, video, the Internet, computer games, and so on, there are *still* children who love to read. And there always will be. Someone once said, "Reading is to the mind what exercise is to the body." Readers are never bored. The same, I can hear someone saying, is true of devotees of the Internet. But contrast the sight of a child absorbed in a book and one hopping about on the Worldwide Web. Not long ago, Gore Vidal was reported as saying that American students "don't know how to read a novel." Not a few of those who *do* naturally turn out to have read *Cricket* when they were young. Long may children have this special help to turn them into lifelong readers! For, as Dr. Johnson famously said, it is literature that enables us "the better to enjoy life or the better to endure it."

Ann Thwaite has contributed to the field of children's literature as an author, critic, and editor. She is best known for her rigorous biographies. Her *A. A. Milne: His Life* won the Whitbread Prize and *Edmund Gosse: A Literary Landscape* received the Duff Cooper Memorial Prize. She has served on the Editorial Board of *Cricket* since 1979.

Felix thought that Biscuit was the tastiest and fattest hamster that he'd ever seen!

As soon as Grandma went shopping, he had a go at opening the cage!

It was not easy!

Biscuit saw a big bundle of fur . . . just right to line his nest!

Felix ended up with a big bald patch, Biscuit with a nice soft nest!

Felix wanted revenge. He went to see Megamog, the big ginger cat next-door, and asked his help.

Megamog was big and strong! Off they went together . . .

Grandma, Felix, and Biscuit the Hamster!

IT DOESN'T SEEM such a long time ago when the first *Cricket* hit the magazine stalls in England! A full-of-fun, zany, little magazine with Trina's wisecracking insects on every page. There has never been anything quite like it for children of all ages. Lots to read, lots to look at and puzzle over with bright pictures on every page.

It was always a joy to receive a script for a *Cricket* story, it made a break from illustrating "heavy" books. It inspired illustrators and editors alike.

The cat door was small, and Megamog was fat . . .

You mean, greedy cat! Now you can just stay right there until I mend the cage!

Thank you, Grandma!

My Oxford University Press editor Ron Heapy loved the new approach, and encouraged me to turn to fun subjects such as the "Dracula" mad stories.

It was a pleasure to produce a new story about my old Hamster. Long live *Cricket*!

—**Victor Ambrus**

185

Happy Birthday, Dear *Cricket*!

by Shirley Hughes

Illustration by
Shirley Hughes

BRITISH CHILDREN'S WRITERS and illustrators are usually the last to hear the latest transatlantic publishing gossip, sitting as we do in our ivory towers. So there was great excitement when, in 1973, the news reached our ears that a brand-new children's magazine called *Cricket* was being launched in the U.S.A., edited by Marianne Carus, emanating from a place exotically named Peru, Illinois. It was Ann Thwaite who first told me about it. This publication was not, she patiently explained, going to concern itself with top test match scorers or England's chances against the West Indies in the coming series, but to be full of children's stories of the very best kind, beautifully illustrated. More encouragingly still, British writers and illustrators were going to be in the running for commissions.

Soon an invitation arrived from Trina Schart Hyman, the art director, and her assistant art director Dilys Evans, to a party at a hotel in London's Notting Hill. We duly arrived, rather nervous. Victor and Glenys Ambrus were among the illustrators there, I remember—probably Fritz Wegner, Faith Jaques, and Quentin Blake, too. We were not nervous for long. Trina and Dilys were friendly and direct. They had a very clear, enthusiastic vision of what they wanted from us, which was good draftsmanship, the ability to work wonders with limited color, and an unfettered imagination. Not bad as a starting point!

Looking through just one early edition of *Cricket* (January 1977), for which I did the cover, I encounter a pantheon of writers and artists I admire: the incomparable Marylin Hafner, the ebullient surrealist Friso Henstra, Troy Howell, Tomie dePaola, Quentin Blake, Fritz Wegner, and of course, Trina herself, who set the whole tone of the magazine with her brilliantly idiosyncratic conversations between Cricket, Ladybug, and Sluggo. It was somewhat awesome for me to follow a previous cover I had seen by Erik Blegvad in his splendidly understated but assured watercolor style. The standard set encouraged you to give your very best.

The encouraging letters which arrived from Trina and Dilys helped a lot. At last, at the Bologna Book Fair, I met Marianne Carus herself. It was the year that my own picture book *Dogger* had just broken through in the U.S.A. She took me to a sumptuous lunch, and we talked about all sorts of things: Bach, Mies van der Rohe, families, Italy, her dreams and ambitions and mine.

It was also through *Cricket* that I met the beautiful Kathleen Leverich, also at a London tea party. She was an editor then, before she metamorphosed into a writer. After we had made polite conversation and said good-bye, I ran into her quite by chance standing alone at a bus stop, wearing a huge turned-up collar, and looking like something out of *The Great Gatsby*! On an impulse, I asked her if she would like to come for a drink with

John and me the following evening, and this was the beginning of a long friendship and correspondence which has lasted until this day.

When Marylin Hafner called on us (I had already acquired a copy of her wonderful *Mrs. Gaddy and the Ghost*), another amazing conversation and correspondence began. I have kept every one of her wittily illustrated letters (and *envelopes*), written occasionally in various richly eccentric personae. And now her Molly and Emmett characters in *Ladybug* are giving enormous pleasure not only to me but my grandchildren, too.

I was always aware that Trina was an assiduous worker despite her laconic, laid-back style. But it was when I stayed in her New Hampshire farmhouse that I got the full impact. She gave the first impression that she did nothing but slope about the place, look after assorted animals and guests, cook, and sit about being hilariously funny. But she could work right through the latter part of the day and late into the night, a perfectionist with a supremely honed confidence in her chosen technique.

Becoming a professional illustrator requires not only talent and an irrepressible desire to draw, but staying power and a certain robust resilience, too. In my own family, it was my daughter Clara Vulliamy who turned out to have these qualities in abundance. I always knew that she had them, though I do not recall ever giving her any advice other than never to let anyone down on a deadline. Now, seeing her going strong in the pages of *Babybug* with her own characters Kim and Carrots is a deep source of pleasure and pride to me, a satisfying rounding of the circle.

So thank you, Marianne and Blouke and all the team at *Cricket,* for giving so many of us a chance to make our varied contributions and for keeping the standard so triumphantly high. Many happy returns!

Shirley Hughes has illustrated more than two hundred children's books, many of which she authored. For her picture book *Dogger,* she received the Kate Greenaway Medal. In 1999 she was named an Officer of the Order of the British Empire (OBE) in recognition of her body of work.

Happy 30th Birthday, *Cricket*!

**by
Fritz Wegner**

*Illustration by
Fritz Wegner*

I WELL REMEMBER how thrilled I was when Trina Schart Hyman first invited me to do some illustrations for a new American children's magazine called *Cricket*.

The style and contents instantly appealed to me. The stories that Trina sent me were fun to illustrate, and it was always encouraging to receive her enthusiastic appreciation, written in her neat capital-lettered handwriting. This, coming from a fellow illustrator/ art editor whose work I much admired, was a particular compliment.

Over the years I produced drawings for a great variety of stories, poems, and puzzles, and perhaps the more challenging as well as enjoyable commissions were some of the covers with seasonal or subject themes, which offered opportunities for fantasy and invention.

I can hardly believe that thirty years have passed since the launch of Marianne Carus's inspired magazine. Unlike *Cricket*, which has remained ageless and full of vitality, regrettably the years have not been so kind to me. Thankfully, there are ever more talented young illustrators who will continue to enhance the pages of *Cricket* and bring pleasure to new generations of children.

Fritz Wegner's career has encompassed advertising, designing stamps, teaching art, and illustrating for books, magazines, and periodicals.

A Message for *Cricket*

from Ruskin Bond

PERU, ILLINOIS, IS a far cry from Mussoorie, India, but the golden thread of storytelling has brought us together—the home of *Cricket* magazine and the mountain home of one of *Cricket*'s long-time storytellers.

I've been writing stories for as long as *Cricket* has been around, and many of those tales and poems appeared in the pages of your favorite children's magazine over the years.

I came to live in the Himalayan foothills in the early 1960s, around the time *Cricket* came into being. I was freelancing—sending my stories here, there, and everywhere. One of the first, "The Day Grandfather Tickled a Tiger," found a home in *Cricket*, and others followed—tales of small-town India, Grandfather and his pets, Granny and her jams and chutneys, and friends, human and animal, that I'd made along the way.

In those early days, not many stories from India were published in America. *Cricket* magazine was a pioneer in presenting tales from many lands and diverse cultures: a multicultural publisher long before multicultural publishing became fashionable.

Another innovation was the little crickets, cicadas, ladybirds, and quaint little creatures who popped up on the margins of *Cricket*'s pages, to explain an unfamiliar word or phrase in a way that was both entertaining and informative.

I get visits from a real live cricket who sometimes comes in at my open window and explores the leafy geraniums that I grow on the window ledge. It doesn't help me with my spelling, but it has a cheerful little chirp or chirrup and its presence helps to brighten up my day.

That's what *Cricket* magazine has done over the years—brightened up the days of many thousands of young readers. So open your windows, friends, and listen to the song of the cricket.

A Song for Cricket

by Ruskin Bond

The simple things in life are best—
A patch of green,
A small bird's nest,
A drink of water, fresh and cold,
The taste of bread,
A song of old.
These are the things that matter most.
The laughter of a child,
A favourite book,
Flowers growing wild.
A cricket singing in a shady nook.
A ball that bounces high!
A summer shower,
A rainbow in the sky.
The touch of a loving hand.
And time to rest . . .
These simple things in life are best.

Ruskin Bond was born in India and is a prolific writer of short stories, essays, novellas, poems, and children's books. Among his honors are the John Llewellyn Rhys Prize for *The Room on the Roof* and the Sahitya Akademi Award. Recent publications include two short-story collections, *Rusty: The Boy from the Hills* and *A Season of Ghosts*.

a true story by Ruskin Bond

The Day Grandfather Tickled a Tiger

TIMOTHY, OUR TIGER cub, was found by my grandfather on a hunting expedition in the Terai jungles near Dehra, in northern India. Because Grandfather lived in Dehra and knew the jungles well, he was persuaded to accompany the hunting party.

Grandfather, strolling down a forest path some distance from the main party, discovered a little abandoned tiger about eighteen inches long, hidden among the roots of a banyan tree. After the expedition ended, Grandfather took the tiger home to Dehra, where Grandmother gave him the name Timothy.

Timothy's favorite place in the house was the living room. He would snuggle down comfortably on the sofa, reclining there with serene dignity and snarling only when anyone tried to take his place. One of his chief amusements was to stalk whoever was playing with him, and so, when I went to live with my grandparents, I became one of the tiger's pets. With a crafty look in his eyes, and

Illustrated by
Jan Adkins

Cricket, April 1974

his body in a deep crouch, he would creep closer and closer to me, suddenly making a dash for my feet. Then, rolling on his back and kicking with delight, he would pretend to bite my ankles.

By this time he was the size of a full-grown golden retriever, and when I took him for walks in Dehra, people on the road would give us a wide berth. At night he slept in the quarters of our cook, Mahmoud. "One of these days," Grandmother declared, "we are going to find Timothy sitting on Mahmoud's bed and no sign of Mahmoud!"

When Timothy was about six months old, his stalking became more serious, and he had to be chained up more frequently. Even the household started to mistrust him, and, when he began to trail Mahmoud around the house with what looked like villainous intent, Grandfather decided it was time to transfer Timothy to a zoo.

The nearest zoo was at Lucknow, some two hundred miles away. Grandfather reserved a first-class compartment on the train for himself and Timothy and set forth. The Lucknow zoo authorities were only too pleased to receive a well-fed and fairly civilized tiger.

Grandfather had no opportunity to see how Timothy was getting on in his new home until about six months later, when he and Grandmother visited relatives in Lucknow. Grandfather went to the zoo and directly to Timothy's cage. The tiger was there, crouched in a corner, full-grown, his magnificent striped coat gleaming with health.

"Hello, Timothy," Grandfather said.

Climbing the railing, he put his arms through the bars of the cage. Timothy approached, and allowed Grandfather to put both arms about his head. Grandfather stroked the tiger's forehead and tickled his ears. Each time Timothy growled, Grandfather gave him a smack across the mouth, which had been his way of keeping the tiger quiet when he lived with us.

Timothy licked Grandfather's hands. Then he showed nervousness, springing away when a leopard in the next cage snarled at him, but Grandfather shooed the leopard off and Timothy returned to licking his hands. Every now and then the leopard would rush at the bars, and Timothy would again slink back to a neutral corner.

A number of people had gathered to watch the reunion, when a keeper pushed his way through the crowd and asked Grandfather what he was doing. "I'm talking to Timothy," said Grandfather. "Weren't you here when I gave him to the zoo six months ago?"

"I haven't been here very long," said the surprised keeper. "Please continue your conversation. I have never been able to touch that tiger myself. I find him very bad-tempered."

Grandfather had been stroking and slapping Timothy for about five minutes when he noticed another keeper observing him with some alarm. Grandfather recognized him as the keeper who had been there when he had delivered Timothy to the zoo.

"You remember me," said Grandfather. "Why don't you transfer Timothy to a different cage, away from this stupid leopard?"

"But—sir," stammered the keeper. "It is not your tiger."

"I realize that he is no longer mine," said Grandfather testily. "But at least take my suggestion."

"I remember your tiger very well," said the keeper. "He died two months ago."

"Died!" exclaimed Grandfather.

"Yes, sir, of pneumonia. This tiger was trapped in the hills only last month, and he is very dangerous!"

The tiger was still licking Grandfather's arms and apparently enjoying it more all the time. Grandfather withdrew his hands from the cage in a motion that seemed to take an age. With his face near the tiger's, he mumbled, "Good night, Timothy." Then, giving the keeper a scornful look, Grandfather walked briskly out of the zoo.

THE DAY GRANDFATHER TICKLED A TIGER

The Cat Who Became a Poet

by Margaret Mahy

Illustrated by
Quentin Blake

A CAT ONCE caught a mouse, as cats do.

"Don't eat me," cried the mouse. "I am a poet with a poem to write."

"That doesn't make any difference to me," replied the cat. "It is a rule that cats must eat mice and that is all there is to it."

"If only you'd listen to my poem you'd feel differently about it all," said the mouse.

"O.K.," yawned the cat, "I don't mind hearing a poem, but I warn you, it won't make any difference."

So the mouse danced and sang:

The great mouse Night with the starry tail
Slides over the hills and trees,
Eating the crumbs in the corners of Day
And nibbling the moon like cheese.

Cricket, June 1982

"Very good! That's very good!" the cat said. "But a poem is only a poem, and cats still eat mice."

And he ate the mouse, as cats do.

Then he washed his paws and his face and curled up in a bed of catnip, tucking in his nose and his tail and his paws. Then he had a little catnap.

Some time later he woke up in alarm.

What's wrong with me? he thought. I feel so strange.

He felt as if his head was full of colored lights. Pictures came and went behind his eyes. Things that were different seemed alike. Things that were real changed and became dreams.

Horrakapotchkin! thought the cat. I want to write a poem.

He opened his mouth to meow, but a poem came out instead:

The great Sun-Cat comes up in the east.
Lo! The glory of his whiskers touches the hills.
Behold! The fire of his smiling
Burns on the oceans of the rolling world.

THE CAT WHO BECAME A POET

"Cat-curses!" said the cat to himself. "I have turned into a poet, but I don't want to make poetry. I just want to be a cat, catching mice and sleeping in the catnip bed. I will have to ask the witch about this."

The cat went to the witch's crooked house. The witch sat at the window with her head in her hands. Her dreams turned into black butterflies and flew out of the window.

She took the cat's temperature and gave him some magic medicine that tasted of dandelions.

"Now talk!" she commanded.

The cat opened his mouth to ask her if he was cured. Instead he found himself saying:

Lying in the catnip bed,
The flowering cherry over my head,
Am I really the cat that I seem?
Or only a cat in another cat's dream?

Margaret Mahy

"I'm afraid it is too late," said the witch. "Your case is hopeless. Poetry has got into your blood, and you're stuck with it for the rest of your life."

"Horrakapotchkin!" cried the cat sadly, and he started off home.

But, five houses away from his own house, a black dog called Max chased him, as dogs do, and the cat had to run up a tree. He boxed with his paw at Max and went to hiss and spit at him, but instead he found himself saying:

Colonel Dog fires his cannon
And puts his white soldiers on parade.
He guards the house from cats, burglars,
And any threat of peacefulness.

The dog Max stopped and stared. "What did you call me? Colonel Dog? I like that. But what do you mean—I fire my cannon?"

"That's your barking," said the cat.

"And what do you mean—I put my white soldiers on parade?" asked the dog again.

"That's your teeth," said the cat.

The dog wagged his tail. "I like the way you put it," he said again. "How did you learn to talk like that?"

"Oh, it's poetry," said the cat carelessly. "I am a poet you see."

"Well, I'll tell you what! I'll let you go without barking at you if I may come and hear that poem again sometime," the dog Max said, still wagging his tail. "Perhaps I could bring some other dogs to hear it, too. Colonel Dog, eh? White soldiers, eh? Very true." And he let the cat go on home to his catnip bed.

If only he knew, the cat thought. I wasn't meaning to praise him. Poetry is very tricky stuff and can be taken two ways.

The cat went on thinking: I became a poet through eating the mouse. Perhaps the mouse became a poet through eating seeds. Perhaps all this poetry stuff is just the world's way of talking about itself. And straightaway he felt another poem coming into his mind.

"Just time for a sleep first," he muttered into his whiskers. "One thing, I'll never eat another poet again. One is quite enough." And he curled up in the catnip bed for a quick catnap, as cats do.

Margaret Mahy is one of New Zealand's most beloved writers for children. She is a two-time recipient of the Carnegie Medal—for *The Haunting* and *The Changeover*—and a six-time winner of the New Zealand Library Association's Esther Glen Award. In 1993 she was named to the Order of New Zealand, the highest honor a New Zealander can achieve.

CATS

by Gina Ruck-Pauquèt

What are their private and secret addresses?
Do their purrs equal our please's and yes's?
How do they produce those purrs?
At night, could they take off their furs?
And why do they sit on the roof?
Are they aloof?
Can they be sad? Do they think very much
About mouse tails and such?
Do they dance the Tom-Tango
and Feline-Fandango,
Or are they far too reserved?
What makes their claws be so curved?
How do they kindle the blaze in their eyes?
Do they wait until moonrise,
And kindle the blaze with a beam?
What do they dream?
And why don't they smile
Even once in a while?
And where do they go when they vanish for days?
Try asking a cat, and see what she says!

Translated by
Doris Orgel

Illustrated by
Erik Blegvad

Cricket, April 1974

201

ERIK BLEGVAD · 74

TOSH

A TRUE STORY

by James Herriot

Illustrated by Beth and Joe Krush

I SUPPOSE TOSH is a strange name for a cat, and particularly for this cat. It is a rough-sounding name, and Tosh was usually an extremely dignified and superior cat. But there was something different about him today.

His owners, Mr. and Mrs. Beveridge, gazed down at him anxiously. "He's gone right off his food, Mr. Herriot," the lady said. "He's been eating less and less for the past week, and now he won't touch a thing."

I reached out and stroked the sleek black head. "Well, that's not like Tosh, is it?" Tosh was really fond of his food as a rule. In fact, I'd describe him as an enthusiastic eater.

Cricket, September 1975

Mr. Beveridge was a butcher, and he brought home the choicest tidbits for his cat. Tosh dined regularly on steak, liver, and kidneys; not content with this, his owners visited the fish shop twice a week so that his diet would not become monotonous. Tosh had it made.

It is not surprising that Tosh grew into a very large shiny cat. He was jet black, except for a snow-white patch under his chin and down his breast that made him look rather handsome. He was always washing himself, especially his big fat face. He would clean his fur carefully, then look around in a self-satisfied way. I think he was somewhat vain.

Tosh was one of my favorite patients. I had treated him several times over his eight years, and he never offered any resistance when I examined or injected him. Cats can be very difficult for veterinarians because they can scratch as well as bite. Sometimes we have to wrap them in a blanket before we can do anything with them. But Tosh was always cooperative and friendly.

I got out my thermometer and took his temperature. It was normal. I sounded his chest with my stethoscope and could find nothing wrong. I felt all over his abdomen but drew another blank. I couldn't pinpoint anything, and yet he did look different.

There was something vaguely unhappy about him. Normally when I examined Tosh, he purred louder and louder till you could

hear him all over the room. But today he only managed a half-hearted sort of rumble, as if he were just trying to be polite.

"Well, there doesn't seem to be anything seriously wrong with him," I said. "But he certainly isn't himself, and he wouldn't stop eating for no reason. He may have a slightly upset stomach. I'll give him a shot of something that ought to help him."

I went out to my car. Sometimes cats getting into middle age can benefit from a vitamin injection, so I took one back into the house. As usual, the big cat made no move when I slipped the needle under his skin. He merely sat there with his head held high—as though he knew he was brave and was proud of it.

I didn't see Tosh for the next few days, although I kept watching for him every time I passed his house. On my rounds I had often observed him crossing the street, and it showed what an intelligent cat he was. He didn't rush out into the traffic, but looked carefully both ways before stalking importantly across. I don't know what he did over there—probably visited friends. I couldn't imagine him doing anything as undignified as catching mice.

On the third day, Mrs. Beveridge telephoned. Tosh still hadn't eaten anything.

When I saw him, I was shocked. The gloss was gone from his fur, and he had lost a lot of weight. He didn't even have a fat face anymore.

"Does he drink much?" I asked.

Mrs. Beveridge shrugged her shoulders. "He does lap some milk, but only a very little."

I went over the cat again with the utmost care, but still could find nothing abnormal. I gave Tosh a different kind of injection to help his digestion, but I did not feel happy about him, and I promised to call on the following day.

When I visited Tosh the next morning, I could see immediately that he was no better. He looked miserable and pathetic, and his white fur was not as clean as usual.

"You know, Mr. Herriot," Mrs. Beveridge said, "he has stopped washing himself. I don't like that."

Neither did I. When a vain cat like Tosh began to neglect his personal appearance, things were bad. I was really worried.

Mrs. Beveridge looked at me, and her lip trembled. "Is he going to die?" she whispered.

"Oh, no, no . . . of course not. It's too soon to be talking like that," I replied. But I was not as confident as I tried to sound. If an animal will not eat, then it will certainly die.

Just then Tosh rose and moved wearily over to his dish in the corner. It held some very tasty-looking chopped fish, but the cat just sat with his nose almost touching the dish. And he stayed like that, motionless.

"Does he always sit over his food like this?" I asked.

"Yes," she replied. "Just as though he wanted to eat but couldn't."

A little bell seemed to ring in my head. "Wanted to eat but couldn't. . . ." I lifted Tosh onto my lap and opened his mouth. And there it was—the cause of all the trouble—a big piece of tartar on one of his back teeth. Lots of cats get tartar on their teeth as they grow older, but this was big and smooth like a pebble. It completely stopped him from closing his mouth and from chewing his food.

I was so relieved that I galloped full tilt out to my car for a pair

WHAT'S TARTAR? ... IT'S HARD BONY STUFF THAT SETTLES ON YOUR TEETH, IF YOU DON'T KEEP THEM BRUSHED AND CLEAN!

of forceps. I squeezed the piece of tartar with the forceps; it cracked and broke away, leaving a lovely, clean white tooth underneath.

Tosh got the message immediately. When I put him down, he went straight to his dish and began to eat, as though determined to make up for lost time. Now and again he looked up as if to say, "That's better. Why didn't you do something about it before?" When I left, he had finished the fish and was starting on some meat.

And of course I *should* have done something about it before. But we all make mistakes, and I made the mistake of looking everywhere but in the cat's mouth. Now whenever I see a sick cat, I look in his mouth first instead of last.

That's what I learned from Tosh.

James Herriot was a British veterinarian and author. He captured the hearts of readers of all ages with his best-selling books, including *All Creatures Great and Small.*

The Cub

by Walter
Dean Myers
*Illustrated by
Leslie Morrill*

"YOU HAVE TO KNOW what it's like, Grandpa," thirteen-year-old Tim Shorter exclaimed. "Motocross is the best! If you could see me ride the trails, you'd understand."

"Sounds dangerous!" Grandpa Shorter stopped walking and looked at his grandson.

"Not if you're careful," Tim said. "Anyway, I'm a good driver."

"I'm sure you are." Grandpa Shorter ran his fingers through a thinning shock of white hair. "I don't know about taking chances just for the sake of doing it, though."

Tim sighed. He'd been spending a few weeks this summer at The Pines, as Grandpa Shorter called his place. It was fifteen miles outside of Helena, Montana, but as far as Tim was concerned, it could have been on the moon. Except for his grandfather's cabin and a small shed they used for supplies, there wasn't a house in any direction for miles. Grandpa Shorter didn't even have a telephone. The only modern thing he had was an old pickup he sometimes drove into town. Tim usually liked visiting his grandfather, but right now he felt that the old man was ready to spend the rest of his life in a rocking chair.

"Let's see what we can catch here at the stream before the sun goes down," Grandpa Shorter said, interrupting Tim's thoughts. "I ever tell you about the time I caught a trout here that was so long we had to send to Sears and Roebuck for a bigger frying pan?"

"Grandpa, where do you get all these stories?" Tim asked.

"We used to do a lot of storytelling when I was a young man," Grandpa Shorter said. "Folks were more sociable than they are now."

Cricket, July 1987

Tim imagined his grandfather sitting by a stove in a country store whittling on a piece of wood and listening to stories. It sounded as exciting as sleeping.

"Anyway, my brother and I were out fishing all that day," Grandpa Shorter continued. "We hadn't caught anything and were just about ready to pack up and leave when I got a tug on my—"

Grandpa Shorter stopped his sentence abruptly and put his hand on Tim's arm.

"What's wrong, Grandpa?" Tim asked.

"Look over there," Grandpa Shorter pointed toward a tree downstream. At the base of the tree, Tim could see a small animal. It seemed to move from one side of the tree to the other and back again.

"It looks like a raccoon," Tim said. "Probably trying to dig up something to eat."

"No," said Grandpa Shorter. "That's a grizzly cub caught in a trap. Old man Jenkins and I have found a few traps around here lately."

"If it is a bear, it's too little to hurt anybody, Grandpa," Tim

WALTER DEAN MYERS

said. "Even you can take that much excitement. I really don't think we have to worry about it."

"Could be. . . ." Grandpa Shorter spoke as if he were talking to himself. "But that cub is no more than a couple months old, so you can bet there's a she-bear in the vicinity. And that much excitement I can't take. A grizzly can run you down and kill you with a single blow. I think we'd better hightail it out of here."

"Yeah," Tim said, looking around him. "O.K., I'm right behind you, Grandpa."

"Keep your eyes open," Grandpa Shorter said. "I don't think that bear will wander off too far from her cub, but you can't be sure."

It had taken forty-five minutes to walk to the stream, but the trip back to the cabin just took them a little over half an hour.

"I didn't think there were many grizzlies around here," Tim said as they reached the cabin.

"Aren't that many," Grandpa Shorter said. "There aren't that many in the country anymore. More important is that they mind their business and don't bother anybody. That cub in a trap changes things, though."

Grandpa Shorter got into the pickup and turned the key. The motor whined, coughed, and died.

"We going into town because of the bear?" Tim asked.

Grandpa Shorter ignored the question and tried to start the engine. Again the old motor whined, coughed, and died. The third time, there was a loud clicking sound and no more.

"The cabin looks pretty sturdy to me," Tim offered.

Grandpa Shorter closed both eyes and rubbed his temples with his hands. Then he looked up, took the keys, and went to the little shed he used for storage. Tim sat on the fender of the pickup and waited while his grandpa banged around in the shed. When Grandpa Shorter came out, he had a rifle in the crook of one arm and an ax handle and a package in the other.

"You going to go out and shoot the cub?" Tim asked.

"Shoot the cub?" Grandpa Shorter had put down the package and the ax handle and was loading the rifle. "No, I'm going to try to free it. Its mother will leave it there for a while, hoping it'll free itself. When it doesn't, she'll either abandon it or gnaw its paw off. Either way, the cub will die. I'm going to try to free it before that happens."

"But I thought you said the mother grizzly could . . . you know."

"Yes, that's right, Timmy." Grandpa Shorter's face was grim. "But you don't leave things to suffer and die if you can help it. Not even grizzly bears."

"I'll go along if you want me to," said Tim.

"I don't really want you to," Grandpa Shorter said. "But since I can't get to town for the sheriff, I guess I'll need your help."

The trek back to the stream took another half-hour. Tim carried the ax handle and stayed close behind his grandpa. As they walked, Grandpa Shorter told him what they were going to do. Tim tried to imagine himself warding off the mother bear, and more than once he thought about going back to the cabin. By the time they reached the stream, the back of Tim's shirt was soaked with sweat.

"You sure this is going to work, Grandpa?"

"No," Grandpa Shorter said quietly. "You scared?"

"Yeah, I guess so," Tim said.

"Good. This is the time to be a little scared. Just try not to panic."

They stood together, looking upstream. Tim could imagine the cub's mother coming from behind one of the trees at any moment and attacking them.

"You see any signs of the mother?" Grandpa Shorter asked.

"No," Tim said.

"Then let's go."

Grandpa Shorter went first, moving quickly toward the trapped bear cub.

WALTER DEAN MYERS

The cub yelped and jumped when it saw him approach. Up close it wasn't as small as Tim had thought. And he froze, horrified, as he saw the cub's paw swing out and its claws make deep, even scratches on Grandpa's arm.

"Don't look at the cub," Grandpa Shorter said. "Watch for the mother, Timmy!"

Tim turned away, holding his breath. He heard the scuffling beside him and his grandpa's heavy breathing. Then he saw what looked like a huge shadow in the bushes fifty yards away. It was the mother bear, and she was lumbering through the branches into the opening between them!

"Grandpa!"

"The firecrackers, Timmy—quick!"

Tim held his arms together to steady his hands as he lit the first firecracker. It exploded less than ten feet in front of him. The second went a little farther.

The huge bear stopped, made a small jump, and started

toward them again, this time more cautiously. Tim saw another bear, a cub as small as the first, behind her. He lit two more firecrackers and threw them toward the mother bear. She took another step, then stopped again and began to circle to her left. She made a noise that was halfway between a growl and a hiss.

"O.K., keep throwing them." Grandpa Shorter's voice was raspy. Tim threw another firecracker, and the huge bear backed away. Then Tim saw the trapped cub scamper toward its mother. Grandpa Shorter had freed it!

Tim looked at his grandpa. The old man was kneeling, and he had his rifle trained on the grizzly. There was blood on his sleeve.

Tim threw two more firecrackers, then felt his grandfather pat him on the shoulder.

"You O.K.?" Tim asked.

"Just a scratch," said Grandpa Shorter. "When we get back home, I'll put something on it. You did a good job, Timmy. I don't think that bear wanted any part of you and those firecrackers. Especially with her cubs to protect."

Grandpa Shorter stopped and grinned at Tim. "She was probably one of those old-fashioned bears. You know—the kind that can't stand much excitement."

Walter Dean Myers is a five-time winner of the Coretta Scott King Award and a recipient of the Margaret A. Edwards Award for lifetime achievement in young adult literature. His *Somewhere in the Darkness* and *Scorpions* were Newbery Honor books, and *Monster* was a National Book Award finalist and winner of the first Michael L. Printz Award.

Owl O'Clock

by Paul Fleischman

Illustration by Anne Hunter

On summer nights I sleep in the treehouse,
far from our grandfather clock's deep chime.
My watch is back in my room. I don't mind.
I see and hear and smell the time.

Frog o'clock,
then first star,
porch lights on,
then jasmine scent.
Cats called in,
then porch lights out,
the evening's final bus
up Ninth,
and then my favorite time of all,
the hour after raccoon-prowl,
the time I love to listen for—
owl o'clock at night.

Cricket, July 2000

213

Dear Marianne

by
Jim Arnosky

I AM FLATTERED to be considered among your first contributors. I remember first seeing *Cricket* magazine. It was an ad with a picture of your first issue, with a color drawing by Trina on its cover. The drawing was a friendly-looking giant reading to children. We were living in a small cabin at the base of Hawk Mountain in the Pennsylvania woods. We had a wood-and-coal stove and a few electric heaters. We had no plumbing. Deanna collected water each day from an aboveground spring. That first year, our heat for the winter consisted of burning wood, which I felled, cut, and split myself. It was a very rugged life. We had one daughter at the time—Michelle.

I spent my days hiking the mountains, learning all I could about the local wildlife. I found bobcats, turkeys, rattlesnakes, copperheads, grouse, wild trout, raccoons, and opossums. One night I heard a screech owl right outside our cabin door, and when I peeked, I saw it sitting on the top rung of a ladder I had left standing against the wall. It was the closest I had ever been to an owl. And I looked for it every night, until finally it found a new perch somewhere in the forest. I could still hear it and I even could call it, and it called back. But it never came to the ladder again.

I would hike ten miles a day in the hills. And at night I sat at my drawing board trying to make sense of all I was seeing in pictures and words. Nobody was willing to hire me then. I just made my drawings and sent out packets of art, hoping I'd get a freelance job to do.

The first packet of art I sent to *Cricket* included some of my early published work. And it was rejected as being not quite what *Cricket* was looking for. But I kept sending until one wonderful day I received an assignment to illustrate Farley Mowat's "Owls in the Family." And with the work, I was given the order (from Trina) to use the payment to get water piped into our cabin. Well, we did use the payment for water, but we didn't have it piped in. We had a hand pump installed.

We lived that way for four and a half years. I did many *Cricket* illustration assignments, and they led to offers from other magazines and publishers. It was at that time that I invented Crinkleroot, and, it's hard to believe that now, after almost thirty years, I am still drawing Crinkleroot! Amber, our second daughter, was born just as we were deciding to move from the cabin to someplace with more space. After a few trips north and east, we ended up in Vermont on this old farm.

It seems so long ago now to think back to those days when I was just discovering all the wildlife of the forest around our cabin and learning the names of all the trees. And working hard on every new *Cricket* assignment Trina sent me. Since then I've been all over the country learning about all the animals that live on this great land with us. But even with all I've seen and all the pictures I've drawn and painted and all the stories I've written and all the books I've had published, I still have a special feeling every time I see a *Cricket* magazine on a library shelf. In fact, I have the first sketch I did for "Owls in the Family" still hanging in my drawing room. It is a drawing of the boy in the story reading a book on the porch with his two pet owls at his side. That porch is the porch of our old cabin at Hawk Mountain.

Thank you, *Cricket,* for all these early assignments and for being such a great magazine for thirty years.

Jim Arnosky aims "to foster an appreciation of nature and a curiosity about wildlife" in his children's books. His Crinkleroot and All About series are among his most popular books.

The Literary Ticket

SO MANY LETTERS, so little time
To celebrate *Cricket* sublime,
So these small memories will have to do
Of sending just two notes to you.

My Dear Ms. Carus, you've sent back
My manuscript, noting its lack.
Rejection from your desk to mine
Is taken as a hopeful sign,
Since you've appended a personal line.

And so I say, Ms. Carus dear,
Rejection I shall never fear,
Your notes are never cruel or mean.
Better than selling to a lesser magazine.

My children tell me that your *Cricket*
Is quite the literary ticket.
In fact my Adam, middle son,
Avows "It's lots of books in one."

He takes it up to bed for fun.

—*Sent with love from* **Jane Yolen**

Jane Yolen sold her first book, *Pirates in Petticoats,* at the age of twenty-one. Since then she has published over two hundred books and been recognized by more than thirty awards committees for her literature. For her body of work, she received the Literary Lights for Children Award from the Boston Public Library in 1998 and an Honorary Doctor of Letters from Keene State College the same year.

*Art by Shirley Hughes,
May 1985* Cricket

My Love Affair with Reading

A Letter from a Reader—by Glenn Robert Gray

I WAS A *CRICKET* kid. Actually, I was reared on equal parts *Cricket* and Lloyd Alexander, whom I regard as not only our finest living children's author but a national treasure. *Cricket* was part of my earliest years. I learned to read a couple of years after *Cricket* started publishing. At approximately the same time, I began reading Lloyd Alexander's books. He was already a Newbery Award winner, and has since gone on to win the National Book Award, the American Book Award, the Regina Medal, and a sackful of other trophies. He was for me then a living legend who also happened to explore the world of myth and legend in his own books. This was intoxicating stuff for a grade-schooler.

To say that I read *Cricket* from cover to cover is not an exaggeration. I even read the masthead, wherein I duly noted the presence of Lloyd Alexander among the editorial staff. Emboldened by his presence there, I wrote him via *Cricket*'s address. They forwarded the letter, and lo, he responded, and a correspondence and friendship ensued that persists to this day. Originally hailing from Reading, Pennsylvania (how's that for a coincidence?), I have been fortunate enough to visit Lloyd in his not-too-distant Philadelphia home, an experience which for me cannot have been unlike his visit with Gertrude Stein in Paris.

It is a sentiment oft-observed that the impact of what we read in our formative years has an incalculable effect on our later life. *Cricket,* and along with it the books of Lloyd Alexander, did as much or more than anything else to foster in me a love of reading. Parents beware! For a long time now, I find that I cannot bear to be without books. The surest way to put me out of sorts is to be "between books," that affliction which affects those of us who have just finished an engaging book and have yet to sink into another one that is as good. The spare moments of my life are a constant seeking out of my next reading material. This love of reading has led to a bona fide case of biblioholism. To live a life in the book world, if only to work near books in whatever capacity, has been an underlying current of my life, so it should come as no surprise that I now work as a librarian.

I can still remember the thrill I felt when I won a *Cricket* story contest when I was eight years old, and it was a greater thrill than my first published article as an adult. Speaking to Marianne Carus, the editor of *Cricket* since its inception, about this article was a thrill in itself—how often do we get to speak with a hero from our childhood?

Thirty years later, *Cricket* is still publishing, and Lloyd is still writing. Over the years *Cricket* has changed, and so have I. Yet I have only to glimpse the cover of an old issue of *Cricket* and I can conjure up its stories in my mind's eye. To this day, I can quote parts of the recording of *Cricket's* first-year celebration, which I listened to exhaustively as a child.

Elsewhere, Lloyd has written of his love affair with music—for me, the sweetest music will always be the flicking of the printed page. In the inaugural issue of *Cricket,* Lloyd wrote of being a hungry reader—to this day, my craving for narrative remains unquenched. I believe Lloyd is right when he observes that the more we read, the more we have the capacity to read. This cauldron of plenty is never dry—nor should it ever be.

So, the thirty heartiest of salutes (or should that be chirps?) to Marianne Carus, Lloyd Alexander, and everyone else involved in this most splendid of enterprises.

Glenn Robert Gray works as an archivist and assistant special collections librarian at California State University.

The Day Mother Sold the Family Swords

A True Story • by Shizuko Obo
Illustrated by Russ Walks

WHEN PEOPLE think about Japan, they either think of Old Japan—people wearing bright, flowing kimonos, living in wooden houses with thatched straw roofs and sliding paper walls, writing poetry on paper lanterns, and practicing the martial arts…or they think of New Japan—everybody wearing business suits, rushing for crowded trains, working fourteen hours a day, making a lot of cars and cameras, TVs and VCRs, but still taking time to practice the martial arts.

I grew up in Japan during a time between the old and the new ways of life—in the final days of the Second World War, when more changes took place in Japan than had taken place in the past thousand years. When I was a little girl, living on the outskirts of Tokyo, I could look out over one of the biggest cities in the world and see nothing but brown, burned buildings and wreckage. There wasn't a tree or a spray of green leaves anywhere. Some of the things I remember about those days were shocking and some of them were also funny, but one of the things I remember most clearly is the day my mother sold the family swords.

Near the end of the war that had started when Japan made a surprise attack on Pearl Harbor, American B-29 planes dropped

Cricket, August 1992
Winner of the 1993 Paul A. Witty Short Story Award

MARTIAL ARTS ARE KARATE, JUDO, AND OTHER FORMS OF SELF-DEFENSE ORIGINATING IN THE FAR EAST.

thousands of firebombs on Tokyo. During this biggest firebombing raid in history, most of the wooden houses with their thatched straw roofs and paper screens burned like stacks of crumpled paper. My mother had taken me and my older brother and sister to live with relatives in the country before this happened. But my father and my oldest brother, Takeo, had stayed home because my father had to work and my brother, who was fifteen years older than I, had already been drafted for the navy and was to begin flight training to become a pilot.

During the last days of the war, my brother Takeo was chosen to be a member of a special attack squadron called the kamikaze. By 1945 Japan was so short of trained pilots that young, inexperienced pilots were asked to dive their airplanes right into the American ships instead of trying to drop bombs on them. The pilots were killed, of course, when they crashed their planes into the ships, which were badly damaged or sunk. These kamikaze were the last weapon Japan had left in 1945, and many young Japanese were willing to sacrifice their lives for their country rather than give up.

Americans found the kamikaze unbelievable. How could you train a pilot to crash his own plane like that? But the Japanese had a long tradition of self-sacrifice. In the olden times, the samurai —who were warriors and also something like policemen—would carry two swords: a long sword for fighting and a short sword to kill themselves if they were disgraced.

During the night in 1945, when the firebombs rained on Tokyo, my brother Takeo was still at home. The bombs didn't hit our house, but fire spread from burning debris, and our house began to burn.

Takeo, who was very brave, ran back into the house to save whatever he could. First he threw the mattresses out of the window to the ground. Then he started to save my father's swords.

My father owned a small factory, but his ancestors were daimyo—a title that was one rank above the samurai. In Old Japan, only noblemen had the right to own or carry swords, and a daimyo was the master of many samurai. My father had kept all of the ceremonial and historical swords from our clan—about twenty of them, two of which dated back to the thirteenth century. These swords were our most precious heirlooms.

Takeo threw the swords out of the burning house onto the mattresses, while the roof began to cave in. My father shouted

KAMIKAZE MEANS "DIVINE WIND."
SAY IT: KAH - MI - KAH - ZEE.

DAIMYO
SAY IT:
DIE-MYO.

DEBRIS IS RUINS.
SAY IT: DE-BREE.

for Takeo to get out of the house—his son was worth more to him than a thousand swords. Finally Takeo jumped onto the mattress after the swords, and a moment later the roof fell in. That was the end of the house I was born in.

In August of 1945, the last bombs fell. American B-29s dropped an atomic bomb

SHIZUKO OBO

on Hiroshima, and another on Nagasaki. Both cities were blown to bits. The Emperor spoke on the radio. He told the Japanese that they must surrender. This was the first time in three hundred years that Japan had ever lost a war. It was the first time in history that Japan would be occupied by foreign troops. Old Japan began to disappear.

My father was stunned. He had never believed that Japan would lose the war. But there was good news for the family. Takeo came back home from the navy. He did not get the chance to crash his airplane into an American ship, because the war ended before he was to make his flight.

Now that our family didn't have to worry about bombs anymore, we had to worry about getting enough to eat. Before the war, Japan had owned overseas territories like Korea and Formosa (now called Taiwan), which produced much of our food. Suddenly we had no overseas territories anymore, and food became expensive. Also, many people were out of work.

My father was a proud man. Still, in order to buy rice, he sold some of his most valuable possessions, one by one. But even when we ran out of food, he never considered selling our family swords. I remember one day when we had no rice, my mother cooked some dandelion leaves and some tender leaves from the shrubbery around our new house. The dandelions tasted like spinach—or maybe we were just hungry.

We had few luxuries. Takeo had not thought of saving the dolls—only the swords that were the symbol of the Japanese warrior—so I just had an American Kewpie doll Mother had gotten me, and I took it with me everywhere until I was about ten years old.

One of the few luxuries adults allowed themselves was to go to a fortuneteller. Japanese loved to have their fortunes told, and many people took them very seriously.

One day when my mother was having her fortune told, the fortuneteller said something that frightened her: "If there is a sword in the family, the family will see blood."

My mother had always said we were a lucky family. Our house had burned down, and we lost most of our money, but nobody had been killed. Even Takeo had come home alive and unhurt. Many families were still waiting for their husbands or sons to return—many never would.

My mother didn't want anyone to die. So she did something that took great courage for a Japanese woman of her time. She ran home and gathered up all the family swords and sold them—to a junk dealer!

When my father came home that night,

A KEWPIE DOLL IS A SMALL, PLUMP DOLL WITH A TOPKNOT.

THE DAY MOTHER SOLD THE FAMILY SWORDS

he was so angry he couldn't even talk. Sometimes he would mutter under his breath, but he never raised a hand to strike my mother—and in Old Japan that was unusual, because a woman had no power, not even to disagree with her husband or to sell his property. My brother Takeo was angry, too. He wanted the swords to hand down to his own sons when he had them. Men were supposed to be warriors.

But I quietly agreed with my mother. I didn't want Japan to fight in any more wars. I didn't want any more bombs falling on my house. And I didn't want to see any blood spilled in my family.

Today, when I look back, I see that many of the things my father believed in were right. He believed in hard work, in keeping his word, and in loyalty to his country. He believed in facing death without fear. But I see that my mother was right, too. She believed that wars were bad and that the Japanese had been wrong in wanting to conquer the world. They both believed that it was important to build a new Japan where people worked hard for peace and not for war—a modern and prosperous Japan.

And that's why I loved both my parents. But I agreed with my mother when she sold the family swords.

Shizuko Obo won the Paul A. Witty Short Story Award in 1993 for "The Day My Mother Sold the Famly Swords."

The Lair of the Demon King

by Jill Paton Walsh ● *Illustrated by Mike Eagle*

Five hundred years ago, when the city of Constantinople had finally been conquered by the Turks, a handful of Greeks were able to flee from the city and return to their Greek homeland in the Morea. (The Morea, now called Peloponnesus, is the main peninsula in Greece.) The Sultan was not content with his conquest of Constantinople. His soldiers invaded the Morea as well, terrorizing the Greek farmers and trying to find the last poor remnants of the defeated Greek army.

Cricket, March 1976

"TAKE ME TO your father," the Captain said in his guttural Greek, his knife at my throat. Then, "How long will it take?" he asked.

"Four hours," I said. "Maybe five. It will be dark before we can get there." My mother looked at me in speechless terror. For my father with his few companions was hiding nearby, an hour away at most.

"We cannot go into the hills with this whelp," said the Lieutenant. "He will lose and betray us."

WHY DID THE DEMON KING HAVE A LIAR, MUFFIN?

NO, NO CHARLIE! A *LAIR* — THAT MEANS A DEN, OR RESTING PLACE!

AND CONSTANTINOPLE WAS..... ooops!...

THE CAPITAL CITY OF THE TURKISH EMPIRE! — IT'S CALLED ISTANBUL, NOW!

I listened, stone-faced, not wishing them to see that I partly understood them.

"So," the Captain said, looking around at the villagers. "In five hours, if he has not brought us to the hideout, we will kill the boy. Have you brothers or sisters, boy?"

I would have lied to him, only Themis, my sister, is so like me, there was no hope once he saw her. He seized her arm. "In five hours, or we kill her, too," he said, glaring.

But I, Nikos, know our hills as well as my goats know them, and I already had a wild thought, a kind of plan. They tied my wrists behind my back and drove me forward on the end of a long cord, like a beast, and I led them out of the village where no path ran, straight up the stony side of the nearest steep. I am light-footed and tough. I set myself to lead them a dance that would tire them out. And while we climbed, they grunting and cursing, their heavy weapons and plated tunics clanking behind me, I thought of a certain place in my mind's eye.

It was supposed to be haunted. Nobody went there, although it was not far from the village and lay above the pine woods on the hillside overhanging us. But once when I was ten or so, and Themis only a toddling babe, my grandmother took us up there to look for a little plant with bitter leaves. Only

the most awesome need would have driven her there, but a man's life was at stake.

Holy George had not been with us long when he fell sick of some fever and seemed likely to die. My grandmother went to visit him, and it was then that she led us up to the haunted place. As we went, I asked her about the path we took, for it was made of smooth white stones where it was not overgrown. She said it was the work of the demon king, whose lair we were approaching.

At last the path doubled back on itself and climbed steeply; across it a wall of stones had been made and a cairn of boulders piled up to support a rough wooden cross. I wondered how we would pass, but my grandmother did not wish to. Instead she found an herb growing by the side of a sweet stream of fresh water that ran there in a glade in the cool shade of the trees. She showed me the plant and set me to help her gather more like it. It was quite hard to find. There were many strange plants growing there, that I had not seen on other hillsides, and chunks of broken white stone lay all around, some of them wrought into leaves and scrolls. While I was searching among them, Themis wandered off, and when I looked 'round I could not see her.

Both my grandmother and I were

A CAIRN IS A HEAP OF STONES PILED UP IN A ROUNDED SHAPE.

226

JILL PATON WALSH

terrified; I, lest she had fallen in the stream, my grandmother, lest the demon had taken her; yet all around me lay a feeling of safety, as though the woods and the white stones were telling me wordlessly that no harm would come to us there. We searched everywhere, and in the end, while my grandmother cried out to me not to, I climbed over the barrier across the path and up farther through the wood, and so came to the heart of the haunted place and stood there astonished and silent.

A shape like half a huge round shallow bowl had been scooped out of the rocks of the hill, and the massive conical dip had been staircased with marble, step upon step of perfect half-circles of stone, rising in tiers to a top rank high above me. Weeds and wild mountain flowers cascaded over the edges and sprouted from cracks, barely softening the stark beauty of the vast shape. Lines of steps low enough to climb with ease divided the great tiers like the spokes of a wheel; at my feet was a kind of threshing floor, ringed by a circle of marble slabs and made of beaten earth. And scrambling halfway up the ascent was Themis. I moved forward a step or two and called her name. But I was awestruck and more than a little scared. The word stuck in my throat, and all that came out was a hoarse whisper.

"Themis!" I croaked. And the whole hillside answered me back in my own voice. It was not an echo, but in the same moment *I* spoke *the place* spoke; loudly and clearly it said in my voice, THEMIS!

"Christ succor me!" I cried in fright, and the place said that, too, loudly and with ringing clarity. In my terror, I dropped my stick, and the sound of it striking the stone disk at my feet rang out clean and crisp all 'round me. I stood rooted to the spot, trembling.

From halfway down the bank of marble tiers, Themis had then called to me, "Why do you breathe so loud, Nikos? Huff, puff, I can hear you!" I didn't believe her, quite. But my curiosity was overcoming my fear. I stood her on the marble disk that marked the hub of the place and I climbed up to where she had been, and beyond. When I reached the back, the highest row, and could see the lovely sweep of the tiers curving 'round below me, I could also hear my little sister's soft breathing, faint but unmistakable, carried to my ears from far below, as clearly as though I stood beside her—no, more clearly, as though the whole hill were breathing. I was still scared, and yet if that place was haunted, it was haunted by a sense of calm and light, and the voices that rang in it were our own.

We found our grandmother praying and shaking, still on the far side of the wall of stones. She seized Themis, traced a cross on her forehead, and looked frantically 'round at me. "What will become of her?" she asked me. "What will become of the child? I heard the demon speak her name!"

"I called her, that was all," I said. "We saw no demon."

But my grandmother had made haste to hobble away downhill, with her right hand full of herbs, and her left leading Themis.

My grandmother made a bitter fragrance, boiling up the plant we had gathered in a pot on the cottage fire, and she took the brew to Holy George to drink, and he recovered quite quickly, though both his smile and his frown were lopsided ever after.

Holy George was very interested in the haunted place. He told me the plants that grew there had run wild out of a

SUCCOR ME MEANS HELP ME!

JILL PATON WALSH

medicinal garden planted in ancient times by wise men of the shrine of Aesculapius, to whom the place belonged. But, said Holy George, this Aesculapius was no demon, but a man, a good doctor, whom the ancients in their error mistook for a god and worshiped. And the great speaking circle in the hills was a theater, he said, where the rituals of the ancients were played out. He said men stood upon the beaten floor in masks, pretending to be what they were not and speaking made-up words to tell a story. And he said that the rings of stones were seats, and that all of them had once been full of listeners.

"Not all the folk in the Morea gathered together could make such a crowd!" I had told him in disbelief. And at that, Holy George told me that our poor country, so ravaged by war and about to be consumed by the Sultan's army, had once been rich and happy—full of fair cities and men who built temples of white stone, and made theaters in the hillsides, and wrote books, and listened to plays, and ran races to honor their gods—and the whole world learned wisdom from them. They did not worship the true god because Christ had not yet come upon the earth; yet they were no demons, but true Greeks. . . .

*　　*　　*

All these memories went through my head as I now trotted 'round the goat runs with my hands tied behind me. I led my party of sweating soldiers 'round and 'round, doubling back again and again on our tracks. Poor Themis stumbled and cried with weariness. In the end one of the soldiers carried her and gave her sips from his water bottle. I wished he had not, for it was simpler to hate them all alike. I kept moving, doggedly waiting for dark.

We saw the blood-red sunset flaming in the sky behind the black shoulder of the mountain. In deepening shadows I led them up a rough track to the source of a mountain stream, where I would bring my goats to drink in the hot summer. Then over the crest and down the other side. And the night deepened overhead, and the brilliant stars shone out. When it was really dark, I led them down the hills again and through the pine woods. I led them through the glade of herbs and over the wall with the cross that was supposed to keep the demon in his lair. One of them saw the cross, even by starlight, and struck it down.

"Are we nearly there?" said the Captain, tugging my rope, as we trudged up toward the theater.

"Very nearly," I said. "One more short climb." But I hung back, as far as the

HOW DO YOU PRONOUNCE THAT GUY'S NAME — THE ONE THE SHRINE BELONGED TO?

SAY IT ES-KUH-LAY-PE-OS!

length of rope would let me. It was very dark, but I thought from the sound of the footfalls ahead of me, by now they must all be within the enfolding hollow of the theater.

"Why are you lurking?" asked the Captain, tugging my rope. "Come on, get us there."

I did my best; I acted, pretending what was not true, speaking prepared words. "I am afraid of this place," I said. "It is haunted by powerful demons. The way lies past their lair." I pitched my voice loudly, hoping they would all hear.

"You idiot!" said the Captain. "On, or I'll start on your sister!"

I moved forward, as if reluctant. Something must have guided me across the arena, for I felt the marble center smooth beneath my feet. That moment I threw my head back and howled, long and loud. Out of the pitch-darkness my cry came huge and vast and from all directions at once. Then I began to mutter and whisper and groan, making ghost voices that grew enormous and flittered 'round the theater like birds, coming from everywhere. I heard the soldiers' cries and screams of fright, their running footfalls up and down. I heard some fall—screaming—from the ends of the tiers of seats onto the stones below; I heard some run past me at top speed and hurl themselves into the woods. I gabbled a prayer at top speed. I tried pulling my rope and found it free—nobody was holding the end of it now. I laughed with triumph, and the laughter sounded back at me, gigantic and crazed, out of the night. Then the night called, "Nikos! Nikos!" as though that were the name of a huge god or of the demon king; Themis was looking for me.

I took her hand, and we went safely home, to be hidden by my mother in the storeroom for a week. But the soldiers never came back for us.

"To save me, you braved the demon's lair?" said my father, when I told him about it.

"There's nothing to fear there, Father," I said. "Only the spirits of men who were Greeks like ourselves. They are on our side against the oppressors. And those stones are waiting, I think, for the time when our land is happy and free again."

"It all belongs to the heathen Sultan now, my son," said my father darkly. "The stones will have a long wait."

"They'll still be there, though it takes a thousand years," I said.

JILL PATON WALSH

Jill Paton Walsh has published more than forty children's books. Her accolades include the Whitbread Prize for *The Emperor's Winding Sheet* and the Boston Globe–Horn Book Award for *Unleaving*. In 1996 she was named Commander of the Order of the British Empire (CBE) in recognition of her accomplishments.

The Innkeeper's Boy

by Diane Brooks Pleninger

Illustrated by Leonard Everett Fisher

RAIN FELL LIKE arrows in the night, hailing down upon the roof of the inn at Clary Crossing until the thatch grew damp and heavy and the roof beams groaned under its weight. The fire sputtered in the chimney, and steaming horses whickered and snuffed in the stalls.

A boy lay wrapped in quilts on a bench by the hearth. It was his job to open the door to midnight travelers. The lazy innkeeper lay abed in an upstairs room, loving his sleep.

At first the boy thought the faint pounding he heard was his dream. On the fourth knock, he awoke and stumbled to the door. Before him stood a tall stranger in a black cloak, an old man pale as death.

"I can go no farther," gasped the man and fell into a chair near the fire.

Luc, for that was the boy's name, hastened to stir the embers and pour a beaker of ale. But the man wanted only to talk.

"The king is dead," he said. Luc was silent, but his eyes grew wide.

"His son, Prince Albion of Picardy, is his rightful heir. But the king's brother, Mogor, the cruel Duke of Artois, covets the throne. He will stop at nothing to claim it."

"Will there be war?" Luc asked.

"Except for this," the man answered, and he held up a small, bright object that glimmered even in the dark room. Luc took it in his hand. It was a gold ring, set with an egg-shaped stone that changed color before his eyes, turning from amethyst to emerald to carmine in the firelight.

"Whoever wears this shall claim the throne of Picardy in peace. It is a song stone. Listen to it."

Luc raised it to his ear and, for an instant, thought he heard a faint sound, like a distant flute.

"The king asked me to carry the ring to Prince Albion at Amiens. But Mogor's henchmen have hounded me at every milepost. I am less than a day ahead of them. And I am growing weak."

"Can you not hide from them?" Luc asked excitedly. "I know many good hiding places in these hills!"

"No one who carries the ring can hide from them. They have captured the silver kestrel, a bird that hears the song of the stone wherever it is and leads them to it. Were it buried in the deepest shaft, they would find it."

The man and the boy sat in silence, pondering this dilemma.

"My strength has left me," said the man at length. "But you are young. Carry this ring to Albion. He will certainly reward you."

Cricket, November 1988
Winner of the 1989 Paul A. Witty Short Story Award

Luc bent to stir the embers. What the man had not seen was that the boy was lame. He walked only slowly and with difficulty. How could he outdistance Mogor's henchmen on their strong horses?

When Luc turned back to tell him this, the man had vanished, leaving only his black cloak on the chair and the cold ring in Luc's hand.

The next morning, Luc rose early, before the innkeeper was afoot. Within his palm lay the ring, its stone changing from azure to amber to coral. He crept into the kitchen and drank a bowl of milk. He must decide what to do.

As he thought, Luc's eye lit upon a small, coarse sack half full of rock salt. An idea began to take shape in his mind. Perhaps there was a way. He took up the sack and dropped the ring inside, burying it in the salt. Then he went to the ale room and gathered up a handful of the corks the innkeeper used to stop his bottles.

Luc filled the sack with corks and drew the strings tight. Then he wrapped himself in the stranger's black cloak and slipped out the kitchen door.

The pale, gold light of morning streamed through the mist. Slowly, Luc made his way to a lake not far from the crossing. It was a small lake, but so deep it had never been sounded. Some said it was an ancient quarry left by the Romans. Others said it was the threshold to the underworld.

Now Luc untied a small boat and rowed swiftly to the middle of the lake. He said a quick prayer that he might be right in his calculations. Then he threw the sack of salt into the deep, black water. In an instant it sank, leaving a string of bubbles and then nothing.

In the late afternoon, the cavaliers of Artois galloped into Clary Crossing. Their gold and scarlet liveries were streaked with dust and sweat, and the hoofs of their foaming steeds struck sparks in the lengthening shadows.

Astride the leathern wristlet of one rode the hooded silver kestrel. The bird gave forth an angry cry as the horses drew to a halt before the inn. The innkeeper came to the doorway and wrung his hands and whimpered.

"What guests did you have last night, man?" cried the leader. "Speak or taste my blade!"

"None, none, none!" gibbered the innkeeper. "Nary a one, one, one!"

"A man in black has passed this way," challenged the leader. "The kestrel does not lie!" And the bird rose up on its talons with a screech.

"Come in, then. Search! Look anywhere you wish. Ask my boy, my only servant. He will tell you. No one stopped last night."

But the cavaliers had no use for a mere boy. Instead, they turned to the mob of villagers that had gathered.

"The king is dead! Mogor shall rule, and his enemies shall perish! A gold sovereign to any of you who can take us to a tall man in a black cape."

A peasant stepped forth. "At dawn this morning, your lordship, I saw a man in black go down to the lake. I cannot say I saw him return."

With a shout, the duke's men hastened to the water's edge.

"Release the bird!" ordered the leader, and the keeper slipped the black hood from the kestrel's head. For a moment, its fierce eyes shone like diamonds. Then with a rush of wings, the bird left its perch and began to soar.

The people watched it climb higher and ever higher over the dark lake. At last, when it had become a mere speck against the sky, the bird folded its wings and with a great, distant, keening shriek fell from the blue like a thunderbolt. Down, down it sped toward the deep black center of the lake, and there it sliced the water like a knife and broke its neck and drowned.

A cry of consternation went up from the crowd, for they saw the cavaliers of Artois turn their steeds back toward Arras and they knew that war was inevitable. Late into the night, candles smoked in the cottages of the crossing as the people gathered their treasures and prepared to hide all that they possessed in hillside caves, away from the plundering soldiers of Mogor.

The inn was the busiest spot of all. There the villagers gathered to await the word of war.

"Where is my salt?" shouted the innkeeper to his boy as he stirred the steaming stewpot. But Luc kept his counsel, saying nothing, and merely threw another garlic in the pot to raise the flavor. Late that evening, Luc rowed to the center of the deep lake and searched the moonlit surface. But he found nothing.

"Where are my corks?" roared the innkeeper the next night. Again, Luc kept his counsel and rolled leaves to plug the ale bottles. Again, he rowed out onto the lake in the moonlight. And again, he found nothing. His heart began to sink. Had he been wrong? Was the ring gone forever? Would there be war?

"Where is my scullery boy?" thundered the innkeeper on the third night. "Luc! Luc! Luc?"

DIANE BROOKS PLENINGER

But there was no answer. For that evening, Luc had rowed to the center of the lake. He had found a dark shape bobbing on the water and had fished it out in silent triumph and pulled open the drawstrings. Among the corks, a tiny moon shining in its onyx stone, lay the ring. The heavy rock salt had all dissolved, and the corks had brought the sack back to the surface.

Some days later, a young lad with a crutch and an oversized black cloak stood outside the palace at Amiens and demanded to see Prince Albion. Everyone laughed, but he insisted. When he was finally admitted, he gave the prince the ring and told him all that had happened. The prince embraced him and led him to his own table. He gave him roast quail, spiced oranges, and sweet puddings to eat, and a bath and a soft feather bed for his rest.

In reward for his cleverness and courage, Luc lived ever after in King Albion's household. There he studied and learned much. And it was soon forgotten that the famous Luc of Amiens, scientist, statesman, and scholar, was once the scullery boy at the inn at Clary Crossing.

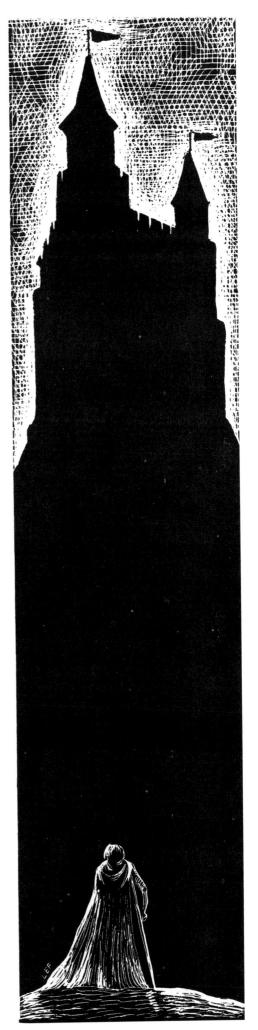

Diane Brooks Pleninger has had three stories published in *Cricket*. "The Innkeeper's Boy" received the Paul A. Witty Short Story Award in 1989.

Dream Maker

The shining silver moon
Is a coin hung in the sky
To pay the old Dream Maker
Whenever he goes by.

by Jane Yolen

Art by Charles Mikolaycak
Cricket, July 1990

YOU WILL HARDLY believe how eager I was to have a big drum like that of Mahmood Agha's. All other wishes aside, the desire to have a drum was my greatest dream. I'll put it this way: I was deeply in love with the idea of a drum and awfully crazy about having one.

Day and night I thought of nothing but the drum. Sometimes I dreamed that I was standing on the roof of our house, resting a brand-new drum on the thatched dome. In the dream I was holding two nicely cut drumsticks in my hands and was delivering hard blows to the drum's bright, shining skin. With every blow the drum made a long, loud noise that could be heard far and wide, ringing through all the streets of the neighborhood, surprising everybody.

When I heard the drum in my dreams, I became overjoyed, and my sleep got sweeter and sweeter. But as soon as I woke up, I would see that there was no drum. Many mornings I found that while sleeping, I had mistaken my pillow for a drum and had given it such hard blows that the feathers inside had scattered all over my bed. Those mornings, with much fuss and very slowly, I would gather the spilled feathers and stuff them back in the pillow, careful not to let my grandmother Bibi know what was going on.

Cricket, June–July 1995

The Drum
by
Hooshang Moradi Kermani

translated from the Farsi
by Teimoor Roohi
from The Stories of Majid
Illustrated by Russ Walks

After that I would get up, go into the yard, and climb the ladder to the roof of our house. I would then go on the roof of our neighbor Mahmood Agha's house and stick out my head and gaze at the closet under the staircase. I would look lovingly at the closet because I knew his drum to be there. I had seen Mahmood Agha bring it out of that same place many a time.

I will not keep it a secret from you: it was Mahmood Agha's drum that made me fall in love with one.

In those days in every district there were a few drums that were beaten on the nights of the fasting month, to wake people up to eat and to say their morning prayers. On mourning days in the month of Moharram, too, the drums would be beaten in front of the crowds of mourners, who would strike their chests in time with the rhythmic sounds.

When Mahmood Agha used to beat his drum to wake people up, my desire for the drum burned deep inside of me. I used to go on the roof and watch Mahmood Agha beat the drum in the dim light of the stars just before dawn. Sometimes I would watch him and his drum in the moonlight.

Once I plucked up my courage and went quietly to the roof of his house and asked him timidly if I could beat the drum. I explained that it was my greatest desire and that I would be very grateful if he would hand the sticks to me and let me give a few blows to see what would happen. But Mahmood Agha gave me an outraged look

and said in a harsh voice, "Impossible! This is not a joking matter, and drumming is not a child's business."

And once I went to a shop where they sold drums and other musical instruments. But the price of a drum was very high. When I asked my grandmother about giving me the money to buy one, she gazed at me, dumbfounded, and then scolded, "You don't say so! What do you want a drum for? Shame on you. Go, sit in a corner and study your lessons!"

Anyhow, my wish didn't come true, and I became a slave to my desire to have a drum. I drew a big drum on a large sheet of paper, painted it, and put it on the wall of my room, but a paper drum wouldn't make any sound. I found two pieces of dry wood, cut them very nicely, and made my own beautiful drumsticks. But I thought it would be a pity to use them on an oilcan. What was I to do then?

Finally, one day, I took the greatest risk I had ever taken. I could not have cared less about being punished or beaten. I took my drumsticks and tiptoed into Mahmood Agha's house. I tried to breathe quietly and less often than usual, and I looked high and low to make sure Khadijeh Khanom, Mahmood Agha's wife, was not around to see me standing there so worried, the sticks clutched tightly in my hand.

If she happened to spot me, I had decided to say hello and ask her to lend me their hammer. But I was lucky enough. She was in the kitchen, and Mahmood Agha was out of the house. There were only a few hens and roosters under a pomegranate tree, poking for food and cackling. As soon as they saw me, they started cackling louder, but I didn't pay any attention. I went round the flower bed and crept into the closet, the doors of which were standing open.

The drum was leaning against the wall, a beam of light from the doors falling on its skin. I stood over the drum and watched it for a long time. My heart beat so quickly, I thought it was going to jump from my chest. I bent and rubbed my hand on the drum's skin. How soft and smooth it felt!

I was tempted. I thought of just tapping on the skin with my fingers to see how it sounded. I set my sticks on the shelf and reached out my hand slowly. My fingers trembled. I gave one very soft blow to the skin. How beautiful the sound was! It caressed my eardrums softly, and my heart filled with joy.

There's nothing worse than drumming secretly, expecting no one but yourself to hear the sound. A drum is made to wake people up, to gather them together, and sometimes to give them a warning; it's not meant for being beaten in secret. Yet

I needed to beat the drum and not let anyone but myself hear the sound. This may be possible if you are in a lonely desert where no living creature is found, not a few yards away from Khadijeh Khanom who was in the kitchen quite close to the closet.

Still, when I tapped on the drum and nothing happened, I became more courageous. I said to myself, "I will tap harder on the drum. No one will hear me." Then I said, "Why not use the sticks, but quietly." I reached for my sticks and stood over the drum, my legs on either side of it, and I held the sticks up. But I was not brave enough to bring the sticks down. I closed my eyes so as not to see what I was

going to do and slowly but surely brought the sticks nearer to the drum. As soon as my sticks touched the skin, the drum made a loud noise. The sound rang inside the room, and almost immediately I heard Khadijeh Khanom's footsteps coming toward the closet.

Surely she was coming to see why Mahmood Agha's drum was beating by itself. I was in a bad fix. If only I could have taken to my heels and disappeared in two flaps of a duck's tail! But it was impossible! Khadijeh Khanom would see me and seize me by the neck and take me to Bibi. And Bibi wouldn't spare me any punishment. She would beat me so hard, I would never forget it all through my life, so hard I would never dare to enter anyone's house on the sly again.

There was no way out, so I knelt down and hid myself behind the big drum like a tortoise. Thank God I was very small. Then

suddenly I had a stroke of good luck. One of the chickens came by, and Khadijeh Khanom thought it was the chicken that had hit the drum. She said some bad words, shooed the bird away, and closed and latched the closet doors, returning to her chores peacefully.

I was left alone in the dark closet, caught in a trap. I was imprisoned with the beautiful, sweet-sounding drum I loved so fondly.

The closet was quite dark. Little by little my eyes got used to the blackness, and by a beam of light coming from the crack between the doors, I could see the drum. I began stroking and caressing every part of it: this was the only thing I could do to the drum in that situation. Although it was warm outside, the closet was cool and damp and called for sleep. Soon I lay down beside the drum, wrapped it in my arms, and drifted off.

I woke suddenly to the *dum, dum* of the drum and saw a mouse jump down from the skin and race to its hole. The mouse had beaten the drum with its tail and was running away frightened. I wished I, too, were a mouse able to beat the drum with my tail and race away as fast as the wind. I said to myself, "It's not good to be big and a human being at such times. It doesn't do one any good."

I got up and peeped out of the closet. It was nearly sunset. I began to be afraid and to resent my wish to have a drum. I squatted in a corner of the closet and said, "How unhappy I am to have such a troublesome wish. It's really childish." Saying so, I felt a great pity for myself and was not far from bursting into tears.

I was lost in thought when I heard my grandmother Bibi calling from the yard. She was quite jittery and was telling Khadijeh Khanom, "Majid has disappeared since noon. I have stopped by every relative's house and have looked everywhere, but I can't find him. I don't have any idea where he has gone or what has happened to my poor little child."

Khadijeh Khanom tried to speak comfortingly. "He might have gone off with one of his playfellows. I'm sure he will be back soon."

Bibi had now started sobbing, and I couldn't bear to hear her any longer. I decided to cry out, "Granny, I'm here," but then the idea struck me to do something out of the ordinary. I said to myself, "Since I'm going to give myself away and pay for what I have done, what could be better than beating the drum and at least fulfilling part of my wish." Without hesitating, I took up my sticks and attacked the drum. As I beat it, I said to the drum, "I suffered all this long, tiresome time because of you. So you must do a good turn for me."

As I played, I tried to imitate a skillful drummer. The drum sounded *dum, der, dum, darum, dum, dum.* I enjoyed every moment of it. I drummed until I was quite tired and then I gave up. As soon as the sound of the drum died down, I heard a lot of screaming and shouting in the yard. I peeped out through the doors. The house was full of people from the neighborhood. Everyone was pointing to the closet, but nobody was daring enough to get close to it. Bibi had fainted, and some women were trying to bring her around by holding rose water and mud under her nose.

Khadijeh Khanom was shivering, saying, "The house is haunted. There's nobody in that closet. I locked the doors myself. Look, they're still locked. Did you hear the drum? There must be genies beating it! Oh, God, I give myself up to you!"

Mash-hady Assadollah, the grocer, was coming toward the closet to open the doors. But as soon as he stepped forward, his family begged him not to do so. "For God's sake, don't cause us trouble. Don't get yourself killed and make your children orphans."

I saw that everything was getting more complicated. I was sitting behind the doors, watching the crowd of people through the crack. I was afraid of them, and they were afraid of me. They believed I was a genie. As I kept watching, I saw three thick-necked, strongly built men, each carrying a big club, heading toward the doors, all the while whispering the name of God. When they were a few steps from the closet, I said to myself, "They will strike me to death before I can prove who I am and why I am here, and they will throw my corpse in the yard." So I put my mouth to the crack and shouted, "This is Majid! Don't beat me, please!"

As soon as they heard my voice, the three men dropped their clubs and ran away. The crowd, too, ran out of the house wailing with fear.

Things were getting worse. If the crowd could get to poor me, they would tear me to pieces. There was only one thing to do, and that was to tell the people everything.

Again I put my mouth to the doors and started giving a lecture. "Don't be afraid. This is Majid speaking. I just came here on the sly to beat the drum. I was caught in a trap. Don't ever be afraid of me. I'm a human being just like you. Trust in me. I won't hurt you. Only open the doors of the closet so I may come out. As soon as you see me, you will understand everything. No panic, please. Believe me—I would very much like to come out of this awful place. I will pray for you not to fall in love with a drum if you open these doors. I will also pray for you not to become as helpless as I am now."

I repeated these things so many times that two, three people—still in some fear of genies—came trembling toward the doors and opened them. I came out quite calmly and smilingly. I still held the sticks in my hand. I stood in the yard near the closet and looked about me. The crowd could not stop staring at me, but no one said anything. I felt ashamed of what I had done. I put my head down and went into the room where Bibi was.

Bibi had just opened her eyes and was taking some syrup. As soon as she saw me, she put the glass down, jumped up, and held me tightly in her arms. "Where were you, Majid? Did you know the sound of the drum was heard in the small closet under the staircase in Mahmood Agha's house?"

"Yes, I know all about it," I said.

"Weren't you afraid?" she asked.

"No, why should I be?"

"Why weren't you?"

"Because it was I who was beating the drum. But of course I was afraid of the darkness," I replied.

Bibi, God bless her, understood that I had been imprisoned in the dark closet for four or five hours and felt a great pity for me. She asked, "Let me see, Majid, did you suffer a lot while you were in there?"

"Yes," I answered, "I suffered a lot. I was near the drum, I had the sticks, but I didn't dare to beat it. Could any suffering be worse?"

Finally, when Bibi had completely recovered and realized what a mess I had made by sneaking into our neighbor's house for the drum, she got mad and went looking for a big stick to punish me. But Mahmood Agha and his wife Khadijeh Khanom both came over to beg Bibi to forgive me.

Little by little other wishes took the place of my wish for the drum, and each of these new wishes helped me grow up a bit more until I became a man and was able to stand on my own two feet.

Hooshang Moradi Kermani is one of Iran's most famous writers. He was born in 1944 in a village near the city of Kerman. He has worked on radio, television, newspapers, and movies, but he is best known for his award-winning stories for children and young adults. *The Stories of Majid* is one of his most popular works.

Teimoor Roohi has translated many of Hooshang Moradi Kermani's short stories from the Farsi.

Nabil Means Wisdom

by Garrett Bodel • *Illustrated by Russ Walks*

Beirut is the capital city of Lebanon, an Arab country on the eastern edge of the Mediterranean Sea. For many years, Lebanon has been torn by fighting among the country's different Christian and Muslim religious groups. If you were ten years old and had grown up in Beirut, there would not have been a time in your life when the people in your city had not been at war. This story tells about Nabil, a young Muslim boy living in Beirut.

Cricket, September 1991

THE SHOOTING isn't bad today, so Mama is sending me to the market. I get to go instead of my sister Malika because yesterday was my birthday!

Mama said to me, "Nabil, you are nine now, a big boy, and that's old enough to go alone. Mind yourself in the streets and stay away from the soldiers." Then she gave me some money and her list of things to buy: white fish, yogurt, dates, bananas, rice, and honey. She didn't even tell me to keep the money safe. She knew I would.

I snapped the money into the front pocket of my overalls and ran out into the street. My sandals clattered on the pavement, and my shadow leaped tall and black against the plain cinder walls. The sun spread over the streets like honey, turning everything to gold.

My papa says that once Beirut was the most beautiful city in the world, and I believe it! Even now, with the houses crumbling to rubble and the pavement breaking between tree roots, it is pretty. One day Mustafa and I will help to make everything beautiful again. We will be architects!

Mustafa is my best friend. He is ten and lives on my street. He comes to have lessons at our house whenever he can. All the children on our block do, because of Malika. Malika's eighteen, and she can remember back before the fighting when there was real school. Malika went and learned history and math and reading. She tells us about it sometimes, but it makes me mad to listen because we don't have a school anymore. All we have is Malika.

When I get to Mustafa's house, I knock on the door to see if he can come out today. Mustafa's mama peeps through the bars on her window before she opens the door. Mustafa's mama is a worrier.

She is afraid because she lost two sons, a brother, and a baby girl in the fighting. My brother Rashid and my brother Ali were also killed. Now only my papa and my oldest brother Khaled fight. That is why there is such a big gap between Malika and me.

But things are better now. We have more children, my little sister Fatima and my baby brother Ezzat, and we have a house. I asked Mama once if she missed my other brothers, and she said yes. But I don't. I don't remember them.

"Nabil Bakkali!" says Mustafa's mama. "What are you doing out by yourself?"

"Mama sent me to the market! Look!" I unsnap the money to show her. "Can Mustafa come, too?" She fusses and tells us lots of streets to keep away from, but in the end Mustafa comes. After all, he is ten, and she has to let him out sometimes.

Mustafa brings his soccer ball, and he and I race each other down the street. We shout excitedly to make the other boys, the inside boys, jealous.

"Nabil," he says to me when we stop to rest under a palm, "let's go down to the docks and watch the ships for a little. We can go to the market on the way back."

I know we should do our errand and

go straight home. I know the docks are not on our side of the city, but the day is so pretty and we haven't seen any soldiers. Besides, I am nine now. So I agree.

We start off down the unfamiliar streets to the harbor and kick the soccer ball between us. I am running in front of Mustafa and looking over my shoulder for the pass

when I crash into someone. The ball shoots past me, Mustafa screams and dives into a doorway, and I fall onto the cement at the feet of a soldier.

He is a Christian soldier with big boots. He wears a gold cross and carries a big gun, which is pointing straight at me. I am too scared to scream. I am too scared to run. I just shut my eyes tight and listen for the bang.

It doesn't come. When I look at him again, he is holding the gun in the air and pinching the sweat out of his eyes. Then he reaches down with one hand and lifts me to my feet. He smiles, just a little.

"Don't stray so far from home, puppy," he says. Then he gets the soccer ball and kicks it back up the street to Mustafa, and the two of us run. We run all the way to the market.

The fighting was bad the rest of the week. The guns were close, and sometimes we could see soldiers running past

the house. We children had to stay inside. Papa and Khaled came home for food and coffee. They were dusty and tired from fighting. After a little rest, they would go out again.

By Friday I was tired of being inside. Fatima and I sat at the table in the kitchen and practiced writing while Malika and Mama cooked supper. The air was thick with spicy rice and fish smells that made my stomach growl. Ezzat was being a pest, tugging at Malika's skirt and whining for a bite. The radio rattled on with more and more news about the fighting.

When Papa and Khaled came in, no one was watching me. I snuck a piece of *halvah* from the bag and slipped out into the darkness. In the doorway I drank in the fresh air and savored the chewy sesame candy.

A small sound made me turn my head, and there beside me in the darkness was a soldier, a Christian soldier. His chest was bleeding, and he was trying to sneak quietly past the houses to the harbor. He was leaning against the wall, trying to catch his breath.

We looked at each other for a long moment. Then he held his finger to his lips and limped off.

I thought of Khaled and Papa in the kitchen with their guns. I thought of the Christian soldier and the soccer ball and I watched silently while this man escaped.

My name, Nabil, means wisdom. I hope someday I will be very wise and I will know if it was right to let that soldier go. I hope someday I will know why they are all fighting in the first place.

Garrett Bodel works for the International Brain Injury Association. She has had three stories published in *Cricket*.

Five Words

by Pnina Kass

Illustrated by Leslie Bowman

More than forty years have passed since the horrible events that are the background to Nettie's story. World War II was fought in Asia, Africa, and Europe. Almost sixty nations were part of the war, and more than twenty-five million civilians were killed. Six million of these were Jews.

By 1941, Adolf Hitler, leader of Germany and the head of the Nazi party, had decided to kill all the Jews in Europe. Hatred of the Jews—anti-Semitism—became the official policy of the German government. As the Nazis invaded Europe, they arrested the Jews and sent them to concentration camps. The most horrible of these death camps was Auschwitz. Here, trains arrived from every part of Europe, bringing Jews to their death.

Nettie's story is the story of many Jewish children, whose parents gave them to strangers or threw them off the death trains—anything to save them. In 1945, at the end of the war, some of these children were found by relatives and taken to live in many different countries.

THERE ARE different kinds of secrets. There's the kind you're dying to tell if someone will just keep asking you, and there's the kind that's so scary that no matter how many times someone asks, you'll never tell. And then there's my kind of secret. That's the one that's so deep inside that you don't even know it's there until something happens.

It was a warm spring day. I sat on the window sill in my classroom, watching all the preparations for the Holocaust Memorial Day. The sounds of the chorus rehearsal drifted up the stairs. David and Mickey were arranging photographs of the Warsaw ghetto, and Naomi and Judith were pinning up maps showing the towns

Cricket, September 1991
Winner of the 1992 Paul A. Witty Short Story Award

and cities where Jews had lived. Danny stuck his head into the room.

"Nettie, instead of just sitting there, you could help."

"And what if I don't want to?" I answered back.

"Then maybe you shouldn't be part of this class!" he snapped.

Naomi dropped the map and walked over to the doorway. She whispered in Danny's ear, and he nodded slowly and went back outside. Naomi came over to me.

"Nettie, it's O.K. Don't pay any attention to him. He just didn't know."

I swung down from the sill. "I really don't know why you think you have to explain about me to everyone!"

"But, Nettie, I didn't mean . . ." Naomi looked as if I had slapped her, but I couldn't stop.

"That's right, no one ever means anything, and that's why everyone in this school feels sorry for me!" I turned around and ran out of the classroom and down the long hall. As I pushed open the school's heavy wooden door, I nearly ran into Mrs. Levy, the principal.

PNINA KASS

"Nettie, where are you running to? What's happened?"

I didn't answer. I just kept on running until I reached the duck pond. I threw myself on the bank, punching my fists into the wet grass. I felt so alone. That same feeling that I had on Saturday nights when there was folk dancing in the kibbutz social hall. Everybody spinning in fast circles with their hands joined and I could never catch anyone's hand. Then someone would see me and say, "Stop, let Nettie in." And then I felt lonelier than ever.

I looked across the pond. There was Griselda leading her goslings into the water for their swimming lesson. I had named her after a beautiful queen in my book of fairy tales. She was graceful and strong and a perfect mother. She backpaddled, nudging the goslings into line and making sure they weren't caught in the reeds.

I moved from the grassy bank to the shade of a eucalyptus tree, leaning back against the broad trunk and stretching out my legs. Suddenly I could remember being dragged through snow with my legs out in front of me and later someone rubbing my legs on the floor of a small house. Sometime, somewhere, long ago. And then the memory was gone. Where had it come from? On the other side of the pond, Griselda was clucking stories to the goslings clustered around her. I shivered with cold.

Past the grove of eucalyptus trees, I saw the small houses of the kibbutz, shuttered from the afternoon sun. One of those houses, tiny from here, was my house. That is, it was Uncle Max and Aunt Sara's house. Uncle Max had found me in Vienna after the war. They told me over and over again, "Now this is *your* house."

I stood up, picking the twigs and grass out of my hair. I pulled it to one side, looping the hair into a thick braid. Again, for just a

second, I could see the past—my mother stood beside me, braiding her hair. "No!" I shouted. "You can't be here now. You left me!" I was sure my heart would break through my skin, it was beating so hard. I started running across the fields and didn't stop until I was home. The house was silent. A note fluttered on the kitchen table. *Nettie—We'll be back in an hour.*

Even though I was alone, I closed the door to my room. I opened my closet and knelt down, reaching way into the back. And then I felt the bumpy texture of the leather. I caught at the handle and pulled out the little brown suitcase.

I sat on the floor, carefully balancing the suitcase on my knees. Attached to the thin red cord hanging from the handle were a key and a cardboard tag with my name: *Klagman, Nettie.* Slowly I untied the cord, and the key fell into my palm. Although the lock was red with rust, it popped open quickly. I lifted up the top.

Five things were inside: two photographs glued to the top, a silver ring with a little bell hanging from it, a harmonica, and a scrap of flowered cloth. It was the photographs that I wanted to see. One was of a man and a woman. The woman's hair was

PNINA KASS

blond, with the sunlight shining through it. She was leaning against the man with her cheek on his shoulder, and you couldn't tell if her hair was short or long. He looked straight ahead with dark eyes that were just like mine. Near the corner, in a slanty script, someone had written *Josef and Mira.*

The other photograph was of the same woman, but this time you could see her long blond braid. There was a little girl on her lap, and they were sitting on a garden bench. The little girl's feet already touched the ground, but still the woman held her tightly. I thought of Griselda circling the goslings.

I held my breath and tried to squeeze myself into that picture, into Mira's arms. Then I noticed something I'd never seen before. The scarf on the girl's head was the same flowered material as the scrap in the suitcase.

Mira held the little girl, squinting into the sun and laughing at the same time. Maybe the little girl had said something funny. The same slanty script read *Mira and Nettie, Spring*.

I leaned into the suitcase, smelling it and trying to bring them back, back out of their photographs. And now I could, I really could! I could hear my father playing the harmonica. I heard my mother singing along as she swung me through the air. I could feel the air rushing past and the sky blue and close. "Don't drop me, Momma. Don't drop me."

Then I thought I could hear inside the suitcase the distant clacking of a train. "You're dropping me, Momma!" The train that took them away and left me behind, with the flowered scarf on my head so I wouldn't get cold.

The next day the whole school assembled in the auditorium. The chorus sang lullabies and folk songs, and there were poems and speeches about the importance of remembering. I sat holding the brown suitcase on my lap. Our class was the last to march up onto the stage. David explained the meaning of the yellow Star of David, and Naomi told the story of the Warsaw ghetto. My hands were sweaty on the suitcase handle. They had finished. There was silence, and everyone was looking at me.

"Nettie?" Mrs. Levy asked.

I stood up and told my secret.

"I hated my mother and father. My father was Josef Klagman, and he liked to play the harmonica. My mother was Mira Klagman, and I remember her laughing a lot. She had a blond braid just like mine." I opened the suitcase. "These are their pictures—this is what they looked like. They threw me off the train, the train that took them to Auschwitz. They didn't want to leave me. I know that now. I know how much they loved me. Somewhere I know they can hear me.

"Momma, Poppa, Nettie is alive!"

Pnina Kass is the author of ten children's books, eight of which are written in Hebrew. She was the 1992 recipient of the Paul A. Witty Short Story Award for "Five Words."

Happy 30th Birthday, *Cricket*!

IN 1973, THE announcement of a new, high-quality magazine for children swept through the children's literature community like a breath of fresh air. The idea that stories for children could be both literary and child appealing was becoming more prevalent, and here was a magazine being designed with this concept in mind. *Cricket*—the title alone was tantalizing—came into being, rich with thought-provoking poems, joyful stories, retellings of beloved folk tales, and art created especially for its readers. Being asked to write reviews for *Cricket*'s Bookshelf was a great honor. For each issue, I was to choose a handful of books from the thousands being published that would tempt *Cricket* readers to extend their reading horizons; it was a challenge but also a delight. On this thirtieth anniversary of the magazine, it is pleasing to know that several generations of children have grown up with *Cricket* and that its mission of combining literature with appeal still holds true.

—**Barbara Elleman**

HERE'S A BIRTHDAY couplet for the Festschrift—sent by a *Cricket* latecomer who's delighted to be part of the bug's latest offspring, Cricket Books.

It's headline fodder fit for the *National Enquirer*'s frothing fictioneers:

"CRICKET GIVES BIRTH TO SPIDER AND LADYBUG, DEFIES INSECT LIFE SPAN, LIVES THIRTY YEARS." CHEERS!

—*With love,* **Paul Fleischman**

LIKE ITS NAMESAKE, *Cricket* soothes and excites. It leaps and bounds, full of adventure and action, and it sweetly sings, meditating on human potential and life-giving nature. This magazine, also life-giving, brings two human beings close to each other every night as before bed, I read from it to my daughter, and she reads from it to me. And, of course, its illustrations inspire.

—**Emanuel di Pasquale**

CAN SUCH A lively, quick-hopping *Cricket* really be so old? In the mucky ocean of stuff put out for kids to read, *Cricket* is a beautiful island with rainbows on it. May it someday have a birthday cake ablaze with a thousand candles! I'm happy and proud to have had a few poems be part of it.

—**X. J. Kennedy**

DEAR CRICKET,
You and I became friends a long time ago. Back at the beginning when you first arrived to put together your collection of stories and drawings and poems for all the world to share, I remember meeting you.

I knew then that you might listen to my stories and poems, and when you finally chirped a welcome to my words that are really my way of talking, I was very happy because that's how I realized that you and I were friends.

I remember, too, listening closely to your many chirps that lined the margins of your books. Some were wise and some made me laugh. We were truly friends as we exchanged our thoughts.

You and I are older now, but one great thing I learned from you. Friends are forever.

Bless you, *Cricket.* Keep singing.

—**Julia Cunningham**

Additional Biographies

Victor Ambrus has illustrated more than two hundred books for readers of all ages. He won Kate Greenaway Medals for *The Three Poor Tailors, Horses in Battle,* and *Mishka.*

Enrico Arno worked as an illustrator, painter, ceramist, and sculptor.

Quentin Blake has received many honors for his illustrations, including the Kate Greenaway Medal, the Hans Christian Andersen Award, and the Whitbread Prize. In 1999 he was appointed England's first Children's Laureate.

Erik Blegvad has illustrated more than one hundred children's books, including works by his wife, Lenore Blegvad. *The Tenth Good Thing About Barney* by Judith Viorst is one of his most popular works.

Leslie Bowman has been a professional magazine and children's book illustrator for over fifteen years.

Nancy Ekholm Burkert won a Caldecott Honor for *Snow-White and the Seven Dwarfs,* the Society of Illustrators' Gold Medal for *The Nightingale,* and the Boston Globe–Horn Book Award for *Valentine and Orson.*

Eric Carle is one of the world's most popular children's artists. His *Very Hungry Caterpillar* has sold twelve million copies and been translated into more than thirty different languages. In 2003 he won the Laura Ingalls Wilder Award for his lifelong contribution to children's literature.

Julia Cunningham is known for her poetry, animal fantasies, and lyrical novels. Her *Treasure Is the Rose* was a National Book Award finalist.

Emanuel di Pasquale emigrated to the United States from Ragusa, Sicily, at age thirteen. He is the award-winning author of several poetry collections and poetry translations from the Italian. *Cartwheel to the Moon,* a collection of poems about his childhood in Sicily, was published in 2003.

Leo and Diane Dillon met at Parsons School of Design and married in 1957, a year after their graduation. They won Caldecott Medals for *Ashanti to Zulu: African Traditions* and *Why Mosquitoes Buzz in People's Ears: A West African Tale.*

Mike Eagle has illustrated many picture books, magazine articles, and advertising pieces. He recently created illustrations for Eve Spencer's *A Flag for Our Country.*

Barbara Elleman, the founder of *Book Links* magazine, has contributed to the field of children's literature as an editor, biographer, and book reviewer. She has received the Hope S. Dean Memorial Award and the Jeremiah Ludington Memorial Award.

Leonard Everett Fisher is the author of many well-known children's books, such as *The Great Wall of China* and *Prince Henry the Navigator.* He has been given the Silver Medallion from the University of Southern Mississippi, the Regina Medal from the Catholic Library Association, and the Kerlan Award from the University of Minnesota.

Paul Fleischman's *Joyful Noise: Poems for Two Voices* was awarded the Newbery Medal in 1989. That made him and his father, Sid, the only such pair to have won Newbery Medals. His most recent innovative works of fiction are *Seek* and *Breakout.*

John Fulweiler is an illustrator, designer, sculptor, and teacher. He has illustrated for *Cricket* since 1984.

Irene Haas is the author and illustrator of *The Maggie B.* and *A Summertime Song.* She has contributed art to children's books, periodicals, advertisements, posters, and record-album covers.

Brett Helquist is the illustrator of the Series of Unfortunate Events books by Lemony Snicket.

Friso Henstra, a widely loved and respected illustrator who lives in the Netherlands, has received many awards, including the Gold Medal from the Society of Illustrators for his work on *The Round Sultan*.

Troy Howell has illustrated many children's books, including *Feast of Fools* by Bridget Crowley and *Favorite Medieval Tales* by Mary Pope Osborne.

Anne Hunter is known for her lovely, detailed illustrations of nature. *Possum's Harvest Moon* is among the books she has written and illustrated.

X. J. Kennedy, recipient of a Guggenheim Fellowship and the Los Angeles Times Book Prize, is the author of several collections of poetry and children's books.

Hilary Knight is the beloved illustrator of the Eloise series and many other children's books, including Lee Bennett Hopkins's poetry compilation, *Side by Side: Poems to Read Together*. He is also a contributing artist for *Vanity Fair*.

Beth and Joe Krush are the illustrators of the Borrowers series by Mary Norton. They have also created art for books by Eleanor Cameron, Beverly Cleary, and Elizabeth Enright.

David Macaulay has earned the Caldecott Medal for *Black and White*; Caldecott Honors for *Castle* and *Cathedral: The Story of Its Construction*; and the Boston Globe–Horn Book Award for *The Way Things Work*.

David McPhail has contributed to more than one hundred children's books. He has created art for works by X. J. Kennedy, Nancy Willard, and Rosemary Wells. The books he has authored and illustrated include *Edward and the Pirates* and *Pigs Aplenty, Pigs Galore!*

Charles Mikolaycak was known for his poignant, romantic illustrations. Among the books he illustrated are *The Man Who Could Call Down Owls* by Eve Bunting and *Tam Lin: An Old Ballad* by Jane Yolen.

Leslie Morrill has contributed illustrations to the Hardy Boys and Choose Your Own Adventure series.

Gina Ruck-Pauquèt has written more than fifty children's books in her native German.

Eric von Schmidt has worked as an illustrator, songwriter, painter, and folk singer. In 2000 he received the American Society of Composers, Authors and Publishers Lifetime Achievement Award. He has contributed art to *Cricket* regularly since 1979.

Mary Beth Schwark is known for her elegant illustrations and paintings. She aims to capture "the poetic truth of a moment" in her work, which has been featured in books, magazines, and art galleries.

Mary Shepard illustrated the Mary Poppins books by P. L. Travers.

Ann Strugnell is the illustrator of the award-winning Julian books by Ann Cameron.

Sue Truesdell has illustrated many children's books, including texts in the I Can Read series by Joan Robins and Betsy Byars.

Russ Walks has illustrated for a wide variety of publications, including *Cricket* and *Ladybug*.

Paul O. Zelinsky won the Caldecott Medal for *Rapunzel* and Caldecott Honors for *Hansel and Gretel, Swamp Angel,* and *Rumpelstiltskin*.

Lisbeth Zwerger has received many awards for her fine illustrations, among them the Hans Christian Andersen Award. The *New York Times* has selected several of her books as Best Illustrated Books of the Year.

Acknowledgments

Grateful acknowledgment is made to the following for permission to reprint the copyrighted material listed below.

Jan Adkins for illustrations accompanying "The Day Grandfather Tickled a Tiger" from *Cricket* magazine April 1974, Vol. 1, No. 8, art © 1974 by Jan Adkins.

Mrs. Paula Arno for illustrations by Enrico Arno accompanying "A Fish for Finn" from *Cricket* magazine, May 1974, Vol. 1, No. 9, art © 1974 by Enrico Arno.

Quentin Blake for illustrations accompanying "McBroom the Rainmaker" from *Cricket* magazine, September 1973, Vol. 1, No. 1, art © 1973 by Quentin Blake, and for illustrations accompanying "The Cat Who Became a Poet" from *Cricket* magazine, June 1982, Vol. 9, No. 10, art © 1982 by Quentin Blake.

Garrett Bodel for "Nabil Means Wisdom" from *Cricket* magazine, September 1991, Vol. 19, No. 1, text © 1991 by Mimi Bodel.

Ruskin Bond for "The Day Grandfather Tickled a Tiger" from *Cricket* magazine, April 1974, Vol. 1, No. 8, text © 1974 by Ruskin Bond.

Leslie Bowman for illustrations accompanying "Five Words" from *Cricket* magazine, September 1991, Vol. 19, No. 1, art © 1991 by Leslie Bowman.

Brandt & Hochman Literary Agents, Inc. for "A Gift from Gertrude Stein" by Lloyd Alexander from *Cricket* magazine, January 1977, Vol. 4, No. 5, text © 1977 by Lloyd Alexander.

Eve Bunting for "A Fish for Finn" from *Cricket* magazine, May 1974, Vol. 1, No. 9, text © 1974 by Eve Bunting.

Curtis Brown, Ltd. for "Dream Maker" by Jane Yolen from *Cricket* magazine, July 1990, Vol. 17, No. 11, text © 1990 by Jane Yolen, and for "Genesis" by Lee Bennett Hopkins, text © 2003 by Lee Bennett Hopkins.

Mike Eagle for illustrations accompanying "A Gift from Gertrude Stein" from *Cricket* magazine, January 1977, Vol. 4, No. 5, art © 1977 by Mike Eagle, and for illustrations accompanying "The Lair of the Demon King" from *Cricket* magazine, March and April 1976, Vol. 3, Nos. 7 and 8, art © 1976 by Mike Eagle.

The Estate of Carole Kismaric Mikolaycak for illustration by Charles Mikolaycak accompanying "Dream Maker" from *Cricket* magazine, July 1990, Vol. 17, No. 11, art © 1990 by Charles Mikolaycak.

Farrar, Straus and Giroux, LLC for "The Fools of Chelm and the Stupid Carp" by Isaac Bashevis Singer from *Cricket* magazine, November 1973, Vol. 1, No. 3, text © 1973 by Isaac Bashevis Singer.

Leonard Everett Fisher for illustrations accompanying "The Innkeeper's Boy" from *Cricket* magazine, November 1988, Vol. 16, No. 3, art © 1988 by Leonard Everett Fisher.

Paul Fleischman for "Owl O'Clock" from *Cricket* magazine, July 2000, Vol. 27, No. 11, text © 2000 by Paul Fleischman.

John Fulweiler for illustrations accompanying "The Day I Rescued Albert Einstein's Compass" from *Cricket* magazine, June 2000, Vol. 27, No. 10, art © 2000 by John Fulweiler.

James Cross Giblin for "Buildings That Scrape the Sky" from *Cricket* magazine, April 1979, Vol. 6, No. 8, text © 1979 by James Cross Giblin.

Harcourt Inc. for illustration accompanying "How Did Mary Poppins Find Me?" from *Mary Poppins Comes Back* by P. L. Travers, © 1953, © renewed 1963 by P. L. Travers, from *Cricket* magazine, July 1990, Vol. 17, No. 11.

HarperCollins Publishers for "McBroom the Rainmaker" from *McBroom Tells the Truth* by Sid Fleischman, text © 1973 by Sid Fleischman.

Harold Ober Associates, Incorporated for "Tosh" from *Cricket* magazine, September 1975, Vol. 3, No. 1, text © 1975 by James Herriot, and for "How Did Mary Poppins Find Me?" by P. L. Travers, text © 1973 by P. L. Travers.

David Higham Associates Limited for "The Lair of the Demon King" by Jill Paton Walsh from *Cricket* magazine, March and April 1976, Vol. 3, Nos. 7 and 8, text © 1976 by Jill Paton Walsh.

Holiday House, Inc. for "Hershel and the Hanukkah Goblins" by Eric A. Kimmel from *Cricket* magazine, December 1985, Vol. 13, No. 4, text © 1985 by Eric A. Kimmel.

Anne Hunter for illustration accompanying "Owl O'Clock" from *Cricket* magazine, July 2000, Vol. 27, No. 11, art © 2000 by Anne Hunter.

Trina Schart Hyman for illustrations accompanying "Great Granddad Stan" from *Cricket* magazine, May 1975, Vol. 2, No. 9, art © 1975 by Trina Schart Hyman.

Pnina Kass for "Five Words" from *Cricket* magazine, September 1991, Vol. 19, No. 1, text © 1991 by Pnina Kass.

Hooshang Moradi Kermani and Teimoor Roohi for "The Drum" from *The Stories of Majid,* English translation by Teimoor Roohi from *Cricket* magazine, June and July 1995, Vol. 22, Nos. 10 and 11, translation © 1995 by Teimoor Roohi.

Hilary Knight for illustrations accompanying "A Hike in New York City" by Sam Levenson from *Cricket* magazine, May 1974, Vol. 1, No. 9, art © 1974 by Hilary Knight.

Beth and Joe Krush for illustrations accompanying "Tosh" from *Cricket* magazine, September 1975, Vol. 3, No. 1, art © 1975 by Beth H. and Joseph P. Krush.

Lescher & Lescher, Ltd. for "A Letter" by Isaac B. Singer-NY-(1973). All rights reserved.

David McPhail for illustrations accompanying "The Fools of Chelm and the Stupid Carp" from *Cricket* magazine, November 1973, Vol. 1, No. 3, art © 1973 by David McPhail.

Walter Dean Myers for "The Cub" from *Cricket* magazine, July 1987, Vol. 14, No. 11, text © 1987 by Walter Dean Myers.

Shizuko Obo for "The Day Mother Sold the Family Swords" from *Cricket* magazine, August 1992, Vol. 19, No. 12, text © 1992 by Shizuko Obo Koster.

Shulamith Levey Oppenheim for "The Day I Rescued Albert Einstein's Compass" from *Cricket* magazine, June 2000, Vol. 27, No. 10, text © 2000 by Shulamith L. Oppenheim.

Doris Orgel for translation of "Cats" by Gina Ruck-Pauquèt, from *Cricket* magazine, April 1974, Vol. 1, No. 8, English translation © 1974 by Doris Orgel, and for translation of "Dreadful Consequences of Absent-Mindedness" by Michael Ende, from *Cricket* magazine, October 1982, Vol. 10, No. 2, English translation © 1982 by Doris Orgel.

The Orion Publishing Group for "The Cat Who Became a Poet" from *Nonstop Nonsense,* text © 1977 by Margaret Mahy from *Cricket* magazine, June 1982, Vol. 9, No. 10.

Diane Brooks Pleninger for "The Innkeeper's Boy" from *Cricket* magazine, November 1988, Vol. 16, No. 3, text © 1988 by Diane Brooks Pleninger.

Gina Ruck-Pauquèt for "Cats" from *Cricket* magazine, April 1974, Vol. 1, No. 8.

Sterling Lord Literistic, Inc. for "A Hike in New York City" from *In One Era and Out the Other* by Sam Levenson, text © 1973 by Samuel Levenson.

Trustees of Leland Stanford Junior University for "Great Granddad Stan" by William Saroyan from *Cricket* magazine, May 1975, Vol. 2, No. 9, text © 1975 by William Saroyan.

Russ Walks for illustrations accompanying "The Day Mother Sold the Family Swords" from *Cricket* magazine, August 1992, Vol. 19, No. 12, art © 1992 by Russ Walks; for illustrations accompanying "The Drum" from *Cricket* magazine, June and July 1995, Vol. 22, Nos. 10 and 11, art © 1995 by Russ Walks; and for illustrations accompanying "Nabil Means Wisdom" from *Cricket* magazine, September 1991, Vol. 19, No. 1, art © 1991 by Russ Walks.

to   Cricket
subject
name Ellie
age   13
comments   Dear Cricket,
I just wanted to say thanks for being there for me ever since I was a really little
kid. Back then, I just loved your magazine for the exciting and interesting stories,
but now I love it for more than that. Your magazine has become for me, a safe refuge
when the world gets to be too much. It is a place where I can go and know that I will
be accepted for me, no matter who I am. Your stories have made me laugh and cry and
wonder and think, and have inspired me to begin a writing career of my own. Your
magazine has taught me hundreds of things about science, history, other cultures, and
the world around me. Even though age-wise I have technically outgrown Cricket, I still
rejoice everytime I open the mailbox and find the latest issue waiting for me. I can
hardly wait to find out what the gang is up to this month, or what new and exciting
tales are waiting for me. Thanks so much for being such a wonderful, entertaining, and
fun magazine.

OCT 1 3 1986

Dear Cricket,
I love your stories!
everytime I get a cricket
magizine I get it right
away. I read it
crichet magizine is still
out when I have kids
because I want my kids
to have a good time
reading wonderful storie's
too. Keep up the good
work! Love, Iland, Age Ten

Dear Cricket,
You've cheered me up on gloo
You're my best friend, you've
lagh and think and wonde
to thank you! You're our fa
friend.
From,
Aimee, age 9

JUN   1985

Dear Eve
I have
a year
a write
why? Be
me a h

Dear Eve
I love "Cr
good thin
times. Ever
"wishing s
on forever

May 24, 1991

Dear Everybuggy,
    I've been getting "Cricket" for a little over a year
now, and this is the first time I've gotten a chance to
write to you.   I'd like to congratulate you on the most
interesting, readable, fantastic, and every other good
adjective magazine.   I'm a bit old to be still reading
"Cricket", 13, but I can't bear to give it up.   And let me
assure you, I'm saving my old "Cricket"s so my children can
read them and their children read them because I think all
the future generations should have the privilege that I've
had in being able to read your magazine...at any age.   Keep
up the fabulous work!
                                          M.H., age 13

OCT 0 8 1991

Dear Cricket,
Your book   is the best book in the
world. Your book is my favorite book in the
world. I just love reading the letters.
I like the stories too. I love the poems.
too, I love the crosswords. I just love your
pictures. Oh how I love your books.
Please write back soon.
            Your number one fan,
            Brandi, age 10

Dear Cricket & Ladyb
    I've been getti
for half my life,
want you to know
been a major fo
shaping my life

Ke
g